The Cull of the
Badgers

Dear Anne,

Enjoy

Lan xxx

L J HARGREAVES

authorHOUSE®

AuthorHouse™ UK
1663 Liberty Drive
Bloomington, IN 47403 USA
www.authorhouse.co.uk
Phone: UK TFN: 0800 0148641 (Toll Free inside the UK)
*   UK Local: (02) 0369 56322 (+44 20 3695 6322 from outside the UK)*

Published by AuthorHouse 04/22/2022

ISBN: 978-1-6655-9574-2 (sc)
ISBN: 978-1-6655-9575-9 (hc)
ISBN: 978-1-6655-9576-6 (e)

Print information available on the last page.

ACKNOWLEDGEMENTS

To my four amazing girls whom I have been blessed with…their love and support are unsurpassable and their wonderful husbands who know, never to come in between a Hargo.

My lovely, dearest, friend Ann, who allowed me to enjoy her penthouse apartment in Spain; sitting by the poolside together, and whilst I was writing away, she enjoyed the sunshine and brought me cool drinks and fresh fruits.

For all my other friends and colleagues who inadvertently played a role defining me as a person.

Most of all to Life for allowing me to enjoy my opportunities, rise from my tragedies, learn from my mistakes and to be a better person.

CONTENTS

The Clans Gather

14.02, in the Year 2014

Somewhere in the southwest of England, snuggled in a sloping valley of luscious, rolling grassland, was a county called Brocklehurstshire. It was bursting with tiny, yellow daffodils and unassuming snowdrops as spring with all its youth and vigour was certainly making its mark on this very special day, whilst winter gracefully retired for a well-deserved rest.

Cascading bluebells and drifts of bright, neon purple crocuses spread thickly over the gentle rocks and merged into dense woodlands of thick old deciduous trees that stood proudly alongside the iconic evergreen pines. Their powerful, thick roots mapped their way forcibly into the slopes of the sandy terrain, wherein lay the home of a colony of twelve badger clans.

On this crisp, chilly February evening, whilst the wind was gently blowing and the tree's branches silhouetted against the perfectly clear blue sky, the badgers of the colony were making their way to congregate at Brockley, to participate in the celebration of the saining of their new cubs. Saining referred to the blessing and naming of the newly born cubs, and to honour this evening's celebration was the colony's spiritual ruler and leader, the High Lord Luminous Snowspirit, and his beautiful, elegant wife; the High Lady Pure Snowspirit of the Brockley Clan. This was the governing clan of the whole colony, and tonight, the High Lord Luminous and his wife took their places at the top of the sacred log table of judgement and protection in preparation of the evening's festivities.

1

The sacred log table of judgement and protection was a strong old tree trunk from the bacacia tree, believed to be over a thousand years old; according to legend, it magically rescued Widejaw the Great, the first chief warrior of the colony.

One evening, as the sun was just beginning to set, Widejaw the Great was making his routine final inspection of all the entrances into the sett when he caught a glimpse of four small tan-and-white dogs, that were frenzied and foaming at their mouths, desperately sniffing at the main entrance of the labyrinth of passages. Quietly and stealthily, Widejaw the Great secured the other passages with thick, thorny holly bushes and glistening laurel leaves. He then lifted his tail and released a strong musk on each entrance. This was known as allomarking; the odour was pleasant to badgers as a welcoming invitation to their setts, but to any other animal, it is most offensive. The dogs balked at the foul, appalling smell and refused to move farther into the passage; Widejaw made a loud, wailing yelp, distracting them from the entrance, and galloped upwards, leading them out of the setts.

The dogs, momentarily stunned by the strong, offensive odour of the musk, snapped out of their stupor and immediately pursued Widejaw, but when the badger arrived at the top, he only found another four dogs and three men with long, wooden spears.

The eight dogs and three men chased Widejaw relentlessly, and to keep them as far away as possible from the sett, he led them to a nearby stream. One of the men threw his long spear, which caught Widejaw in the shoulder, and it began to bleed. He bravely continued forward, diverting their attention from the main sett, but soon found himself surrounded by all the dogs. Without surrender, he pushed himself valiantly towards the dogs, but by some miracle, a large tree trunk lying across a bed of rich moss engulfed him, harbouring him from his attackers' hot pursuit.

Whilst inside the trunk, which seemed filled with a potpourri of wonderful, comforting scents, he began to calm down and feel protected. He could hear the muffled yelps and barks of the dogs climbing and scratching all over the trunk, but they sounded like they were miles away.

After what seemed like an eternity, he heard one of the men say, "Come on, you silly mutts, there is nothing here. There are no holes or entrances in this dead tree trunk, and we are wasting our time. We have lost him.

Let's take the dogs somewhere else. In fact, it is too late now, and the dogs need a rest, so we had best feed them, or else they might eat us for a meal. Ha ha. Let's go."

Widejaw waited about half an hour and then began to wonder how he was going to get out; magically, the trunk opened and gently lifted Widejaw out.

Waxy, thick, heart-shaped leaves appeared on what seemed a dead tree trunk, and then droplets of a sap poured down between the leaves. Instinctively, Widejaw reached out and applied the sap to his wound; the bleeding stopped, and his wound was healed. Filled with awe, he realised that this was the work of his ancestors; he knelt down and began to scratch the earth, as all the badgers did when they were worshiping their ancestors or thanking them for their good favour, and with deep gratitude, he began to recite his thanks, "Oh, great ancestors, I am truly indebted to you for your protection and believe my purpose here is not done. Give me the strength to do your bidding at your command."

Widejaw then got a whiff of aromatic, fragrant flowers, and to his amazement, an ivy vine edged with tiny red flowers began to climb around the trunk, and a radiance of tiny orbs began to hover over the old dead tree trunk. It was the most beautiful thing he had ever seen. The tiny orbs spiralled in a great speed, and suddenly four silhouettes appeared before him.

Widejaw stood paralysed in wonder and elation to have witnessed this revelation of the ancestors. The four badgers had different coloured robes; one was white, the second was red, and the third was a black and white pelt; the fourth diminutive badger was a female. Despite being the smallest, it was she who spoke in a firm but gentle tone.

"Widejaw, we represent the north, south, east, and west of all the colony. We have given you a worthy charge; your mission is to secure this spot as sacred and worthy of worship and celebration to congregate for the blessings of all future events. There will be great changes that you will not witness yourself, but today marks the spot of a future gathering that will change the balance between man and forest. This log which concealed you will be known as the Log of Judgement and Protection, or LOJAP. Go now, and spread this proclamation."

With that message, the four figures disappeared into the night, leaving an ambiance of celestial blessing. Feeling enlightened, Widejaw returned to the sett and told all the badgers what happened. From that evening, the log of judgement and protection was worshipped as a sacred venue and referred to as LOJAP. The ceremonies included the coupling of young badgers, the sad celebration of a badger's passing, and most important, the saining of the young cubs, together with the annual rituals of worship to their ancestors.

One auspicious evening, it was not just the saining of the cubs of the twelve clans or the annual honorary ancestor worship, but also the celebration of all the clans to witness the saining of the newborn heir to the High Lord and High Lady Snowspirit. It was the first time in twenty moons that a high lord had his own son and heir. For several years, the high lord's position was passed on to a white-pelted badger of integrity and outstanding qualities, but tonight, High Lord Luminous stood in complete elation and pride, welcoming the arriving clans and guests; he couldn't wait to present them with his own heir.

The High Lady looked around and felt a great pride for all the wonderful work that the leaders' sows and she had done in the last week to prepare for this evening. She looked across to Brit Clawdigger and marvelled at her amazing strength, disguising the recent tragic loss of her only boar cub.

Badgers from the twelve different clans across Brocklehurstshire lumbered in earnest to watch the cubs receive the blessing of regdab, the sacred sap from the bacacia tree. The sap marked the cubs with a scent recognisable by all the clans to protect them against their enemies. To honour this double celebration, all the forest animals, including polecats, otters, weasels, moles, deer, foxes, and rabbits, came to pay their respects and lined up according to importance, forming an arena looking onto this great event.

The leaders of each species sat in harmony at a table close to LOJAP; they looked out to ensure that each of their military councillors was attentive and paying attention to any misgivings in view of last week's brutal, cruel tragedy of the badgers.

The owls were perched above the treeline, whilst the smaller birds with their keen predacious nature kept watch, looking for unwelcomed guests. The crows, with a keen visual of their surroundings, flew through the crowd, spying and picking up any conversation that might explain what happened last week. Their biggest task was to go back and forth between man and forest and report their findings to their leader, the Grand Councillor Oscar Owl, High Lord of all birds and respected for his wisdom and experience.

The military forces of all the animals stood in unison with the red pelt badgers. Tonight, it was not just a night of festivities but also a mission of protection and security. Their friends, the badgers, were being persecuted and slaughtered, and every effort had to be made to help them.

Councillor Clawdigger made a quick account that all was as he planned and approached Councillor Widejaw, confirming he was satisfied and the celebration could commence.

Sadly, not all the forest animals were welcomed. Years ago, the hedgehogs and moles had a small territorial dispute, and the badgers were asked to intervene to make a fair judgement. Under the reign of leader at that time, the High Lord Morning Light, the moles were awarded the rights to the territory, as the High Lord deemed that their activity burrowing holes benefitted the badgers in building their setts more easily, and the process also guaranteed a ready supply of earthworms, with very little effort by the badgers to work to get them.

The hedgehogs found the decision most selfish and unfair; they were infuriated. In anger, their High Lord Harold rolled himself into a ball and catapulted himself into High Lord Morning Light, striking him between his eyes and killing him instantly. An immediate uproar and bloodbath followed, with the badgers locking the smaller hedgehogs in between their jaws, killing them instantly. During this slaughter, the badgers discovered that the hedgehogs' coats were filled with the tastiest bugs and mites; after killing them, they feasted on their coats. The feud continued, and for many years, hedgehogs kept as far away as they could and remained enemies to both the badgers and the moles.

The moles were forever indebted to the badgers but sadly, always felt that they were treated subserviently and used as a huge part of unpaid labour, initiating setts for the badgers. They also lived in fear of the hedgehogs and preferred to stay underground but were reassured that they had the lifelong protection of the badgers.

The councillors of the governing clan began to make their way to LOJAP. Their lovely sows were seated across the sacred log, nursing their cubs by a large font filled with regdab. The councillors helped their sows get comfortable by the font and then made their way to their seats at LOJAP. There were eight distinct chairs, and the seating was arranged according to importance.

The High Lord was responsible for defence, infrastructure, and education, whilst the High Lady was responsible for health, environment, housing, and lettings. To the right of the High Lord sat Councillor Widejaw the 7th, military counsel. He was of a fiery red pelt and leader of all the warriors. Proud to bear the name of Widejaw and living up to his ancestor's honourable name, he never rested and was constantly on the lookout for trouble or unrest. Law and order of all the clans was always in check as Widejaw ate, breathed, and slept. His breed, of the fiery red pelt, like the High Lord's pure white pelt, was distinct to the others of the black-and-white pelts, as they were only allowed to couple with their own kin. The High Lord's kin, boasting a pure white coat, are unique and endowed with magical powers of the sixth sense and perception. The chosen one from the badgers with the white pelt was also able to shapeshift, and with this divine intervention, the High Lord made several trips into the world of humans as one of them. With these spiritual gifts and abilities, the gifted badger of a white pelt was always chosen to lead the colony.

To the right of Widejaw sat Councillor Clawdigger, a handsome boar of the regular black-and-white pelt. He was chief civil engineer of the Brockley Clan but originally from the Brockhall Clan. Clawdigger was the genius behind the infrastructure of the different setts and tunnels. The construction of tonight's setup was masterminded by him, and the visitors were impressed by how well organised it was. Like his wife Brit, he masked his tragic loss of their young cub with a brave face and smiled politely as the badgers nodded in sympathy. All the badgers and animals were so proud of him and Brit. However, Brit struggled to find the right words to respond to their wishes of sympathy and only offered her gratitude for their kind thoughts through lowered lids and a small smile.

On Clawdigger's right sat the kind, caring, lovable head of academia, Councillor Wisepaws. Unlike the other athletic councillors, poor Wisepaws lumbered from one sett to the other. He was on the plump side and was teased by several of his peers. However, his mind was more alert and intelligent than any of the other badgers, and both young and old loved this amicable, rotund wise professor and had confidence that no other could teach and nurture their young ones as Wisepaws could. Even the older badgers still sought his advice, and all regarded him affectionately as their beloved oracle. The younger badgers took great joy in mocking their teacher for all his clumsiness and eccentricity but cherished their precious maestro.

To the left of the High Lady sat the impeccable Councillor Pharmacia, who was responsible for all health matters of the clans. Unlike the rest of the clan, who are all Eurasian badgers, he is an American badger and very over-the-top regarding health and hygiene, but the High Lady had assigned the right person to the job, as he was totally conscientious of the health and well-being of the clan. Pharmacia worked very closely with Councillor Flash, who was sat on his left.

Flash oversaw all the cleanliness and housekeeping of the setts and latrines. Like Pharmacia, he was obsessed with health and cleanliness, and both got on like a house on fire. However, they struggled to work with Councillor Bodger, who was responsible for housing and letting. Sadly, Bodger did not share the same ethics or morals as Pharmacia and Flash, which caused a lot of arguments amongst them. Bodger, a good-looking boar and a charmer, always manipulated all the badgers around him and got away with murder. Sally, his sow, was everyone's sweetheart, and they forgave him and put up with his antics for her sake. He spent far too much time on the decaying fruit pile, getting intoxicated, did not give his job the fullest attention, and neglected Sally. (Badgers get very intoxicated eating decayed fruit, so this is forbidden and frowned upon, especially for a councillor.)

On this very important evening, Bodger had still not made his appearance, and Flash could see Sally was anxiously looking out for him.

Why did you couple up with that selfish drunken fool? Flash thought.

He turned and saw that the High Lady was also looking out anxiously for Bodger, so he stood up and approached the High Lady. He said, "My dear High Lady, the High Lord is in such good spirit, so why don't you suggest that he begins his speech before he notices the absence of Councillor Bodger?"

The High Lady turned to her favourite councillor, whom she had known for many years before she arrived at Brockley, and nodded in agreement. She whispered to her husband that all the clans had arrived, and it was a good time to start his speech.

The High Lord replied, "My beloved Pure, I am quite aware that you are trying to distract me from the absence of your impudent Councillor Bodger, but as always, my love, you are right. I will commence my speech, but I warn you, that I cannot condone to this behaviour and urge you to reconsider his position."

The High Lady replied, "You are right, my love. I will deal with him severely on the morrow."

The High Lady gave a gentle nod to Brit, who opened the ceremony with a beautiful a cappella song, followed by a melodic orchestral harmony of the polecats and weasels ensemble, which also included a choir of last year's cubs. All present looked in awe and listened to their emotional medley telling the tale of the forthcoming war against man and the badgers, and the need for mothers and fathers to prepare their young cubs to face this with all their strength and unity. Clawdigger looked at his wife with so much pride, knowing she was filled with grief for their recent loss. There were tears in the eyes of their elderly parents, anxiety in the eyes of the young mothers and sows, pride and strength in the warriors, and confusion in the eyes of the young cubs, not understanding the ambience around them except that the music was soothing and comforting. As soon as Brit finished her medley and the overwhelming applause ceased, the High Lord stood up with pride and dignity and began his speech.

The High Lord's Speech

The High Lord Luminous stood up and looked into the crowd; everyone was filled with anticipation of what he was going to say. Embracing his colony, he raised his arms and slowly stretched them back as far as he could. Lifting them as high as he could manage, he began to move slowly to the right and then to the left with his palms cupped into a tight fist. The tightly cupped fist symbolised an unbreakable bond of friendship and unity, and as their leader was welcoming everyone's presence with this symbol, the congregation responded by cupping their fists as well and acknowledging each other with this gesture of harmony.

Dusk boldly made its presence whilst the sun slipped into a long slumber for the winter's evening. The bats quietly made their presence, sneaking into little gaps they could find amongst the birds. The frogs, who generally filled the soundscape of the forest with their crescendo of nuptial calls, stood close within the inner circles to get a better view. However, no one could stop the unseen katydids and crickets, who seemed oblivious to what was going on and continued to harmonise their lovely evening chirps.

The High Lord Luminous began his speech: "Welcome, most honourable clans and loyal friends of the forest. Tonight, as we remember our ancestors, we thank them for blessing us with our new cubs and continuously guiding and protecting us from our enemies. Whether you are from Brockhoist or Brockville, a white albino kin like me or red kin like our warrior leader Widejaw, or the majestic black-and-white pelt as most of you are, tonight, we stand as one united family, and this extends to all our friends of the forest.

"Our ancestors have held the setts of this colony together for over a thousand years," he continued. "Tonight, a night of rejoicing has been tarnished by last week's tragedy, and we are here to ask our ancestors for guidance and strength in the war waged on us by man. They are animals like us. They find love like us, couple like us, and have young ones like us. They hunt, feed, and nurture their young ones like us. They live in a shelter and protect their loved ones from nature's elements, but sadly, they have been exploiting us with no sense of remorse, other than pure sport. We have lost family and friends in this meaningless game. This cruel sport of baiting us out of our setts, pinning our tails down, and setting dogs to brutally attack us whilst we were entrapped was harsh enough, but now, they have gone a step too far."

He turned to look at Councillor Clawdigger, whose eyes brimmed with tears, and softly continued, "Too far. We are all aware that traps are being set up in the forest to capture us, and then we are taken away to be gassed or killed."

He turned to Brit Clawdigger, who held her head up high despite tears streaming down her cheeks; she tightly held onto her cubs. The High Lord slowly continued, with an increased anger in his tone.

"I am sure you all have heard of the loss of our innocent cub last week alongside some elderlies of our colony. They were lured into man-made traps, brutally killed, and left to die."

He paused and turned to Brit, who looked at him with a small nod of approval for him to proceed.

"By the thousands, we have been condemned as disease-spreading carriers and sentenced to be killed and gassed. This time we cannot, we will not accept the injustice of man."

The High Lord's voice grew louder above the crowd's chants and cheers of support.

"My clans, tonight I will commence the saining of all our cubs and ask for the strength of our ancestors to help create a wiser, stronger generation. I ask for wisdom to lead you away from the danger and the guidance to keep my clans and forest friends safe. I ask that we live with harmony and equality with all creatures, and help defend and look out for each other. Let us all be one and join as one true race of animals against man."

The congregation of all the badgers and friends of the forest clucked, chirped, wailed, and yelped in unison at their leader's words of encouragement.

"Tonight, my clans and my friends, we stand completely united. Our relatives, the polecats, otters, mink, moles, and weasels, and our friends, the fallow deer, rabbits, and foxes, will stand together and protect each other, with the help of our feathered friends, who keep a tight vigilance from above. Our new cubs, with the guidance of Councillor Wisepaws and our warrior leader, Widejaw, will help avoid bloodshed in this forthcoming war with their wit and strategy, rather than obliteration and destruction."

Unhappy at this nonviolent plan of action, an uproar arose in the crowd.

"What? No killing them, like they killed us?" shouted the Broxton Clan, four circles away from the High Lord.

These were the fiery red pelts, bred as warriors and angrily scratching their strong paws into the ground, as if ready for battle on the frontline.

They angrily shouted, "We saw sixteen of our kin mercilessly shot in those traps and left to die. We cannot accept your civil strategies. We want revenge. Revenge!"

A wave of anger and unrest swept across the clans, and one by one, the badgers from all the clans began to pound their feet and unanimously chant, "Revenge! Revenge! Revenge!"

Widejaw and his military leaders tried to restrain the angry crowd, but they could not quell the slow uprising.

"They are all evil," shouted the clan from Brockhedge, echoed by the clan of Brockville.

"They kill us for game and pleasure," screamed the clan from Brocknook.

"Gambling at the cost of our lives," cried the clans of Brockmeadow and Brockrook.

Aware that the clans were fuelled with rage brought on by the tragedy last week, the High Lord Luminous knew he had to resort to his magical abilities. He looked towards his High Lady, who gave him a nod of approval, and climbed on top of LOJAP. He shrieked a long, loud resounding yelp and transformed himself into what looked like a giant waterfall, glistening with cascades of water.

The crowds stopped in their steps and gasped at the beauty in front of them, whilst wisps of vapour slowly dispersed into the air, releasing wonderful scents of basil, lemon, and lavender. The vapours flowed towards the outer circles, creating a calming euphoria, and the aggression of the crowds slowly dissipated into tranquillity. In the meantime, Widejaw and his warriors guided the clans back to their correct positions, and order was restored.

The High Lord resumed his natural form, and many of the clans and forest friends who had never witnessed a transformation gasped at such a wonderful feat.

He then turned to his colony and said humbly, "No, please, my clans, we must not kill or regard ending one's life as a means of justice. We must maintain our morals and defend ourselves, or else we will be no better than them. We must always value our ten sacred inscriptions, which we will recite later during the saining. I promise I will always look out for you, so please hear me out."

Apologies came from all around the circle; they murmured that someone with such magical skills must be trusted, and they grew silent, allowing the High Lord to continue.

"I believe that most of you are aware that the Councillor Claudius Crow, military advisor and personal assistant to the Grand Councillor Oscar Owl, has been working closely with me between man and the forest. Please stand, Councillor Claudius."

Councillor Claudius Crow stood and took a brief bow, and High Lord Luminous continued, "Councillor Claudius Crow has informed me of what man call campaigns to eliminate the badgers; they refer to this elimination as the cull."

A cold shudder went through the whole forest, and all the animals looked at each other with forlorn expressions, confused at this merciless human-made mission.

The High Lord Luminous continued, "I made my transformation as a man last week and went across to their land, where I discovered that this cull is a cruel attempt to kill all the badgers, eliminating us by the thousands in a very short space of time. We need to protect ourselves and avoid being tricked and seduced by their traps, but believe me, there are some good man as well out there, who are arguing our case and fighting for our right to live in the forest in peace."

His speech was interrupted once again by the clans' further uproar and disapproval.

Widejaw turned to the crowd and shouted, "Show respect for your lord, or you will be removed from this gathering and severely dealt with by me."

Fortunately, the calming vapours had made their way to the outer circles, and the High Lord continued, "Yes, believe me, there are good man out there, trying to help us, so we must not be prejudices against all of them. They are working very hard for us, for no material gain other than wanting to protect us. If these man have faith and believe we have the right to live here, do you really want to prove them wrong? Don't live up to their general, unfavoured opinion of us as disease-carrying vermin who deserve to be eliminated. I say no. No, we show them that we are sensitive, loving, and caring animals who belong in our forest."

The crowds cheered and applauded at the High Lord's words of wisdom.

He continued, "I have plans to meet up with these man when the time is right, to work together and help them understand our way of life and show them we can live together in harmony and respect."

In the middle of their applause, the crowd fell silent, and a path opened up between the badgers and other forest animals, who made way for a very unexpected visitor.

The Unexpected Visitor

Unaccompanied by any of his warriors, the High Lord Henry Hedgehog entered the arena. Dressed in his full royal regalia, adorned with acorns and berries in between his walnut-coloured quills, he boldly walked towards the High Lord Luminous. What sets High Lord Henry against the other hedgehogs is his pure white belly and rich coloured quills, unlike the characteristic furry brown bellies of his clan. He was, of course, of an African aristocratic heritage, and although the badgers were five times bigger than him, he bravely approached LOJAP. Being proud of his own high-ranking position, he did not bow, but stood respectfully in front of the High Lord Luminous, who diplomatically acknowledged the High Lord Henry's position.

As the High Lord Henry was about to offer his greetings to the High Lady Pure, Widejaw jumped in front of him, blocking him from coming any closer to the clan's spiritual leader and his sow, bellowing, "How dare you come and disrupt our celebrated evening?"

He was just about to take him in the firm grip of his jaws when the High Lord Luminous stopped him.

The High Lord Luminous turned to his councillor and said, "Widejaw, it is clear to see that the High Lord Henry comes in peace, as he is totally unarmed and without any of his warriors."

Widejaw stood aside, secretly admiring the hedgehog's incredible bravery. The High Lady gently stroked her High Lord's arm with approval and asked the High Lord Henry Hedgehog to continue to speak.

"Thank you, kind lady. My honourable greetings; blessings and peace come with my visit. My clan and I are gifted with a keen sense of hearing, and we have all heard of the troubles that your colony are facing and of the dreadful elimination that man have plotted against you. My warriors and myself sadly witnessed the massacre last week, and this became the deciding factor that made me come and approach you. What we witnessed was a fate no animal should have, and despite our very long feud, we have come to offer support and comradeship. There are several things we can teach you for this forthcoming war which will protect your clans from elimination.

"As your High Lord said earlier about unity, we too are forest animals but have lived in continued fear of the badgers, and therefore I suggest a treaty of friendship and unity between our clans. We request that we are no longer regarded as prey and would like to be acknowledged as part of this kindred of forest animals. Do we not deserve to be part of this wonderful family? Now, when this prejudice has been inflicted on you, can you not empathise how we have felt for all these years, hiding and living in isolation?"

He looked directly at Widejaw and continued cautiously, "We can offer you our strategy in warfare against man. I would be happy to demonstrate our skills."

Widejaw bellowed, "Do you dare insinuate that our warfare strategies are inferior to yours?"

"No, councillor, not at all," Lord Henry replied, bowing respectfully to Widejaw.

He turned to the High Lord Luminous and continued, "Most honoured Lord Luminous Snowspirit, with all due respect, in a confrontation of one of us against one of you, we are clearly no match, being only a fifth of your size and weight, but let me demonstrate our skills, and I hope you can then use your imagination of the impact of my demonstration multiplied by all of us. May I please stand on your sacred table so you can all witness what we can do?"

The High Lord nodded for him to proceed. Lord Henry turned to the crowd and politely asked them to stand aside.

He continued, "Please observe our skills and kindly observe that fourth tree with thick branches fifty metres from here, next to the small hillock on the right."

The crowds turned around to observe the tree; Widejaw walked over to the hillock and leaned against the tree.

Lord Henry hollered, "Honourable councillor, I would recommend that you keep your distance from that tree."

Widejaw whispered to himself, "I am sure that I am in grave danger."

Lord Henry rolled himself into a tight ball, and all his spikes interlocked, resembling a flail used in the wars of the medieval times. Slowly he began to make a puffing, hissing noise, sounding like a snake. As he released a loud shrieking yelp, he ejected his spikes with such velocity and amazing accuracy that every spike catapulted in a uniform curve, landing in the trunk of the specific tree he had targeted.

The crowd gasped at the hedgehog's demonstration and slowly backed off, wondering how they had managed to escape this archery of spikes. They quickly lost their appetite for these creatures, and a murmur of approval passed through the crowd.

"Goodness, I do not think I'll desire a hedgehog as my delicacy ever again," one of Widejaw's warriors called out.

A ripple of laughter ran through the crowd.

Another badger shouted, "Definitely want them on our side."

Widejaw was very impressed, already imaging how to add this means of defence to their strategy, and he gave the High Lord a nod.

High Lord Henry did not miss the sign of approval and unrolled himself; with more encouragement, he began to explain to the warrior chief, "Our ability to use our entire bodies to aim and target, as I have just demonstrated, will help in your defence against man. This must make us an asset and an advantage for you to have us on your side."

A warrior of honour, Widejaw approached the High Lord Henry and bowed in respect, saying, "High Lord, that was an incredible display of your skills, and I would be honoured to have you and your clan as part of our forces protecting ourselves against man."

High Lord Henry nodded to Widejaw, turned to High Lord Luminous, and added, "A plight amongst my clan is that our coats are infested with mites and insects which ultimately eat into our coats and kill us. We'll allow you to consume these mites and insects, as we believe they are a great delicacy for your clan. There is no need to skin us alive. Relieving us of our constant plight of the mites will enable us to be more worthy soldiers and comrades to help in this impending war. We have lived in the forest in fear, occupying areas away from the badgers, and have always been outsiders. We beseech you, tonight, to start a new beginning by accepting us as part of the family of the forest."

A large roar of consent went through the clans of all the circles and forest animals, and just as the High Lord put both hands out to the High Lord Henry to seal the new friendship, another interruption arose.

"Discarding your coats and eating your mites was far more exciting and delicious," slurred Councillor Bodger, who was completely intoxicated.

He appeared from nowhere and was accompanied by Willy the weasel and Paddy the polecat; the three of them had obviously just returned from the forbidden heap of fruit.

Bodger stumbled and continued to slur, "We do not need these vermin."

Before he could say another word, Widejaw grabbed him by the neck and dragged him away.

The High Lord Luminous sharply dismissed his remark and shouted, "Please remove yourself and your companions from this ceremony immediately. You are a disgrace to your clan and have no right to be here."

Sally Bodger looked at her little cubs, who were so confused as to what was happening and embarrassed to hear the sneers across the clans whispering about Bodger. She bravely stepped forward, and in a second, Flash stood beside her to help remove her drunken mate. She turned towards the High Lord and begged him for forgiveness on behalf of her mate.

"I am so sorry, my High Lord, and my deepest apologies to you, High Lord Henry. My cubs were so excited about this evening's celebration; for their sake, please will you allow their father to take his place to witness their saining? Please, my lord, it is a moment I could never give them again. For their sake, kind lord."

The High Lord Luminous was insulted by Bodger's outburst, but he looked at Sally and felt that this night was going to be remembered as a night of forgiveness and new beginnings. He asked her to rise and allowed

Flash to assist Bodger, the bad apple of the clan, to take his seat. Bodger did not even show any remorse, as he was totally inebriated.

The High Lord Luminous turned to Lord Henry and said, "Tonight is a night of new friendship and forgiveness. However, Lord Henry, could you also mend your feud with High Lord Maximus Mole?"

Owing to his poor vision, the High Lord Maximus stood up and meekly sniffed out the position of the High Lord Luminous. He was very nervous and feared that the High Lord would be very upset with the revelation he was about to make; the last thing he needed was to be facing in the wrong direction when he spoke to him.

His loud short sniffs and rapidly squinting eyes made everyone in the congregation smile. As he began to talk, or rather stammer, High Lord Paddy Polecat had to move him slightly to the right as he was swaying away from the direction of the High Lord, whilst Councillor Claudius Crow had to keep moving him to the left, to keep him in the centre. The crowd tried to supress their laughter as they watched this comical scene.

High Lord Maximus Mole took another big sniff, and now confident that he was indeed facing High Lord luminous, he began to stammer nervously.

"High Lord Luminous, forgive me, but High Lord Henry came to see me after he had witnessed the massacre and discussed how he wanted to help you. We as moles have always felt responsible for the feud and believed it was time to end this feud and were instrumental in burrowing a safe tunnel for him tonight to come before you and offer his treaty of friendship."

With more confidence, he began to stammer less and continued, "Forgive me if you think I was conspiring against you. Although we are blind, the only thing worse than being blind is having sight but no vision. True vision does not require the eyes, and I believe you are a leader of vision and can see the rewards of ending the feud."

The High Lord Luminous was impressed by High Lord Maximus's words of wisdom. He said gently, "High Lord Maximus, you are loved and respected amongst all of us, and we believe that you only had the best intentions. Please sit yourself down and continue to enjoy the evening."

He turned to High Lord Henry and said, "Please stop and enjoy the festivities with us and take your seat by High Lord Maximus."

A faint cheer was heard in the distance, and before he went to his seat, Lord Henry turned to the High Lady Pure and said, "I am sorry for the loud cheers, but my clan are happy that the meeting has proven to be victorious. As I said before, we can hear everything."

The High Lady gave him a small smile and replied, "We all have our gifts, Lord Henry. Please invite your clan to come and join us in our celebrations."

Little did Lord Henry know that both the High Lord and High Lady were expecting this reunion, and little did he know what a huge role he was to play in the cull.

The Saining of the Cubs

Dressed in a flowing, regal robe made of lush, green moss and wearing a crown made from bacacia leaves, decorated with snowdrops, juniper berries, and crocuses, the High Lord knelt and scratched the ground, asking for the blessing of their ancestors. He rose and took the urn of regdab in his right hand; in his left hand, he took a branch of leaves from the sacred bacacia tree and began the ceremony.

The High Lord made his way to the farthest outer circle. He began a chant of purrs and chirps, blessing the cubs of the Brockmeade clan. The elders of this clan fell before the High Lord, apologising for Bodger's insolent behaviour and thanking him for forgiving him.

The High Lord insisted they get up and then said, "You have not failed him; we all missed signs where he needed our help, and together, we must help him find himself again."

It was a law amongst the badgers that everyone was equal, but those who were respected for their outstanding achievements were recognised for their leadership and assigned responsibilities in the governing clan. Bodger was no exception. As a young badger, he displayed a high degree of business acumen and had amazing social skills. With these combined attributes, he sealed many business deals with skilful negotiation, and his integrity earned him the respect of being landlord of the colony, supervising housing and lettings.

The High Lord continued to sain the cubs of the remaining circles, Brocknook, Brocksworth, Brockhedge, Brockmeadow, Brockrook,

Brockville, Brockhoist, Broxton, Brockhaven, and Brockhall, until now there was only one circle left, the Brockley Clan. The whole colony and forest friends waited with bated breath to see the young cubs of the ruling clan of the badgers. Those in front allowed the hedgehogs to stand in front of them so they could witness this wonderful celebration.

The choir of last year's cubs began to chorus together with the rabbits, minks, and otters, whilst the owls provided a strong baritone, alternating with the shrilling wails of the vixens, creating an extraordinary medley of music, accompanied by the orchestral ensemble of the polecats and weasels. The highlight of the evening finally commenced.

These events did not miss the attention of a certain Mr. Geoffrey Grimes, wandering in the woods that evening in search of badger tracks.

Geoffrey was a gangly young man of six foot, two inches with a shock of uncontrollable red curls. He had a complexion like underbaked pastry, with a mass of freckles being the only sprinkle of colour on his face. Just short of twenty-two years old, he recently joined a graduate scheme within the Department of Environment, Food, and Rural Affairs (DEFRA), and one of his assignments was to search for evidence of badger tracks. His boss had given him and his team a very hard time for not tracking down any evidence of badger tracks in Brockley after a whole week of investigation, so he decided to come out this evening and see what he was missing.

As Geoffrey was carefully shining his iPhone torch on what he identified as badger footprints, he was suddenly immobilised, and then to his amazement, he heard an incredible agglomeration of sounds, harmonising with the magical sky above him. He looked down between the bushes and wiped the steam off his glasses, using the sleeve of his crumbled shirt, to witness an incredible gathering. He stood in wonder as if in a dream, watching a huge ring of animals looking at a smaller crowd of badgers and their young cubs.

"Oh, my goodness, this is incredible," Geoffrey said. "What's going on in there? I must get this on my iPhone."

As he slowly moved his mobile phone into position to capture this extraordinary event, he inadvertently stepped on a twig.

"Oh, no," Geoffrey he cried, wincing as he saw an enormous red badger turn and slowly make his way towards him.

He stood, frozen, and was convinced that he was in trouble, as he could not outrun what looked like an army of badgers. Paralysed and not sure of what to do, he remained dead still, and after a minute or two, which felt like an eternity, the red badger made his way back into the circle.

As someone brought up in the northwest in Lancashire, he thought, *Oh, my goodness, how am I going to convince anyone of what I am seeing? Trust me to be on my own and in the perils of death. These southerners already think I am the geek from the north; I just hope I live to tell this tale.*

Geoffrey continued to observe a sequence of events that he could only compare to a ceremony. For some reason, it had an air of formality and ordinance, and as he took in this phenomenon, he said to himself, "I am convinced that all the animals from the forest are here. Jeez, look at the birds above."

The first family to approach the High Lord was Clawdigger and his lovely sow, Brit. They presented their four beautiful female cubs, Power, Sharp, Speed, and Drill.

Wisepaws and his sow, Brooke, proudly brought their four handsome male cubs, Wizz, Clev, Gene, and Bril. Widejaw and his handsome sow, Bellatrix, brought forward two fiery red male cubs, Mercury and Dynamite, and a beautiful female cub they called Bojana. Pharmacia and his sow Molly also had two male cubs, Buzz and Bawson, and their girls were named Minx and Mindy.

Bodger managed to sober up and stood, embarrassed, by poor Sally's side to present their cub Brad and their lovely female cubs, Polly and Poppy.

Flash and Sparkly proudly followed with their three handsome cubs, Bristle, Blitz, and Sheen. Finally, the High Lady Pure Snowspirit, dressed in a flowing robe of snowdrops spilling over with bluebells, glided towards the High Lord with their three female cubs, White, Snowdrop, and Glisten, and their male cub, Fire Snowspirit (heir and next leader of the twelve clans). The crowds applauded for such a blessing from their ancestors of such fine young cubs and their new heir.

The seven main families of the Brockley Clan turned to face all the other clans and friends of the forest, whose roar of cheers and goodwill had to be quelled by Widejaw. The High Lord, meanwhile, gently swept a branch of leaves from each cub's their tiny nose to their foreheads, anointing them with the sap of regdab. The behaviour of the cubs was exemplary as they wanted to giggle, as this was most ticklish part of the ceremony, but they had been severely reprimanded during practise by Wisepaws and knew they had to be very good. However, there was always an exception: Speed Clawdigger.

She affected dismay with a frown on her furry face as the High Lord swept her nose, pretending that it was not ticklish at all. In response to the frown, the High Lord winked and pinched her nose as he observed that she had the most remarkable jade green eyes.

He turned to Brit and said, "This one is a little beauty, indeed, my dear Brit; I believe she is going to be quite a handful."

Speed did not quite understand what he meant, but she remembered that Councillor Wisepaws said she had to remain quiet and behave. Instead, she began to churr and yelp uncontrollably, as it was too ticklish to remain composed, and from that day on, everyone knew the High Lord developed a soft spot for Speed.

Finally, the moment came for the High Lord to sain his own cubs, and with great joy and pride, he repeated the same ceremony. After praying over his three female cubs, it was time to sain Fire Snowspirit; he raised his young heir for all the crowd to see. The sun had set, and dusk had replaced the clear blue sky with a dark velvet rug, with a scattering of bright stars peering out of its rich folds. The moon was full, providing a perfect spotlight for their new heir. The birds continued to sing in various choruses, with all the animals celebrating this wonderful night. The hedgehogs also joined in, feeling very proud and happy to be part of this new bond between all the animals. They rolled themselves into balls and performed spectacular gymnastic routines, impressing their new friends, who unsurprisingly backed off slightly, after witnessing their adroit dexterity of shooting their quills.

The High Lord raised his arms once again and repeated the cupping of his palms in clenched fists and said, "Tonight has been a wonderful celebration of welcoming our new cubs and rekindling our friendships."

He turned to the High Lord Henry, nodded to include him in their prayers, and continued, "Now we need to praise our ancestors and thank them for always looking after us. Let us fall on our knees, so they may look down and see us pay them respect. Let us now recite our ten sacred inscriptions, which tonight holds true for love, forgiveness, and friendships."

The colony bowed down on their knees and scratched their strong claws into the ground as a symbol of awakening their ancestors. The deep scratching noises resounded into the early evening, and the air began to fill with dust, releasing a musky scent mingled with a hint of the sap of regdab, not dissimilar to that of eucalyptus. It was like an ecclesiastical phenomenon as the High Lord led the clan members in a chant:

The High Lord began, "Be guided by the wisdom of your High Lord, as he is your chosen leader."

The clans responded, "To this we do obey."

"Respect and love yourself, for without this, you will never be able to love others."

"To this we do obey."

"Work together for the benefit of the forest."

"To this we do obey."

"Obey your parents, as they only mean to protect and guide you."

"To this we do obey."

"Take responsibility for your actions, and be prepared to protect the innocent."

"To this we do obey."

"Decayed fruit is forbidden, as it will cloud your decisions."

"To this we do obey."

"Respect the earth and all that dwell on it."

"To this we do obey."

"Respect our fellow animals, and offer kindness and friendship."

"To this we do obey."

"Protect the young and innocent, as they cannot comprehend evil or bad."

"To this we do obey."

"Only with pure heart and repentance can we call on our ancestors for guidance and help."

"To this we do obey."

As the sacred inscriptions were recited, the stars in the sky merged to form four silhouettes of badgers, all with raised arms and cupped fists, looking down onto their descendants. The unity of the stars above created an illumination of rays of light on the whole colony. The colony felt inspired, filled with wisdom, renewed by the belief that all will be well.

The hedgehogs were astounded at what they were witnessing; they felt a surge of warmth go through them and rejoiced that they were now part of this family. After the final inscription was read, the illumination slowly faded into the dark sky, and one by one, the clans rejoiced that their pledges had been acknowledged. The retreat to their own setts began, and as a customary gesture, the visiting badgers and forest friends were given a pack of nuts and berries as a sign of appreciation for their attendance.

Widejaw reminded all the badgers to stay on the main track and not be lured by any treats on their way, as this bait led to the traps. Last week's tragedy was a bitter reminder that he had to be more vigilant to protect the clans. Widejaw and his warriors monitored the retreat, and all the clans left in an orderly manner. He was too busy organising law and order to worry about the presence of a stranger.

However, at the end of the ceremony, he turned around and whispered to himself, "It's okay. Tonight, you might escape me, but not the next time."

Geoffrey Grimes stood in a dreamy enchantment as he watched the bright light shine on all the animals. Gasping in astonishment, he said, "Magical. What have I just seen? If I did not know better, I could have sworn that I just witnessed a gathering of all animals celebrating an event. Goodness, what am I thinking? I must be losing my mind and going crazy. I must speak to Sarah and Shams; hopefully, they will believe me. I have had a full week of a program to slaughter these creatures; I do not think I can go through this."

He kept very still until the coast was clear. When he could hear nothing but the comforting sounds of the katydids and crickets, he took note of the surrounding landmarks; one thing he observed was a tree with a startling amount of what seemed like chocolate quills in its trunk.

"I must try to take note of the number of my steps to the roadside and make my way back here again with Sarah and Shams," he said to himself.

As soon as he was out of sight and safely back on the roadside, he checked his phone and made a note that it was 5,547 steps, so just over a mile. He also made a note of his location and wished that he had been brave enough to mark his location earlier. He noticed a pub across the road and reckoned the location of the ceremony was about southwest from where he stood.

Hmm, the Dog and Gun, he thought. *I'll remember that.*

Looking at his phone and realising that it was just after six o'clock, he decided to grab a pint, have some tea, and try to piece together what he had just witnessed.

What Geoffrey was unaware of was that he, too, like High Lord Henry Hedgehog, was going to be very instrumental in this forthcoming war of the cull of the badgers.

The First Inscription

Be Guided by the Wisdom of Your High Lord, as He Is Your Chosen Leader

The National Farmers Union in England lobbied hard for a badger cull, as they believed the animals were spreading tuberculosis; the government agreed to pursue this policy, in spite of scientific evidence that culling the badgers would not have an impact on reducing the disease and disregarding the fact that the primary means of transmission is cattle to cattle. However, in Wales, they developed a program vaccinating the badgers and disputing the possibility of badgers transmitting bovine tuberculosis (BTB). In spite of all these facts, the government still pursued the cull, and the Department of Environment, Food, and Rural Affairs (DEFRA), headed by the ambitious Jeremy Fischer, campaigned for a big operation.

Geoffrey Grimes had just attained his bachelor of science in agriculture at the University of Lancaster, but much to his father's and grandfather's disappointment, he accepted a graduate position near Bristol with DEFRA. His entire family, going back to his great-great-grandparents, had worked on a large dairy farm in the lush countryside of Whitewell, a quaint hamlet in Bowland, up in the northwest of Lancashire. These farmlands, approximately nine square miles, belonged to the Duchy of Lancaster, and Geoffrey never understood why his family worked so hard as tenants on the farmlands, as all the proceeds benefitted HRH Queen Elizabeth.

The Grimes family were true royalists and totally dedicated to the

Crown and monarchy. Geoffrey was raised amongst commemorative plaques on the dado rail going back to the reign of Queen Victoria.

His mother, originally from Scotland, had her own opinion of the monarchy; inadvertently, she may have influenced Geoffrey not to feel as loyal to the royals as his grandparents would have preferred.

The day Geoffrey announced he accepted his job, Luke, his dad, said in his thick Lancastrian accent, "I carnnot work out why you car'nt stop up North and 'elp out on t'farm. T'whole family were in tears t'day you got your degree, and this is 'ow you trat us."

His father shook his head in disappointment and continued, "If I'd a-known you were goin' to let us down, I woulda put my foot down instead of letting you go swanning off to some fancy university. We always worked for t'Queen and her family, and she 'as always seen us right, but now my only son is going south and ending the family tradition."

Luke Grimes, a small man with a rotund stature and a weather-beaten complexion, was truly heartbroken, but Geoffrey's grandfather, old man Joseph, tall and lean with a slight hunch caused by old age, was even more upset.

He said in a hoarse whisper, "Son, you proper let us down, and now we will have to get your sister Gail running the farm for us, as we have nay choice. She should be getting some bairns in, whilst she has time."

Gail, Geoffrey's younger sister, was small and plump like her father; she looked at her brother affectionately, raised her eyebrow mockingly at her grandad's remark, and responded, "Don't you worry, Grandad. Mom has taught me a trick or two running the farm, and do not forget, is not our Queen a strong woman whom we work for on the farm?"

The whole family began laughing, and Joseph gave her a loving, toothless grin. For a moment, it took the sadness away from Geoffrey's leaving.

Geoffrey could not argue with his lovely family. All his life, he had seen how they honoured the Queen and regarded her as their leader and a role model of honour and integrity. Although he did not feel the loyalty or patriotism they did, he would never detract from the unquestionable respect they had for their leader.

The next morning, as he was getting ready to set off to Bristol, his mother insisted that he take her pride and joy, her white Golf GTi, which she called Zola.

"You be looking after my Zola," she said as she gave him a playful nudge. "I always knew you were eyeing her up." Mary hugged him and continued, "You don't be listening to your dad and grandad; just go make your mam proud of you. Working for the government and all, that is something that makes my heart burst with joy. I love ya, my gingernut. Now get going, and let me know when you arrive safely."

Mary was a good head taller than Luke. She was originally from the Outer Hebrides in Scotland, and Luke had fallen head over heels with this red-haired beauty, who was also a farmer's daughter. He brought her to the northwest twenty-five years ago, and she has remained the strong woman behind him. She was not just a wonderful wife but a loving, supporting, and caring mother of their two children.

Geoffrey gave her the biggest hug he could manage and made his way down south. He remembered how homesick he was, leaving home to live on the campus of Lancaster University, but this was his actual big move to becoming independent and away from his family. He was not quite sure what the job entailed, but he was ready to make a difference in his life and hoped one day, his grandfather and father would be proud of him.

Traffic down the M6 and eventually the M5 was horrendous. After four and a half hours, he finally arrived, exactly on time, for the orientation interview with Mr. Ollie Gunner, the head of the department.

Ollie had a very full head of hair with not one strand of it out of place; he was of medium stature and impeccably presented in a suit and tie. His whole demeanour was fastidious, and Geoffrey self-conscientiously wondered if he should have had a bit of a wash before the meeting.

Ollie looked at Geoffrey from head to toe and said, "Good afternoon, Mr. Grimes. I am delighted that you are on time and hope your journey was not too tiring. You are one of the twelve graduates we have recruited to form my squad; our mission is to eliminate these pests, the badgers. There are thousands, and I want the numbers severely reduced. Save going through everything individually, please read these brochures and kindly prepare this questionnaire for tomorrow, so I can assess how much you know about these animals. I assume from your background that you shoot and destroy the badgers up in the North to protect your cattle?"

Before he had a chance to answer, Ollie continued, "It does not really matter, because here in the south, we are taking charge of this whole ridiculous problem. Please avoid reading articles from the League.Org, Change.Org, and others, as I do not want any opposition in the operation room. You are basically one of us or simply out of this operation. Have I made myself clear?"

Once again, Geoffrey was not given a chance to respond but was dismissively told to report at nine in the morning in the operation room, where he would meet the rest of the squad.

At nine the next morning, Geoffrey arrived at the operation room; after reading his notes, he knew the key code to enter the door was "BTBK1LL." The other recruits arrived at the same time; they were of a similar age to himself. However, there was one recruit who was already in the operation room; he turned and looked smugly at all the others coming in, as if they were late. He was called Richard Nicks, and in no time several nicknames were assigned to this very unpleasant individual. Medium built with a good physique, it was obvious that he had trained at the gym regularly. He sat in the front row with a protein shake in his right hand and not once acknowledged any of the recruits coming in. Soon, all twelve recruits arrived and sat themselves meekly away from the front row, unlike Richard.

Five out of the twelve candidates were ladies, and an attractive redhead had caught Geoffrey's eye immediately, but sadly, she took one look at his full head of shocking red curls and heavily freckled face and only offered him a small polite smile. She was called Sarah MacBain. Geoffrey could not stop looking at her amazing, fiery hair. They began introducing themselves, and Geoffrey learnt Sarah had come all the way from Duddingston near Edinburgh; to his delight, he heard Sarah say that her family were caretakers of Holyrood Park, leading to the Palace of the Holyrood house, a place the Queen frequented on her trips to Scotland.

Hmm, Geoffrey thought, smiling to himself. *Just wait till I tell her about my family's royal commitments, a nice icebreaker.*

Another recruit, Shams Aziz from Birmingham, sat timidly in the back of the room. Geoffrey remembered how he was never invited to be a part of anyone's groups in his younger school days and so decided to sit next to him.

Ollie Gunner arrived with his hair swept into a perfect quiff and wearing a pristine suit and tie. Without any delay, he took his position at the front of the meeting room and said, "Good morning, everyone. After meeting all of you yesterday, I have no time to listen to you introducing yourselves to each other, so please just put these name tags on."

He began to give everyone a name tag, and when he saw Richard Nicks holding his shake, he said, "There is to be no breakfast dined in my operation room. Please ensure that no food or drink is ever brought into this room again."

Richard moved very uncomfortably in his seat, not sure as to whether he should get rid of his shake, but thought he had better sit still until instructed. The others all shared a small smile.

Ollie handed out a questionnaire and said he would return in ten minutes. Geoffrey wished he had read the literature thoroughly instead of his usual skimming. He felt that Ollie was somehow going to make him pay for his lack of diligence. Ollie returned with a projector and slides and carefully set up his presentation.

When he finished, he simply snapped, "Stop everybody and please exchange your papers and mark each other's work."

Without another word, he began to put all the answers on the board.

Geoffrey looked at Sham's immaculate handwriting and feared his partner could not read his dreadful illegible scribbles.

Geoffrey began ticking off everything as correct on Shams's worksheet, looked at Shams, and embarrassingly put his hands over his face.

Shams gave him a smile and deliberately turned Geoffrey's answer sheet upside down, as if it would help him read his scribbles better, and in that moment, they instantly hit it off and became friends. It goes without saying that Shams had got the best score, much to Richard's disappointment, who was awarded second place, followed by Sarah.

After Ollie reviewed the answer sheets, he turned to Geoffrey and smugly asked him if he was sure he understood why he had applied for the position at DEFRA.

"I hope you realise that we are very serious about this operation and its success to improve the environment."

Ollie then began presenting a series of slides depicting evidence of tracking down badger tracks, and the presentation totally enraptured

Geoffrey's interest. He was fascinated by the intensity of Ollie's knowledge and expertise.

Ollie impressed the team with his amazing detective work of tracking down badgers and his overwhelming knowledge of their lifestyle and habits. The team soon learnt what intellectual animals they were, literally with rules of organisation and hygiene within a sett. Food was never allowed within a sett, fresh hay was brought into a sett once a month, and they made their litter outside the sett, like a communal latrine. He also pointed out that older setts were generally unused and were mostly occupied by foxes and rabbits, so it was important to notice what footprints they were observing when tracking the badgers.

Geoffrey was intrigued by these creatures and loved everything he was learning about them, but he was uncomfortable about the cold nature that Ollie displayed towards culling these animals.

Ollie said, "There is an explosive increase in these animals, and they are reducing the hedgehog population and endangering the bees. Most important, the farmers have implored us to reduce their numbers as we believe that they are transmitting tuberculosis to cattle. I am sorry, but my vote goes to saving the cattle."

Sarah raised her hand and asked, "Why can't we offer the vaccination to the badgers, like they do in Wales?"

Ollie hissed slowly and said, "Your job, young lady, is to help track the badgers and report their location so we can set the traps. If that is a problem, please leave now, as I consider this is a foolproof operation, and I do not want any interference in my mission. We believe there are at least ten thousand badgers within an area of 300 square kilometres, and I want all of you to help me make sure it is down to five thousand as soon as possible. In fact, my target is to eliminate five thousand within six weeks."

There was a very silent gulp amongst all the recruits, except for the smarmy Richard, who responded, "Yes, sir."

Ollie looked across Richard with an approving smile and thought, *Yes, this one has redeemed himself. I can see a lot of myself in him.*

Turning to the rest of the group, he continued, "I am dividing you into three groups. Mr. Shams Aziz, you had the highest score, so I want you to team up with Mr. Richard Nicks, Miss Sarah MacBain, and please can you accommodate the weakest link, Mr. Geoffrey Grimes. I have read his CV, which appeared very promising, so I hope some of your discipline rubs off onto him."

He looked around and continued, "Darren Whitworth, I would like you the head the group and please team up with Andrew Morris, Beth Greenwood, and Rita Mesina, is it?"

A young woman smiled broadly and said in her rich Ukrainian accent, "Mosina, Mr. Gunner."

"Apologies, Miss Mosina, I hope everything is clear in my instructions and correctly interpreted by you, as I appreciate that English is your second language."

"Crystal, Mr. Gunner," she replied with a polite smile, as she looked directly at this condescending person.

Both Darren and Andrew graduated together at Nottingham. Beth seemed very timid and quickly latched onto Rita.

Ollie reviewed the list of recruits and continued, "Martin Caton, Dan Morley, Jade Gardner, and Maria Cox, you are team three, and by no means does this suggest that you are the weakest link. You have not been selected by qualification, as at this moment, you are all equal recruits, but I am a man about results, and I will soon be recognising only those with results. Martin, I would like you to be the team leader."

Before Martin had a chance to respond, Maria, a very bubbly and confident girl, asked politely, "Mr. Gunner, is there a reason why none of the girls have been chosen to head a team?"

Without disguising his feelings towards her, Ollie responded smugly, "Miss Feminist, the positions will be rotated as the weeks go by."

Completely taken by surprise, Maria started to say something, but Ollie continued, "Let's take a recess for thirty minutes so you can acquaint yourselves with your groups."

Maria looked around and said sarcastically, "Nice to know we have an such inspiring leader."

The groups left the room, but the consensus of each group was that they were very disappointed with their leader. They all felt the same, apart from Richard Nicks.

The Second Inscription

Respect and Love Yourself, for without This, You Will Never be Able to Love Others

With the three groups now assigned, Ollie spread out a large map of the southwest of England on the white board. Using a large red marker, he circled approximately ten areas. He then turned to his teams and said, "We believe that county Brocklehurstshire is rife with badgers; for all those not from around here, you can gather from the map that all the various town names, that is Brockley, Brockhall, Brockville, Brock whatever, indicate that badgers live in the area."

"Why is that, Mr. Gunner?" asked Jade, a beautiful but very timid girl.

"Because, Miss Gardner, the word *badger* is believed to derive from 'Brock.' Have I enlightened you today?"

Jade's face brightened into a deep blush, and Maria gave her a sympathetic look and mouthed the word "mean." This put a smile on Jade's face, but unfortunately, their communication was observed by Ollie.

He looked at the two girls and snapped, "I do hope I have recruited two adults as opposed to two children, but if you would rather leave the room or stand in a corner, that would suit me fine."

Ollie did not realise that apart from Richard Nicks, all the other recruits were building up a resentment towards his harsh, dismissive attitude.

Continuing to make bold red marks on the map, he encircled the area once more and continued, "This is what we term the pilot zone; the entire southwest is infested with them, and we need to reduce this badger population."

Without an ounce of remorse, he continued, "Well, today, February 7, 2014, my other division advised me that in the last half hour in Brockley, we managed to trap about thirty to forty badgers, including a young cub; like taking candy from a baby."

He smirked under his breath but loud enough for all to hear and continued, "Might as well end its life now, before it starts breeding. Traps have been set within a hundred-kilometre radius, so I hope to have trapped at least five hundred today, and there's another four thousand five hundred to go. With your training of tracking them down and the second squad setting the traps, I am … I mean, we are going to hit our target in no time."

Once again, Sarah raised her hand and asked, "What happens to the badgers once they are trapped?"

Ollie gave her an undisguised look of disapproval and asked, "What do you think happens? Do you think we put them up for adoption?"

Richard interjected with a laugh and replied on Ollie's behalf, "They are gassed or shot, whichever is easiest or cheapest."

This sent a shiver down Sarah's spine, and she began to question why she had ever signed up for this job. She looked across at Geoffrey and could sense that he too felt uncomfortable, and as they both caught each other's glances, they decided to discuss more of what they had just learnt together.

After Ollie Gunner finished what he called his morning drill, he announced, "Right, I have given all of you your assignments, and we will meet up next Friday. I now must bid you adieu, as I have a live television interview with ITV later this afternoon. So see you in our next meeting, where I hope you will have some good news to report to me. I want GPS locations and no excuses; a full week concentrating on your assignments should be very fruitful."

Shams turned to his newly assigned team and suggested they discuss a plan of action for next week. Richard arrogantly said he had some ideas he would like to put forward, but Sarah made it quite clear that Shams was the team leader, and all plans were finalised by him.

Shams thanked her for her support and said to meet in an hour at the Costa Café next to the BP station across the road.

Sarah was walking just behind Geoffrey and speeded up to walk next to him and Shams. She instinctively felt she should be careful of any comments she made in front of Richard, but somehow, she felt she could trust Geoffrey and Shams.

She thought she would test the waters and said, almost sheepishly, "So guys, what do you think of Hitler?"

Geoffrey was gobsmacked that she was being so friendly; he just stopped and looked at her without responding.

Shams turned and said, "Yes, he does seem somewhat militant in how he addresses us. Anyway, see you in half an hour."

Sarah responded, "Yes, see you shortly." She turned to Geoffrey and said, "I was referring more to his genocide approach to the badgers."

Geoffrey was just about to make his response when Richard caught up with them, so he quickly changed the subject.

"I have always been lactose-intolerant and love the soya latte at Costa. It's fabulous, and I can finally enjoy an alternative milk latte."

Sarah smiled and played along, saying, "What a coincidence, I am also lactose-intolerant. I'll give it a try based on your recommendation."

Richard caught up and did not even say hello; he reluctantly sat down, saying, "So, where's our leader? Checking that his Maserati is still intact?"

"What?" Sarah asked.

"Haven't you seen that flashy motor on the campus?" Richard asked smugly. "Like to know how his family made that kind of money."

Geoffrey sensed the tension and said pleasantly, "Well, which one of you will join me for a soya latte?

Sarah smiled, replying, "I will, please." Turning to Richard, she added, "Well, I think he is the most down-to-earth person I have met, and now that I know that that is his motor, I am certainly going to ask for a spin in it."

Richard gruffly replied, "Probably just a daddy's boy."

The conversation came to an end as Shams made his way towards them, oblivious of the tittle tattle that just expired. Shams was very much a leader in the making. Tall, slim, and despite being impaired with a slight lisp, he was very well spoken. He arrived with printed-off maps designating a specific area for each team member. Shams always removed his glasses when he addressed anyone, as it made him feel more comfortable if he could not make out their faces looking directly at him.

Shams meekly addressed his team and said, "Guys, it's been great to be assigned leader of our team, but I am very much of the attitude and belief that we are all equal. I do not regard myself better than any of you and want us to work closely together. Geoffrey, I believe you have a farming background. Have you any personal knowledge regarding the badgers infecting your cattle?"

Geoffrey responded, "To be honest, the only problem we ever had up north was the foot-and-mouth disease."

Richard rudely interrupted, "What's our past or background got to do with any of this? We all have been given a specific task, and that's to track the badgers."

Sarah turned to Richard and said politely, "I think it's good to know what kind of experience we can bring to the table, so I'd like to know a little about you. What's your background?"

Richard sheepishly responded, "Er, my mother sells shoes in Torquay, and like I said, I can't see how it should affect me being here."

He shifted vey uneasily in his chair and grew anxious at the questions.

"Not at all, Richard," Sarah said. "I don't understand why you are being so sensitive. One would think you had a secret personal mission."

"Everybody, let us just calm down," Shams said. "Richard, what did you have to share with us that you mentioned earlier?"

With a big grin on his face, and now feeling in command of the team, Richard looked around carefully, lowered his voice, and leaned into the group, whispering, "Well, considering we are to hunt them out, and that Ollie is expecting good figures, my uncle knows someone who owns several Jack Russell terriers who could sniff them out."

Sarah stood up and nearly knocked him down, shouting, "We are not badger baiting, and that is final; it's not what we're here for."

Shams and Geoffrey unanimously agreed with her, and Shams turned to Richard and said, "Let's stick with the agenda and remember that our job is just to track the evidence of their whereabouts."

Looking concerned, he continued, "Richard, I suggest that you do not attempt to sniff them out. I come from a place called Bordesley, where we have a problem with urban badgers. I cannot really call it a problem, as some of my friends and neighbours feed them in spite of the large holes they create in their gardens. But what I wanted to say is that the badgers are quite big, up to about eighteen kilos, and gallop quickly, so you really do not want to endanger yourself. They are magnificent, and my neighbours have actually said they tap on their back doors for food. They actually enjoy looking out for them."

Richard looked at them and sinisterly thought to himself, *Don't preach me about the dangers. I know full well what these animals are capable of.*

"Oh, my goodness, that's incredible," said Sarah. "I am meeting up with a friend, whose parents do just that. I've been hoping for an invite so I can see an actual badger."

Shams continued, "The most important thing I want to stress is for us to work together. I feel that safety in numbers is key, so I suggest that we work together all week next week, and when we understand the tracks better, then we can split up into two groups."

"Agreed," Sarah said, looking directly at Geoffrey to make quite clear that she refused to be partnered with Richard.

Shams did not miss the blatant hint that Sarah made and continued, "Well, considering it's Friday afternoon, shall we call it a day, as I need to visit the mosque. Let's meet up on Monday here at Costa at nine in the morning. I have seen the boardroom timetable and noticed that Mr. Gunner has blocked the meeting room on Friday next week at three in the afternoon, so I am assuming that will be when he wants to see us. It would be great for us to be prepared with some information and give him some definite co-ordinates and sightings."

Geoffrey turned to Shams, who smiled and said, "Don't worry, Shams, I will not let you down, and even OG will be so impressed with me."

They all laughed except for Richard, who stood up before Shams said the meeting was over and was out the door without even as much as a goodbye.

"Well, he was in a hurry," Sarah said, making her feelings towards Richard quite clear. Turning to Shams and Geoffrey, she asked what their plans were for the weekend.

Shams reminded her that he was going to the mosque, and Geoffrey said he had no plans. Shams sensing a chemistry building between Sarah and Geoffrey, smiled and said, "Well, I will leave the two of you to it and hope you enjoy the weekend."

Geoffrey went into such a deep blush as soon as Shams left but felt this was actually a chance to ask Sarah out, so he said, "Do you want to go for a drink somewhere?"

Sarah felt genuinely upset for letting him down and replied, "I am so sorry, Geoffrey; can I take a rain check on that? I am meeting a friend who lives in Bristol, and I said I'd make my way there this evening so I could be back early Sunday. Like I said earlier, his family has a big garden, and he told me that when the sun sets about four, the badgers come into their garden and eat the fruit that his parents leave out for them. I just want to see them. I am so excited."

Sensing the awkwardness that Geoffrey was assuming her friend was a boyfriend of a romantic nature, she continued, "Why won't you come as well? Freddie would not mind at all."

Sarah could not understand why she was feeling the need to clarify the fact that Freddie was just a friend. She nearly spelt it out that Freddie was her gay best friend from the University of Newcastle.

"Oh, no, not at all," Geoffrey said. "I could not impose. I am actually still exhausted from that long drive yesterday, and we have had so much to take in these last two days, so I think I'll just chill out and read my notes that I should have done yesterday. I cannot let Shams down; he seems to be a great guy."

"Yes, lovely and very intelligent," Sarah replied. She then looked at Geoffrey and said, "Well, let's catch up on Sunday evening for a quick drink, and I will tell you about the badgers; that is, if any show up. I really do want to chat about Ollie Gunner, so please say yes."

Geoffrey smiled and said, "Of course. I would love to. Let me walk you to your car."

He walked Sarah to her car and made his way to his own car, smiling and already looking forward to seeing her on Sunday evening. He was keen on getting back to his room, as he was in total rapture of these amazing animals and wanted to do as much research on them as he could.

Hmm, need to go through my notes, he thought. *These badgers have got me totally intrigued.* He then looked at the map Shams handed to him and said to himself, "Fascinating."

Geoffrey walked across the road to the retail park, where his car was parked. As he walked past Curry's PC World, a big electronic entertainment departmental store, he caught a glimpse of Ollie Gunner on about ten television screens inside the shop.

He walked in and heard Ollie Gunner saying amidst a protesting crowd, "This morning, I met with my twelve new recruits, whom I have termed my squad. Together, our mission is to eliminate five thousand badgers within the next six weeks, and I cannot see any obstacles in our way. My target is secured."

Geoffrey left the shop and began to walk back to his car. He switched on his ignition and looked at the fuel gauge.

Oh dear, he thought. *I am running very low on fuel. I best fill up.*

He drove back across to the BP station, and as he was filling up his car, a pale, pasty-faced man walked past him. As he turned to walk into the shop to pay, much to his surprise, Geoffrey saw a large, white badger make his way round the station back into the woods.

"Blimey," he said. "A white albino badger, like Ollie was explaining this morning. Oh, my goodness. What an amazing coincidence. Wait till I tell the rest of the team.

He stepped back out and walked around the back to see where it had gone, but as Shams said, they were quick, and in an instant, it was gone into the woods.

With a big smile on his face, he walked into the shop and said to the fuel attendant, "Just seen a badger."

The fuel attendant grimaced and grunted, "Seventy-two pounds. Please enter your pin. Vermin, as far as I am concerned."

"Are there many of them here?" Geoffrey continued.

"They are all over, but the sneaky sods know how to cover their tracks. Can't wait for that Ollie Dollie to sort them out."

Geoffrey paid and left the shop, smiling and saying to himself, "Ollie Dollie, ha ha."

The Third Inscription

Work Together for the Benefit of the Forest
07.02 in the Year 2014

On this lovely Friday morning in February, in spite of the crisp chill in the air, the newly born cubs were frisking in the fields, smelling the flowers and sneezing from the pollen on the blossoms. There were some less fortunate ones who were running back to their mothers, crying with bee-stung snouts, only for their mothers to say that that will teach them a lesson, not to poke their noses into the unknown. For now, it was all about play, but these were the first steps for these cubs to become future warriors and leaders.

The High Lady, Molly, Sparkly, and Sally were all busy preparing for the saining ceremony next Friday and were slowly and carefully extracting the sap from the bacacia trees. It was important to get enough so as not to damage the trunks. They then had to gently sift it into the ceremonial font, crushing juniper berries into the sap and mixing it with their own musk, allowing it to set into a pliable gel. This process needed a week to be perfected, so today, it was important to ensure that the sacred sap was processed and ready to be gently rubbed onto each cub's forehead next week. The High Lady was compelled to participate in this process, as the sacred bacacia would not release its sap unless drawn by a spiritual leader or his sow. The High Lady's claws were quite sore with the gentle but strong scratching of the thick bark, but even after four continuous hours, she never once complained.

Brit, Brooke, and Bellatrix went more afar to gather as much food as possible for the celebration. Bellatrix, who was astoundingly beautiful, with her fiery red pelt, was stronger and faster than any of the other sows and gathered twice as many earthworms, nuts, and berries. Brit and Brooke tried hard to keep up and finally begged her to slow down.

"Bellatrix, you are embarrassing us," Brit said. "Please wait."

Brooke joked, "You are just showing off."

Bellatrix replied, "Sorry, girls, but living with Widejaw is one constant living exercise routine. "

The sows all laughed, imagining Widejaw commandeering a militant routine within their sett, and the three little cubs standing to attention. Bellatrix continued laughing and said, "You may laugh, but he never switches off."

Brit turned to Bellatrix and said, "Why don't you start a keep fit class? It would be great for all of the sows to get together and have some fun instead of just having this one day when we all work together."

Bellatrix laughed and said, "You know, Brit, that is a wonderful idea; it's time we did more things together. It's a shame that we are all living together, yet we still do things separately as different pelt colours, except for this one event every year."

Brooke replied, "I could not agree more. I will definitely put a little seed of thought into my dear sweet Wisepaw's ears. He is wonderful, and I thank our ancestors for coupling him with me. "

Brit and Bellatrix smiled, and Brit looked at the little cubs and said, "That's the best way to start. They are so innocent. Look at them; they know no difference or distinction and are not bothered about the colour of their pelts, just having a great time together. How wonderful. Now truly is a time for big changes."

Filled with a new sense of unity, the sows carried the food slowly back to the others.

The High Lord Luminous was nowhere to be seen today, but his clan knew that his absence meant he was away in the land of man.

That morning, the High Lord walked to the edge of the woods and arrived at his portal, a place called BP, which we know to be a fuel station. He lumbered over to a giant burgundy cup with the words COSTA on it, and as he knelt, he began to scratch the ground, whilst chanting the sacred words, *"Sekarang saya jadi orang."*

He transformed into a man of small stature with extremely pale skin, wiry thick hair, and beady little eyes. With his white loose attire and waddling gait, he crossed the street and walked into the big bright shop called Currys. There were huge screens with pictures and voices. Beautiful plants and animals were on the screens, but the High Lord had learnt that he could use a small gadget to change the screen and search for the news. The sale assistants knew to ignore him, calling him a time-waster, as they all knew this pale, beady-eyed man only came in to change the channels and listen to the news.

Adam, one of the sales assistants saw him enter the shop and told his colleagues, "Alert! Alert! That strange musk-smelling man walked in."

All the other colleagues laughed and avoided the man, whom we know as the High Lord Luminous Snowspirit.

This did not perturb the High Lord; he was glad to be left alone. Today, he had learnt that besides Andy May, a famous musician who was against the cull, two other men, Barry Odie and Manuel Gonzalez, were actively creating communities, campaigns, and petitions pushing to protect and conserve the badger population. The High Lord felt a sense of reassurance that all was not lost, and it was so wonderful that these man cared and were trying to help.

He watched as the news presenter reported, "Change.org, the world's platform for change, announced 326,000 new signatures on the recent petition to renounce the cull. The League.Org, another supporting organisation, is also gaining more opposition to the cull, and with the increased resistance and high levels of social media, the Department of Environment, Food, and Rural Activities, commonly referred to as DEFRA, is under severe pressure to rethink their current campaign."

However, in the next television clip, the press was interviewing Ollie Gunner, who said arrogantly, "This morning, I met with my twelve new recruits whom I have termed my squad. Together, our mission is to eliminate five thousand badgers within the next six weeks, and I cannot see any obstacles in our way. My target is secured."

The crowd of farmers sent up a massive cheer in support of Ollie Gunner; also in the crowd were a group of opposing activists from the League.Org and other people who were upset about the campaign, shouting, "Cruelty! Murder!"

Ollie ignored the resistance and smiled as they were roughly pushed aside by the police. He continued, "We are ready and prepared. Our first target area is in the surrounding county of Brockley. Traps have been set, and I am, I mean, we are happy to report that we have just received results of a successful entrapment."

More jeers and protests broke out from the opposing crowd.

"This is pure cruelty and inhumane," shouted Barry Odie, leader of the League.Org.

Ollie could see that the loudest protest came from a gaggle of activists in the far right, and when he looked harder, he realised it was Andy May, the famous rock star from Her Majesty. He was making a lot of noise and had a strong following.

Ollie could hear Andy shout, "Save the badger! Stop the cull! Save the badger! Stop the cull." Andy and his supporters continued to chant as they were pushed aside, away from the cameras.

Sadly, their cries were muffled by the rising cheers of the farmers supporting the cull. These farmers voluntarily helped to fund the cull, so DEFRA were meeting all their demands.

It was approaching three in the afternoon, and the sun would soon be setting. The High Lord decided it was best to return to the forest. He left the shop and returned to his portal across the road. Filled with an alarming sense of grief, he had to return to his clans to tell them of the disparaging news he had just heard.

He crouched down and chanted, "Sekarang saya jadi binatang."

Orbs of light surrounded him, and within a minute, the High Lord transformed back into a badger and carefully made his way towards the woods.

Back in the colony, Clawdigger, Pharmacia, and Flash were creating the seating arrangements for next week's saining ceremony. It was going to be a big congregation of all the colonies and the friends of the forest. Clawdigger was an engineering genius when it came to infrastructure. He masterminded an ideal setup of concentric circles going up into the treeline. He wanted the birds to umbrella the top, creating a canopy for that evening.

The ceremony at LOJAP was near a small stream, so the otters and polecats could attend and be seated near water. They brought in a lot of hay and old leaves and twigs for the little cubs to rest through the long ceremony, and whilst Clawdigger, Pharmacia, and Flash galloped as fast as they could back and forth, Bodger was nowhere to be seen.

However, he could be heard joking and laughing with the foxes, rabbits, polecats, and weasels. Bodger was the landlord of the colony, and it was his role to lease out the unused and old setts to these animals in return for fresh food as their rent. However, on most occasions, he accepted decayed fruit as payment, purely for himself, which was forbidden. The decayed fruit produced alcohol, which resulted in intoxication, and this was against the inscriptions of the colony.

Clawdigger shouted in frustration, "Where are you Bodger? We could really do with your help here."

"Calm down, old friend," Bodger replied, winking at the weasels and foxes. "I am working here, sorting out new leaseholds."

He eventually turned up to assist, but in no time, the others felt it was better when he was out of their way as his sluggish, lethargic assistance was more annoying than helpful.

Widejaw and his warriors were monitoring the perimeters of the forest, looking out for unusual or suspicious activity, whilst Wisepaws was in a tizzy, with the cubs running about and enjoying just being cubs.

"Okay, little ones, can we please have one more rehearsal?" Wisepaws shouted as loudly as he could.

Widejaw was not very far away, as one of his responsibilities was to watch over Fire, the little heir, and seeing that Wisepaws's commands were barely being acknowledged, he gave a stronger, louder command which caught the attention of the cubs and brought them to a halt.

Wisepaws did not appreciate his position undermined, but he merely said, "Okay, cubs, ten more minutes in this lovely sunshine, and then you must all return to the nursery."

With squeals of delight, the cubs ran havoc once again, tumbling and chasing each other.

Fire Snowspirit was close by his sibling White Snowspirit, whilst Snowdrop and Glisten stood as closely as they could, watching Widejaw's cubs play-fighting as warriors. He approached the High Lord's cubs and stood amongst them with a keen eye on his own cubs.

White turned to him and said politely, "I am looking after Fire, Councillor Widejaw; you can do your other jobs."

Taken back by the young cub's maturity, he smiled and said, "You are a wonderful sibling, White, and I am proud to see what good care you are giving Fire."

Fire was the youngest of the High Lady's litter and was quite a weak cub. The cubs had to take turns with their feed, but White always insisted that Fire went first, and she made sure that he was full before letting the others feed from her mother. The High Lady was so touched by White's love for young Fire and often said to her, "White, you will make a very fine High Lady one day, as your heart is pure and white, just as we named you."

On the other hand, Clawdigger Junior, the eldest cub of Clawdigger and Brit Clawdigger, enjoyed being the head of the litter and the attention he got from his mother being the only male cub. His siblings quickly ganged up against him, playing tricks whilst he was asleep. They would put flowers and berries around his head and laugh when the bees stung him. In spite of being just a young cub himself, he would play all the games with his siblings and always let them win, all but Speed, whom he knew wanted proper competition. His siblings idolised him, and even at such a young age, he gathered a lot of respect from the other younger cubs.

Mercury, Dynamite, and Bojana, the fiery little cubs of Widejaw and Bellatrix, also played amongst themselves, and it was quite sad how they felt they were different from the rest of the clan. Like the High Lord's cubs, pelts of a different colour played amongst themselves, which made them a very minority group.

The red cubs sparred with each other under Widejaw's watchful eye; he chuckled to see Bojana, his female cub, beat her siblings all the time. After a while, instigated by Molly, Pharmacia, Buzz, Bawson, and their little siblings Minx and Mindy came to join them. The fiery red cubs stopped in their tracks and looked confused as they were told constantly they were not allowed to play with pelts unlike themselves.

Widejaw thought, *Hmmm, American badgers, always a rule to themselves, but we live in new times today.* And with that thought in mind, he gave an approving nod to his cubs and smiled hesitatingly at Pharmacia.

Mercury, Dynamite, and Bojana looked at each other and with a massive squeal played with the black-and-white cubs as if they had known each other forever. Within seconds, White led her siblings into the circle of fun, and the screams and shouts sounded like a bonfire of fireworks going off. The other cubs heard the excitement and joined in the fun without hesitation.

As Brit, Brooke, and Bellatrix arrived back at the colony and saw all the cubs playing together, they looked at each and held their paws together, saying that now they were truly all one clan, working together.

Wisepaws came out from the nursery and saw all the cubs playing together; in all his years as head of academia, he never felt a greater moment of pride.

He shouted as loud as he could, "Okay, cubs, your ten minutes are up. Now let us see who can run fastest into the nursery."

Wisepaws counted the cubs as they returned to the nursery; Fire and White were the last ones in, and he realised that Little Clawdigger was missing. Leaving the cubs under strict instruction to practise being quiet for ten minutes, he went out to look for Widejaw.

The sows happily walked to their boars, discussing what a happy day and a new beginning today was going to bring, when all of a sudden, Brit looked around, and her heart skipped a beat as she saw Widejaw and Wisepaws looking anxious as they walked towards her and Clawdigger.

Trying not to panic, she pulled away from the crowd and started to look for her son. Slowly losing her composure, she began to shout, "Junior! Junior!"

With no response, she began screaming, "Junior! Where are you? Please come back now; this isn't funny. Junior! Clawdigger Junior."

Clawdigger, Flash, and Pharmacia walked a little farther into the woods to look for Little Clawdigger but stopped when they saw the High Lord approach them with his head lowered.

The High Lord felt limp and swallowed deeply as Ollie Gunner's words ran through his mind: "Traps have been set, and … we just received results of a successful entrapment."

He summoned Widejaw and whispered what he had heard on the news, and in an instant, Widejaw and his warriors galloped off through the fields.

The High Lord took both Brit and Clawdigger into his arms and told them what he had heard.

Brit and Clawdigger stood in shock and horror as their worst nightmare began to unfold.

Widejaw returned from his inspection of where the incident had happened as advised by the High Lord, and in his calmest demeanour began, "I am so sorry, Brit and Clawdigger, but there are traps out there, and little Clawdigger and several elderlies are in the traps." Before he could continue, Brit collapsed and screamed, "No, not my Clawdigger."

Clawdigger felt paralysed and asked quietly, "Where is he, Widejaw? Where is my cub?"

"I am so sorry, Clawdigger, I cannot let you see him."

Widejaw had to restrain Clawdigger, who shoved past him and his warriors, fighting to get through to find his cub.

Widejaw held him firmly and said, "I am so sorry, Clawdigger, but we must leave now, or else we will endanger the entire colony."

The High Lord approached Brit and Clawdigger and gently coaxed them back to the sett.

"Come, my dear ones, come and let the warriors do their job," their leader said gently, feeling every ounce of pain the poor Clawdiggers were feeling.

The warriors gathered as many branches as they could and brushed away all traces of their tracks. Even Bodger pulled his weight; after recovering from the shock of the horrific loss, he summoned his friends, the rabbits, weasels, polecats, and foxes, to help the warriors make new tracks to put men off their tracks. The birds and forest animals helped collect twigs, big leaves, and branches to conceal the venue for next week's celebration, and all the animals worked till late into the night to ensure the venue was hidden.

Once Widejaw was confident that the venue was secured, he made his way back; with a sunken heart, he looked at the outskirts of the forest and said tearfully, "I am so sorry for letting you down, little Clawdigger. I should have been there looking out for you. I failed you, young one, but promise I will never let your father and mother know how you were cruelly left to die in those traps. You are now with our ancestors; be at peace, dear little one, but I will avenge your death."

Widejaw knelt and scratched the ground and asked the ancestors to take the spirits of their lost ones with them.

"Ancestors, give me the strength to look out for my clans, and I beg the forgiveness of the elderlies and young ones who we let down today."

What started as such a beautiful day to a new beginning, working in unity as one, ended with a deeper resolution to stand together and bring this cruelty to an end.

The Fourth Inscription

Obey Your Parents, as They Only Mean to Protect and Guide You

A group of elderly badgers huddled together in their usual tranquil spot; high above, clouds that looked like half-melted marshmallows that were whipped by the swirling winds across the crisp blue sky. Sitting happily and content in their usual rendezvous, hemmed between the fields and peaks, they began reminiscing their old days as they basked in the winter's sun.

Grand Artemis stretched his paws and began one of his tales that he had repetitively recited on every occasion:

"Just as the ferocious dog came down the sett, I was ready and waiting for him. When he turned on me, I opened my jaw and trapped him in one swift movement, and all I could hear was his small yelp."

The other older badgers chipped in their tales whilst chewing on some old hay and honeybee combs. These honeybee combs had been allowed to ferment and so had an inebriating effect if consumed in excess, but these elderly badgers were all retired and earned the reward of a small consumption to relax on this lovely afternoon. Each of their tales recited were greater and more exciting than the last.

Little Clawdigger had been told a million times by his parents to stay close by the colony, but he decided he wanted a bit of an adventure today. He could hear the chuckles and throaty coughs of the older badgers, and his curiosity led him towards a big holly bush in front of their gathering. As he clumsily peered in between the holly bush, he pricked his small snout on the sharp-edged leaves and let out a small yelp, "Ouch! My nose."

One of the older badgers pricked up his ears and called out, "Who is behind those bushes?"

Little Clawdigger peeked around the bush and meekly replied, "I am sorry. I have been naughty looking for an adventure, and now I am lost."

Pretending to be angry, Grand Stuart raised his voice and asked, "And why aren't you working with your family in the fields?"

Little Clawdigger, trying so hard not to cry, replied, "I'm so sorry. I just wanted to see what was going on here."

He then looked at the older badgers, who all seemed to be very crossed with him, and his eyes filled with tears, and he began to cry.

"Now, then," Grand Artemis said. "There is no need to cry; come and sit with us, and tell us where you are from."

In between his small sobs, Little Clawdigger stuttered, "Mama s-s-said I must never s-s-speak to strangers."

"Mama is right, young one," the older badger said, "but after we tell you who we are, you can tell us who you are. I am Grand Artemis, and this is Grand Stuart, Grand Victor, and last but not least, Grand Alexandria."

Little Clawdigger began to smile and asked, "Why do you all have the same name, Grand? I am just Clawdigger Junior, and my papa is …"

But before he could finish, one of the older badgers interrupted and said, "Ah, you are Clawdigger's and Brit's little one."

They began to hug and squeeze him, saying what an honour it was to meet the cub of the greatest civil engineer in all the colony.

"We were looking forward to seeing you at the saining next week," Grand Artemis said.

Beaming with delight, he continued, "We are all called Grand because we are very old and allowed to retire and enjoy the day with no responsibilities. One day, you will enjoy such a luxury. But for now, come sit with us and chew on some hay."

Little Clawdigger looked with interest at the honeybee combs, but before he could say anything, the older badgers unanimously laughed, and Grand Artemis said, "Not today, young one. Since it's only three hours before sunset, we will set off and accompany you back to your clan, as we do not know what danger lies ahead for such a young one."

Sarah arrived at Freddie's house about four o'clock that afternoon. He lived with his parents, in a large, detached stone house with a balcony flanking off the lounge, overlooking a magnificent garden. Both his parents were retired, enthusiastic gardeners who loved nature. The garden was landscaped so that the banks contoured gently into the stream that flowed by their house. The banks were supported by swales which acted as bowls to hold the water. A variety of grasses, comfrey, berry bushes, and herbs clung onto the sides, whilst delicate early purple petunias, primroses, violets, pansies, and snowdrops stumbled and fell carelessly onto the next step.

A wooden bridge made of old pallets yet designed with an Asian flavour flanked from one end of the stream to the other, with an ornate gazebo built across the other end of the stream. Chinese lanterns, lit by small bulbs, hung off the pergola by the side of the gazebo, and a small chiminea was kindling a fire. As Sarah entered the lovely lounge with an immediate view of this breathtaking garden, Freddie's parents gently waved her to come and join them on the balcony.

"Nice to meet you, Sarah," said Mrs. Odie, Freddie's mum, tapping the seat next to her for Sarah to sit on. "I am Ann and so glad to finally put a face to a name."

Ann was a statuesque lady with big blue eyes framed behind a pair of designer tortoiseshell glasses. She had just a hint of blush on her cheeks, and her blonde hair was casually swept back by a simple Alice band. Sarah was totally in awe of her effortless beauty and elegance.

Her husband, Barry, was a tall, handsome silver fox; he walked towards Sarah and said, "I'm Barry; would you like a glass of wine?"

"Yes please," she replied.

Sarah was overwhelmed with excitement as Ann explained how the badgers appeared just before sunset every evening, knowing there will be vegetables and nuts left out for them.

"How many come out?" Sarah asked as she reached out for the glass of Sauvignon Blanc. "Ooh, lovely, thank you. New Zealand as well, my favourite."

"Well, we get as many as twenty sometimes," Barry said. "They come and take their food and lumber away. One night, Annie and I were out and came back half an hour later than usual, and can you believe it? One of them came tapping at the back door."

"Oh, my goodness," Sarah said, "only this morning, one of my colleagues was telling me exactly the same thing."

Barry continued, "Apparently, they are older ones, from what me and Annie have learnt, and I am surprised only six are out there tonight. There are generally more of them. Here, take my binoculars and watch how gently they come and take the food."

"Oh, they are beautiful," Sarah exclaimed. "Amazing. Freddie, come and look."

"Are you joking?" Freddie asked. "I have seen them all my life; you enjoy. My parents are badger spotters."

Sarah was excited to watch the badgers and said, "This is magnificent. I cannot wait to tell my colleagues."

"Lovely, Sarah," Ann said. "Freddie mentioned that you had taken a job down here; so what is it that you are doing?"

Without realising the consequences, Sarah replied, "I was accepted as one of the recruits for DEFRA."

Barry was aware of the recently promoted recruitment boasted by Ollie Gunner only this afternoon, and without hesitating, he stood up and snapped, "What? With Ollie Gunner? You are one of his squads?"

Ann and Freddie turned to Sarah, hoping this was not true.

Sarah replied sheepishly, "Yes, I am."

Barry said angrily, "I am sorry, Miss MacBain, but you must leave my home immediately. You are collaborating with a man we regard a butcher. Only an hour ago, he announced he had trapped dozens of these harmless animals, and you come in my home and say you want to witness the badgers coming into my garden. We are compassionate about these animals and wanted to share this beautiful experience with you, not teach you about their habits to enhance your job opportunities."

Sarah tried to explain that she did not agree with the way Ollie worked, but her words fell on deaf ears.

Ann turned and walked away, and Sarah thought she saw her cry as she left the room.

Freddie turned to his father and said, "I am so sorry, Dad. I honestly had no idea."

Freddie picked up Sarah's bag and walked her to the door. He said, "How could you take advantage of our friendship? I never thought to ask who you were working for, but you should have known that my dad leads the League.Org, supporting the petition to abolish the cull. Goodness, Sarah, didn't you do your homework?"

Without giving her a chance to explain herself, he opened the door and showed her out.

Sarah stood outside the door and broke into tears. Confused, she walked back to her car and began her drive back to the campus at DEFRA.

Geoffrey was feeling a little peckish after he filled his tank up and started thinking of his mother's meat and potato pie. He smiled as he reached out for his phone and called her number.

"Mum, how are you?" he said. "Only two days away, and I already miss your tattie pies."

"Aww, your mam is missing you too, gingernut," his mum said, "but I know you too well, so what's the real reason you are actually calling me?"

"Oh, I don't know," Geoffrey said. "I just feel so confused about the responsibilities of my new job."

"Give it some time, love," his mum said, "and if it's not right for you, you come home. You hear me?"

"Oh, I'll make the right decision, Mum. Anyway, there is a gorgeous girl in the same recruitment intake, so it is probably more interesting than I am leading you to believe."

"Brilliant! She must be something special, 'cause this is the first time you've ever mentioned a lass to me. Now you take care; you were always brought up to do the right thing, and I know that is exactly what you will do. Love you, son."

"Love you too, Mum."

After Geoffrey hung up, he thought about how uncomfortable he was with Ollie Gunner's methods. By now, he was starving and stopped in at the supermarket. His intention was just to grab a pizza and some bits, but he ended up spending a fortune.

"Goodness," he said, "that's the last time I am shopping when I am hungry."

Geoffrey went home, put his pizza in the oven, and went upstairs to grab a shower. He switched on the news, and just as he was dishing out his pizza, the doorbell rang.

Who could that be at this time of the night? Geoffrey wondered as he went to the door.

"Oh, Sarah, what are you doing here?" he said after opening the door.

He looked at her and was shocked to see her sobbing; she was distraught.

"Oh, my goodness, please come in. What has happened?"

Just as Sarah walked in, the newsreel from earlier in the day flashed onto the television screen, and she could see Barry Odie, clear as live, leading the protestors against Ollie Gunner.

"Oh, my goodness," she cried. "How could I have been so insensitive?"

"Calm down, Sarah," Geoffrey said. "What is going on?"

Sarah told him what had happened at Freddie's and how stupid she was not to have known Freddie's father was associated with the League. Org's campaign against the cull.

"I insulted my friend and his family, Geoffrey, and like an idiot, I didn't even put two and two together. I tried to tell them I was having doubts about what we're doing, but they just kicked me out."

"Sarah, listen, it's only been two days; we are all getting emotional. We'll have a full week next week, and we can think like professionals and assess the situation. Let's just sit down and have my delicious pizza I prepared earlier, with extra red peppers as fiery as your red hair."

With that, Sarah laughed, stopped crying, and sat down to eat with Geoffrey.

The old badgers slowly made their way to the Brockley Clan, and whilst they lumbered along, Little Clawdigger galloped back and forth, shouting, "I think I know the way. I think I know the way."

"Go on then," Grand Artemis shouted, but after a few minutes, he realised Little Clawdigger had gone astray.

Little Clawdigger started sniffing something that he could not define, but he knew he was starving, and these smelt incredibly good. They looked like tiny little pieces of wood but smelt so good, so Little Clawdigger started to eat them and followed the trail of this delicious food. (We know these as peanuts; the traps were set with them as bait to entice the badgers into a cage.)

"Where has the little mischief gone now?" Grand Alexandria asked.

"Clawdigger," they shouted.

"Over here," he squealed.

The atmosphere seemed a bit surreal to the old badgers, too silent for comfort. Suddenly, they heard Little Clawdigger release a loud yelp and screech, and as they began to run towards him, their paws were caught by foothold traps, and they found themselves unable to move. Within seconds, cages fitted with sharp knives came down from above and further trapped them in situ. The knives that came down in the cages sliced their bodies and faces. The animals screamed in pain and agony.

Bravely ignoring his severe pain, old Artemis shouted out to Little Clawdigger but received no response. Old Victor stretched his neck and shook his head, as he could see Little Clawdigger, lying limp in a cage with three or four other badgers, not moving at all and covered in blood. The four old badgers were immobile in a cage big enough for three but heroically held on to each other. As their lives slowly ebbed away, they could see dozens of other badgers that were all trapped and slowly tormented in this cruel manner.

Grand Artemis reached out to his friends and said softly, "To you we arrive, great ancestors, please bring little Clawdigger along with us."

When Widejaw arrived, the badgers were bleeding to death; he felt helpless, as there was nothing he could do. The kindest thing he and his warriors could do was to close the eyes of those who had died with them still opened. The warriors and Widejaw were filled with shock and horror at this brutal massacre. They approached the cage that held Little Clawdigger; he was lying limp in the trap, unaware of what had happened to him. Widejaw sat by the cage and held his little paw, as he knew his death was only minutes away.

He looked at the cub's confused eyes and said, "Today, you have become a hero, and your adventure is not over, as you will be going to see our ancestors, and they will tell you how brave you are. I will let your mother and father know how strong you have been, and I will look after them and your siblings for you. I am so sorry I did not see you leaving the field."

A small smile appeared on his face, and then his eyes lost all expression. Widejaw knew that life had left him; he released his paw and closed his eyes. He turned to see an elderly badger smile at him, in spite of his excruciating pain.

Old Artemis looked at Widejaw with a weak but brave smile. Widejaw commanded his warriors to all kneel down and honour the dying badgers.

Widejaw and his warriors scratched the ground with such vindication and begged their ancestors to take the dying badgers quickly, to end the cruelty inflicted on them. Widejaw turned and saw how brave and proud the dying badgers were. Despite their cruel and painful plight, not one was crying out for help, which would have endangered the colony. Maybe they just surrendered, as they knew it was the end. Widejaw could see that Grand Artemis was trying to say something. He got as close as he could to him, and the old badger was miming, "Peanuts," and darting his eyes at the ground. Widejaw nodded that he understood and stayed with him till his final moment.

After Widejaw and his warriors went round and comforted all the badgers in their last dying moments, he looked around and saw the trail of nuts and berries leading to the traps. He instructed his warriors to remove all the nuts and berries, and brush away all evidence of any badger tracks.

Badgers were coming from all directions to make their way to the saining ceremony in a week, and he did not want them lured to this execution site. The tracks were prominent as the older badgers were heavier, and their slower gait left very strong imprints of their tracks, so Widejaw and his warriors had to work very hard, covering them up with branches and leaves. Once Widejaw and his warriors carefully removed all the traces of the badgers and the enticing bait, they returned to the colony as fast as they could to report the tragic, brutal slaughter to their High Lord. There was a lot to do before the saining ceremony, and he needed to prepare a stringent security plan to ensure there were no disruptions for next Friday.

Later that afternoon, after his interview was aired and delighted with the reports he received, Ollie Gunner went into the woods to visit the site where he had organised the traps.

"Mr. Gunner, we have trapped about fifty to sixty badgers within the Brockley area," one of the squad members said, "and we have the same amount again in the other pilot zones of our operation. Most of them are severely hurt, and we should really shoot them now. What is your instruction? We have the equipment to gas them, if you prefer, or we could get our shotguns out."

"What would happen if we just left them?" Ollie asked.

Very uncomfortably, the worker replied, "I would say for the amount of blood they have lost, they would be dead in about an hour."

With no conscience or remorse, Ollie said, "Leave them, and in an hour, empty the cages and set the traps for the next catch."

"But sir, that is not the protocol as dictated in our manual," the worker said.

"Do I have to repeat myself, young man?" Ollie shouted. "What is your name? I do hope you realise whom you are trying to contradict?"

"I am sorry, sir. My name is Nick Panay, and yes, I will carry out your instructions, sir."

Nick gathered his team and announced, "Mr. Gunner has instructed that there is no need to gas or shoot the trapped badgers. We are to leave them a further hour before we empty them out of the cages and into the sacks."

"What about the Wildlife and Countryside guidelines?" Steve Foley, a member of his team, asked. "We need to ensure that they are all humanely dead. And furthermore, foothold traps should have never been used, nor should blades have been put into the cages. I am really not happy with how this operation is going."

Nick replied, "Listen, we are just doing as instructed. I don't like doing this, either. We are not even supposed to cull the poor sods till after May, but who are we to say anything, if Ollie Dollie has just given the word?"

Nick contacted all the other target areas of the pilot zone and passed on Ollie's instructions to the rest of his team.

The Fifth Inscription

Take Responsibility for Your Actions, and Be Prepared to Protect the Innocent

Nick Panay, Steve Foley, and four others returned an hour later to the site, as instructed by Ollie Gunner. They were horrified at what they saw. The poor badgers had bled to death, and the ground was soaked in blood.

"I really don't want to be part of this, Nick," Steve said. "This is not the job I signed up for. Look at the poor animals, left to suffer and die in pain. It's disgusting."

Nick looked at the caged badgers, lowered his head, and told Steve, "You are right, mate, but what can we do? He's the boss, and he's in charge. Let's just clear the cages, reset the traps, and go home."

"Wrong, Nick," Steve said. "We can do something about this. For starters, I refuse to reset these traps for the next slaughter."

Mick Jones, originally from Wales, was another member of the team. Sensing that Steve needed some support, he said, "Hey, Nick, Steve's right, this is not on. We do not practise culling in Wales, never mind mercilessly slaughtering these animals. It sickens me that we are not complying to any of the humane killing that we were trained to do. As our section leader, I am begging you to do something about this, as I cannot go home tonight and rest peacefully, knowing full well that I have been part of this massacre."

Dale Matthews, a new member of the team, also chipped in a similar protest; Nick did his best to quell the increasing discontentment amongst the team.

He raised his voice above the team and said, "Alright, let us just empty these cages and clean up the area. You are all correct; we can do something about this, and I certainly agree not to reset the cages. I will report this to Jeremy Fischer and see what he has to say. Let me first take a video of this, so he will see the actual footage as it is."

By the bright light of the strong industrial lamps, Nick, Steve, and the other men emptied the cages, heaved the dead bodies into massive rubble sacks, and then loaded them into a skip. Their hands and clothes were soaked in blood, and they felt as if they were part of a crime scene, as opposed to doing what they had been trained to do. These men were all trained marksmen able to kill a badger with a single shot to the heart and lung area, and now they all felt their operation was compromised and against all DEFRA-approved standards.

Widejaw returned to the colony and requested an emergency meeting with the High Lord Luminous.

"High Lord, I have never in all my years witnessed such a cruel slaughter of our kin," the warrior leader said.

Built with an exterior like steel and a strict military discipline, Widejaw was never seen as an emotional badger, but as he continued his report to his leader, his eyes were brimmed with tears, and as he began to speak, he gasped and sobbed.

"Our elders were guillotined as the cages, fitted with sharp blades, came down whilst they were trapped, immobilised by the footholds secured in the ground. Some of them were dismembered, and Little Clawdigger was lying there, terrified, and I could not do anything for him but hold his paws for the minutes he had left. I'll never forget the fear in his eyes."

Widejaw struggled to continue, and after fighting his tears back, he continued, "I am numb with grief, High Lord, and I want revenge."

High Lord Luminous looked at his strong warrior, broken to pieces by this tragedy, and sat him down.

"My dear Widejaw, the answer is not revenge. I have no explanation as to why it has come to this. But believe me, there are some truly good people out there who are looking out for us. I want you to work on a strategy to defend our colonies, not attack man. The High Lady told me that today was a day of true unity amongst our own. The pelts of all colours played together with no prejudice or discrimination, and today's tragedy highlights the need for not just us badgers to work together, but also for us to respect all the animals in the forest and stand together in harmony. Go and rest, my dear warrior, as the whole clan will want to hear your report tomorrow. But I'd ask you to put aside your thoughts of revenge. Please trust me that it is not the correct approach for our future."

Widejaw left the High Lord's sett, and a few seconds later, Clawdigger approached him from around the corner. Widejaw looked at the handsome badger, who seemed completely lost. Clawdigger's eyes were red raw with all the grieving he had done for the death of his cub; he pleaded to Widejaw, "How did my cub die? Please tell me the truth."

Widejaw gave him a strong hug; unable to look at him in the eye, he continued to hold him in a firm grip and said, "Like a brave hero who made you proud and who we will always remember."

He gently led Clawdigger towards his sett and said, "Come, my friend, you need your rest, and your family need you more than ever now. We have enemies out there, and we must work hard to protect each other. We must somehow find the strength for the big day next week."

Ollie Gunner arrived at what he called Plot CULL1. This was located five kilometres from the Brockley Clan, and he was happy to see, by the light of his iPhone's torch, that the cages had been emptied. However, his happiness turned to displeasure when he realised the traps had not been reset. He walked carefully around the plot to avoid the footholds and further noticed that the footholds had also not been reset.

"What's going on here?" he asked. "Why hasn't he reset the traps or the footholds?" He dialled Nick Panay's number.

It was half past nine in the evening, and when Nick saw on the caller ID it was Ollie Gunner, he decided not to answer, thinking to himself, *Forget it, it's Friday night. I have done my overtime, and it's way past my office hours.*

Ollie was infuriated that his call was not taken. There was nothing that he could do until Monday, so he angrily made his way back to his Range Rover.

Unknown to Ollie, the High Lord Henry Hedgehog and a few of his warriors had witnessed what had happened to the badgers earlier in the day, and despite their feud with the badgers, the High Lord Henry could not condone such a tragedy. Before Ollie got back to his car, the hedgehogs released several sharp quills into each of his tyres. Ollie got into his car and switched his ignition on, but the car would not move. Confused and annoyed, he jumped out and shone his torch to see what was going on.

"For goodness sake," he shouted.

As he shone his torch on his tyres, he could not believe it. Not only one, but all four of his tyres were punctured. Just as he was checking his fourth tyre, his iPhone ran out of battery and his torch went out, and he was in complete darkness. To make things even worse, he felt sharp small arrows piercing into his bottom and started hopping up and down, yelping like a crazed man. In the dark, he slipped on an uneven surface and fell onto what felt like a bed of spikes. He got up and stumbled and fell again into another bed of spikes.

"Ouch," he yelled. "Ouch, arrrrrh! Ouch; what is going on?"

He finally managed to get back into his car and switched the engine on again. He put his phone on charge, switched his lights on, and tried to see what was happening. He caught a glimpse of an army of about thirty hedgehogs scuttling away, but that confused him, as this was certainly not hedgehog territory.

"What are all those hedgehogs doing in badger territory?" Ollie asked. "Where have they come from? And surely, they could not have played a part in this nightmare."

Stranded in the middle of the night, Ollie waited for his phone to be partially charged; when he finally had a signal, he placed a call to the AA.

"I am sorry, sir, but we cannot be with you for at least another two hours," said the AA operator.

Ollie was furious, and despite of all his aggressive threats, he had no choice but to wait alone in the dark woods.

Shams Aziz returned from the mosque and spent all evening planning his team's itinerary for the next week. Ollie had given each team a big area to work on, and he thought it best for him to spend Monday and Tuesday together with Geoffrey, Sarah, and Richard before splitting them into two teams. He already decided he should team up with Richard Nicks, as Sarah made her feelings towards him quite clear. Satisfied with his plan of action, he switched on the television and saw Ollie Gunner on the screen, boasting of his new squads and confident of his success in reaching his target.

It had been a strange day, and Shams was trying to take everything in. No one he knew reacted to badgers with such aggression. He was aware of what he signed up for, but like Sarah and Geoffrey, he was uncomfortable with Ollie's approach. Against Ollie's instruction, he began to read all the bulletins promoted by the League.Org. By the time he went to bed, it was nearly two in the morning; he was relieved he had a weekend to chill out before Monday.

Richard Nicks contacted his uncle Shamus and arranged to meet him at five o'clock at a local pub near the campus.

When he entered the pub, a cheerful laugh rang out from the corner; a stout man hobbled over on a crutch, shouting, "Tricky Dicky, how have you been keeping, son?"

"I am doing well, Uncle Shamus. Got myself enrolled on the team with DEFRA to track down the badgers, and I am very well connected and in the top team of the cull operation."

"Great news, son. Well done, but please be careful, as you know how those badgers killed your father and grandad and left me with one leg." A dark shadow fell on his face as he began to shudder, reminiscing that fateful evening.

Richard's grandad, Shamus Nicks Senior, had two sons: Shamus Nicks Junior and John Nicks. Originally from Ulster, it was believed that Shamus Senior was part of the Hardcore Terrier Men. This was an international organisation that practised badger baiting as a sport, earning a lot of money from the bets taken. In spite of this being totally illegal, Shamus Senior and his sons captured, raised, and trained young badger cubs.

They also trained their Jack Russell terriers to hate the scent of a badger; they bought the dogs from Mark Ashley, who sold the dogs under the guise that they were farm trained to kill rats and fend off foxes.

Shamus Senior would drug the badgers before a fight and take bets from the spectators, who would naturally back the badgers, based on them being bigger than the dogs. He would then deliberately starve the dogs before a fight, and when they were released into the artificial den, they would mercilessly seize the drugged-up badgers and attack them till they fell defencelessly.

John, his son, would act as a timekeeper, allowing the dogs down for a certain amount of time whilst the spectators looked on through the glass window from above. Before the badgers could regain their senses, he would stop the fight and take all the winning bets of those who backed the badgers and prepare the second fight for the evening.

The spectators, impressed with the dogs, would then back the dogs, but the effect of the drugs administered to the badgers would have now worn off, allowing the badgers to now have the upper hand and literally rip the dogs apart. The poor dogs were then abandoned on the road as if knocked down by a car. Many times, the badgers were also left by the roadside as if it were another roadkill accident. It would have been less cruel for the badger to be knocked down by a car.

Shamus and his sons made a lot of money doing this. Not only was this sport illegal, but he was also cheating the participating spectators (not that they deserved any sympathy). Both parties were evil, enjoying a sport and gambling at the poor animals' expense.

However, one night, Shamus and his sons faced a comeuppance which was befitting for such cruel people.

On this fateful night, after the spectators left, whilst Shamus Senior was counting all his takings, Shamus Junior gathered up the surviving terriers and led them back to the cages at the back of their pickup truck, where he gave them a well-deserved meal. In the meantime, his brother, John Nicks, went into the arena to clean out the blood-sodden hay from the previous fights and replace it with fresh hay. With an iron staff fitted with a knife at one end, he also threw some fruit to the badgers and prodded them to antagonise a reaction. Convinced that they were still quite drugged up, he took his time shifting the hay about, but suddenly, the biggest badger they had, nicknamed Hercules, charged at him and bit his leg. He screamed in pain, and his father dived down to rescue him, but the six badgers had massacred his son within minutes and soon approached him.

Shamus Junior heard the loud screams and cries but was helpless above as he tried to find the heavy metal lid which was used to seal the artificial tunnel. There was no room for him to go down into the tunnel to help his father and brother, and as he looked around for the lid, it was too late, as Hercules and the five others rushed up from below and charged at him. Hercules seized him by his thigh, and his jaws remained obstinately clamped into his leg. Luckily for Shamus Junior, Tommy Balls, one of the spectators, was not far away when he heard the loud screams and ran back to the fighting ring. He grabbed the heavy lid and beat Hercules off Shamus Junior. He helped Shamus as much as he could and then rang for the ambulance.

Tommy turned to Shamus, who was now bleeding profusely, and said, "I am sorry, Shamus. This is the best I can do. I cannot wait around and risk being arrested. I am sorry."

When the ambulance arrived on the scene, they quickly worked out what had happened and contacted the police. Shamus Junior was treated but subsequently arrested and ultimately served a ten-year prison sentence for badger baiting. Richard, a young boy at this time, was left to be raised by his young mother, and from that day, he was fuelled with hatred for badgers killing his grandad and father.

"Don't you worry, Uncle Shamus," Richard said. "I am going to avenge my grandad and father and execute as many of those creatures as I can, and it will all be legal and above board. I have waited for this day and will not let Papa or Dad down. Do you still delve in badger baiting?"

"No way, son, don't even mention it. I relive that dreadful night, helpless that I could not do anything to save my father and brother. I believe someone up there spared me and gave me the chance to make amends. Listen to me, Dicky, what we did was wrong and cruel, very wrong, and very cruel. I have lived every day regretting it, and the terror of that evening has haunted me every moment of my life. Do your job, and enjoy your revenge from their elimination, but keep away from them. Are you listening to me, son?"

Uncle Shamus shuddered and continued, "You were just a child, robbed of your dad, but your mother used the dirty money we made and gave you a brilliant education. I am proud of you, but please find some peace in your heart and live a good life with all these great opportunities ahead of you."

Richard believed his uncle meant well. He was aware that Uncle Shamus had given his mother all the money they had made to set her up with her own shoe business, and a successful one, at that. Cara Nicks, his mother, was mortified at the whole incident and ashamed by her husband's activities. She moved to Torquay and remarried, making a new life for herself and Richard.

James Wilkinson, his stepdad, was a very loving, caring man who supported him throughout his childhood, but he missed and loved his father and all the exciting tales he had told him.

Richard knew he was not going to get any information about baiting from his uncle but continued to pry.

"Did you ever keep in touch with Tommy Balls?" he asked.

Uncle Shamus smiled and said, "Owed him my life, I did, and yet he keeps apologising for abandoning me. I never grassed on anyone, son. Did not tell the police anything. My lips were sealed."

He sighed with so much grief and regret; he looked across at his nephew and said with a big hearty smile, "I bet he would love to see you, young Dicky.

"Come to think of it, it's time to catch up with him again. Strange guy, only drove Saabs. Silver ones at that. I see him now and then at the Dog and Gun."

Richard could not conceal his pleasure that Uncle Shamus had taken the bait so easily.

"I would love to call him. Would that be possible?"

"Absolutely. Here is his number, son, but I honestly beg you not to get involved in anything which leads you into trouble. But we could go to the Dog and Gun now for a proper pint of Indian pale ale, and you can tell me more about your new job."

"I would love to, Uncle Shamus," Richard said, "but I need to dash off to meet an old friend. I could meet you about eight o'clock next Friday, okay?"

"Brilliant, lad," Uncle Shamus said. "Now you go and have fun, and I will see you next week."

He made his way out of the pub as quickly as he could, and as soon as he was out of sight of his uncle, he immediately called Tommy Balls.

"Six p.m. next Friday will be fantastic, Mr. Balls."

"Please, Tommy will be fine, and I am honestly looking forward to meeting you, young man. Now, it's called the Dog and Gun, and it serves the best Indian ..."

"Pale ale," Richard interrupted with a chuckle." Yes, Uncle Shamus already told me. Thank you once again."

The Sixth Inscription

Decayed Fruit Is Forbidden, as It Will Cloud Your Decisions

"A whole week has gone by, and none of you have any evidence to present," Ollie Gunner shouted across the room. "Have you been on a holiday or simply forgotten the purpose of your mission? What is going on?

"Mr. Aziz, your group was the most promising. What sorry excuse have you got?"

Shams took his glasses off and replied politely, "I can honestly tell you that we worked together all week, and the ground was absolutely clear of any badger tracks. Strangely, however, we found more than the usual hedgehog tracks. It was like there were more hedgehogs in the predetermined badger areas. If I did not know better, I would say that the badgers emigrated and the hedgehogs took over their territory. From what you have told us and what we have researched, where there is a hedgehog, it is unlikely there are badgers, but in the area we were assigned, there are simply no badger tracks."

The other groups echoed in agreement as they were in the exact position as Shams and his team.

"Do not be so blooming ridiculous," Ollie retorted. "I've spent years doing this job and jolly well know the blooming badger's habitat."

He took a deep breath, calmed down, and added, "I did, however, experience a strange phenomenon myself last week, and now that you mention it, I saw a lot of hedgehogs where I was."

Shams nervously continued, as he explained that many other animal tracks were prominent, and if the tracks were unidentifiable, they could have been deliberately swept clean.

Martin Caton, section leader of the other group, spoke up from the back of the room and said sheepishly, "My guys and I actually felt that we were being watched."

He felt tremendously relieved when Darren Whitworth, section leader of the third group, piped up, "I know exactly what you are saying." He turned to Rita and said, "Rita, share with the group what you saw on Wednesday."

Rita Mosina stood up, gave a small nervous laugh, and continued in her lovely foreign accent, "Well, I feel somewhat crazy saying this, but Wednesday afternoon, I pointed out to Darren that there were birds of all kinds perched in the trees; they looked down at us as if in preparation to swoop down and drive us away. The crows were perched at such a low height in the trees, as if to eavesdrop on our conversation. An unusual number of rabbits were diving from all directions, distracting our investigation, and moles were burrowing through the ground and coming up, unafraid of our presence. It was a rather eerie experience, and we felt like intruders and without doubt we were being chased away."

Ollie went red in the face with exasperation and shouted, "For goodness sake. You all sound like some freaked-out kids in a Friday night horror film. If I don't see results next week, you'll all need new jobs, as I am not accepting this poor performance."

Completely flustered, and without looking at the rest of the class, he snapped, "We will reconvene next Friday."

As the groups left, Richard Nicks held back and cleared his throat softly, to catch Ollie's attention.

"Yes? Have you something to say, Mr. Nicks?" asked Ollie.

Richard was quite embarrassed that his group had seen his attempt to obtain a private word with Ollie, so he said softly, "Have you a minute, Mr. Gunner?"

"Not really," Ollie replied, "but with your recent poor performance, I might as well see if I can help you with anything."

"Well, sir, I really do not know how to come out with this, but in view of our failure to track the badgers down, I was wondering if I could suggest using the assistance of one of my uncle's friend, Tommy Balls. He …"

"Goodness, Mr. Nicks," Ollie interrupted. "I certainly know who he is."

There was an uncomfortable moment of silence, but Richard could see that he had planted a seed of thought in Ollie's mind.

After what seemed an eternity, Ollie turned to Richard and said, "Do not mention this conversation again. Do you understand? I hope you have a good weekend."

He walked away, stopped suddenly, turned back, and said, "Mr. Nicks, I think we both are on the same path for the same goals. See you next Friday."

Richard left with a smile on his face, knowing that Ollie was certainly thinking in tune with him.

Ollie walked away, dreading his report to his superior on Monday. Ollie was an ambitious young man and a candidate earmarked by his boss, Jeremy Fischer, for DEFRA's next executive director. Jeremy Fischer was more than likely to be nominated secretary of state, and he was putting Ollie and Michael Richardson to a test for the next six weeks to see who was the better candidate for when he moved up.

The test was brutal: who could eliminate more badgers in a short period? Jeremy liked Ollie's ruthlessness, as he reminded him of himself at that young age. Michael was an expert and very competent, with every rule and regulation under his belt, but Jeremy felt he got too emotionally attached to the animals, and this was a negative, in Jeremy's opinion. The ultimate result was to see who did the better job, and that was his main concern.

If you want a blooming job done right, you just have to blooming do it yourself, Ollie thought to himself. *Jeremy is going to be so disappointed. I had fantastic results in the first week and now absolutely nothing. What is going on with my teams? Squad 1 is just not responding as requested. Squad 2 cannot even find me tracks. I'll tell Jeremy the squads need changing and fire the lot of them.*

Wiping his smile off his face, Richard came face to face with Geoffrey, Shams, and Sarah at the end of the corridor.

"You look very pleased with yourself, Tricky Dicky," Geoffrey said.

"Who told you that's what my family calls me?" Richard asked, wondering what else Geoffrey knew about him.

"Just a guess," Geoffrey said. "Anyway, we're a team and should share all our information with the team."

Going very red in the face, Richard lied and said, "It was a personal favour which required permission from Ollie Gunner and nothing to do with the project."

"You are not a good liar, Richard," Geoffrey said, but Shams interrupted and said, "We were just waiting to confirm that we will get together at ten o'clock at North Wessex Downs near Brockley on Monday. Is that okay with you, Richard?"

"Perfect. I will see all of you there."

As usual, with not as much as a goodbye, Richard turned and walked away.

Shams was going back to Birmingham for the weekend, and Sarah was also going back home for her mum and dad's wedding anniversary. It was getting quite dark in spite of it being only four in the afternoon, and since Geoffrey had no plans of his own, he took a walk into the woods before returning to the DEFRA campus.

Brad and Poppy were running round their dad, whilst Polly climbed on his back. Sally looked on and felt such a great sense of love to see Bodger; when he was sober, he was so wonderful with his cubs. Bodger looked up and caught his sow's eye. He felt embarrassed and looked away. Sally came up to them and gently pulled the cubs away; while they played together on the hay, she said, "Bodger, you make me so happy when you are like this, and I love you so much for being a wonderful father."

He replied, "Ha, you say that, but I know I am not the chosen boar that Flash would have made you. I can still see the glint of love that he has in his eyes for you."

Sally could not deny that Flash was her first love and that it was the choice of the leaders uniting the clans which made her couple up with Bodger.

She said, "Bodger, that was a long time ago, but as soon as I first laid eyes on you, my heart skipped a beat, and I promised to devote myself completely to you from that day onwards. Have I ever caused you to doubt me?"

"I'm the laughing stock of this clan," he said bitterly. "They all talk about the great love between Flash and Sally, the beloved darling of the clan. I bet Sparkly feels as big a fool as I do."

"Bodger, that's an unfair, cruel thing to say," Sally said, trying to fight back her tears. "Sparkly is my friend, and she has never made me feel guilty or as uncomfortable, as you do. I do everything to please you, and all you do is turn to forbidden fruit with your good-for-nothing friends and use me as an excuse for your weakness."

"Weakness? How dare you. My job requires it, and the socialising I do ensures that the setts are rented out to what you term my 'bad friends.' How dare you upset me on this day?" Bodger stormed out of the sett.

Sally put her face in her hands and let out a soft cry, forgetting that her young cubs were still nearby. Brad, Poppy, and Polly were confused but sensed that their mother was sad; they quickly came to her side and licked her all over her face. Sally pretended it was just a game and pulled them close to her, tickling their bellies until they squealed with giggles.

"Come on, my sweet cubs, we need to get you ready for your big night: the saining ceremony."

The High Lady Pure Snowspirit made her way to visit Brit and gently tapped at the entrance of the sett. She could hear a gentle but swift gallop towards her, and in a small voice panting with excitement, Speed looked up and said, "Hello, who are you?"

The High Lady laughed and picked up Speed, gently passing her back to Brit.

"My dear Brit, I cannot find the words to tell you how I admire you for getting on with all these activities in preparation for tonight."

She grabbed Brit's paw and could hear a tremble in Brit's voice as she replied, "Thank you for your kind words, my Lady; both Clawdigger and

I have been on autopilot, trying to look after the young cubs, and I am so grateful they have no comprehension as to where Little Clawdigger has gone. They understand that he is with the ancestors but cannot understand why he will not be coming home."

Brit had to turn away as she could feel that she was going to lose control. She composed herself and bravely continued, "There has been so much to do, and that has kept me occupied."

The High Lady gave her a hug and asked, "Are you sure you are up for performing your beautiful solo tonight?"

"Yes, my Lady, it will be sung as a tribute and honour to my cub," Brit said, turning to Clawdigger, who entered the room.

"My Lady, what a pleasant surprise and honour to visit our sett," Clawdigger said.

"Please, Clawdigger, I am humbled by both your bravery and strength. The whole colony is in moaning for you and in awe of your continued relentless efforts all week, for tonight's celebration."

Clawdigger, who barely kept his tears back, replied softly, "Thank you, my Lady; both Brit and I look forward to seeing our cubs being sained tonight, and we will take the opportunity to beseech our ancestors to look after our Little Clawdigger."

The High Lady grabbed his paw and gave him a hard squeeze, and then she went to Brit, gave her a big hug, and said, "Well, I will leave you in peace. I am glad to have had this moment with you both. Once again, you are loved by all the colony, and the High Lord and I are truly in awe of your courage. I will see all of you later."

Bodger left the sett and walked into the woods, regretting once again the harsh words he said to Sally. "Why can't I control myself? I truly do not deserve her. How can I hurt someone I love so much?"

Just as he was in the depth of clearing his thoughts and trying to work out how silly he was to be so jealous of Flash, two dark figures jumped out of nowhere and pulled him down to the ground. They began to wrestle. He started to fight back till he heard the giggle of his two friends, Willy the weasel and Paddy the polecat.

"Are you crazy? I could have hurt the two of you with one bite," Bodger yelled.

"Just having a bit of fun," Paddy squealed. "You should have seen your face; one minute, you were in a deep thought, and the next minute, you were wondering what was going on."

Willy looked around and whispered, "By the way, what's going on? I know it's a special night tonight, but I have never seen all those red coats go up and down, bossing everybody around so much."

Bodger looked up and replied, "You were not around last week, but sadly, many of my kin were killed, including a cub. Widejaw and his warriors are doubling securities and trying to erase all our tracks to avoid man from finding us."

"That's sad, Bodger," Paddy said. "That explains why he insisted we went over our own tracks several times before coming into the woods. Anyway, you look miserable, and both me and Willy need to cheer you up."

"Not tonight, guys," Bodger said. "I cannot let my cubs down. I have got to be on best behaviour for them."

He began walking away from his friends.

"Steady on," Willy said, dragging him back. "They certainly don't want a miserable dad at their saining ceremony. Come on, we just found a heap of some very decayed fruit, and it's sending off some fantastic flurries that my nose cannot resist."

"Come on," said Paddy. "Only a small bite, and then we'll attend the big ceremony together."

Sadly, Bodger had a problem of not being able to control his urge for the forbidden fruit; he gave in and went off together with Willy and Paddy.

Tommy Balls was at the Dog and Gun, just on the edge of the Brockley woods, at six in the evening, as arranged with Richard Nicks. He was just about to order a pint when his phone rang.

Of a burly build, Tommy had a scraggly beard with missing bits and a distinctly big nose which was dotted with blackheads. He sported a combover but was very smartly dressed in a pair of chinos and Pringle jumper.

In a raspy deep voice, he answered, "Hello."

"Hi Tommy, it's Richard Nicks. I am outside, but I just saw Uncle Shamus walk in, and I really don't want us to meet in front of him. I said I would meet him at eight, but he is obviously early. Can we go somewhere else?"

"Leave it with me," Tommy said. "Give me a couple of minutes, as he is walking towards me." He hung up.

"Look what the cat dragged in," he said, giving Shamus a big hug.

"How are you keeping?" Shamus replied. "Come on, come on, let's get you a pint."

"Shamus, pal, I would love to," said Tommy. "But I was just coming off the phone with the boss, and she has summoned me home. Another time?"

"Absolutely," said Shamus. "Ha ha, that's why I never got me no ball and chain. Good to see you, pal, and let's hook up together soon. By the way, I gave your number to John Nicks's son, Dicky. I'm actually meeting him in a couple of hours but thought I'd get a couple in before he arrived. He might be contacting you, and for the sake of his dad, please keep him out of mischief if he does."

Feeling uncomfortable around his collar, Tommy replied, "Oh, for sure, Shamus. We don't want to be going down that road, do we? And let's definitely get together soon."

As he was putting his coat on, Shamus asked, "Are you still driving a silver Saab?"

Tommy laughed, gave a big wave, and said, "As always. See you, pal."

Tommy made a quick exit, looking around to make sure no one was watching him as he walked over to his silver Saab.

"Bingo," Richard said to himself. "Mr. Silver Saab."

Richard walked towards the silver Saab and said nervously, "Hey Tommy, glad you could make it."

Tommy turned around, looked at him, and said, "By gum, you are the spitting image of your dad."

"Thanks, Tommy. The good news is that I have spoken to my boss, and I think I have sparked an interest. I believe he will be wanting to use your dogs."

"Like I said, Richard, it will cost a bob or two," Tommy said, looking around again.

Geoffrey was just coming out of the wood, still mesmerised by what he had just witnessed, when he suddenly saw two men talking by a silver Saab. He stopped short in his tracks when he realised it was Richard Nicks and a man he did not recognise. Instinctively, he got his phone out and took pictures of the two of them. Carefully, he strained his ears to catch the gist of their conversation.

"Don't you worry about the cost," Richard said, "and with Ollie Gunner involved, I am sure he will swing it round to look very much above board. Tommy, just be ready for my call, as I have three colleagues who are watching me like hawks, so you can't call me."

Tommy nodded and replied, "Not a problem, Richard. I can't get over how much you look like your dad. Good to have met you."

He shook Richard's hand and got into his car.

"What the heck is Tricky Dicky up to?" Geoffrey asked. "I knew he was collaborating with Ollie Gunner about something. I just don't trust him. I need to speak to Shams and Sarah before Monday morning."

Geoffrey hung back and saw Richard walk into the pub. It was now about half past six, and he was definitely ready for that pint. As he entered, he saw a big man with a crutch hobbling towards Richard, bellowing, "Tricky Dicky, you are early; must have been thinking the same as me, ha ha. Let me get you a pint of that good ale I promised. You'll never believe who you just missed by a couple of minutes."

Richard feigned ignorance and responded, "No idea, Uncle Shamus. Who?"

"Tommy, and the biggest laugh is that he is still driving a silver Saab. I can't believe he only drives that make of car. At least have a change of colour. I tell you what, he has put some timber on. Anyway, I came in earlier as I wanted to have the fish pie, which is honestly incredible. Shall I get some for you?"

"So uncanny, Uncle Shamus, but I would not know who he was if he jumped in front of me." Richard laughed, lying through his teeth. He continued, "And no fish pie for me; I cannot afford the extra timber. Can I have a Caesar salad, please, my body being a temple and all that."

He was glad his uncle was walking ahead of him and couldn't see how red he was in embarrassment for lying, but Geoffrey did not miss any of this conversation and made note of the name Tommy Balls. He knew

Richard was lying to his uncle, as he had seen him with the stranger by the silver Saab.

Without thinking it completely through, Geoffrey went to the bar, stood next to Richard's uncle, and struck up a conversation as to what was best on the menu. Voluntarily, Uncle Shamus recommended the fish pie, and Geoffrey thanked him. He insisted on helping him with the extra pint he was carrying and pretended to be surprised when he saw Richard at the table.

"Richard, what a coincidence," Geoffrey said. "Is this your father, as I can see a strong resemblance?"

Jovially, Uncle Shamus said, "No, I am his uncle. How do you know each other?"

Richard looked at Geoffrey and said simply that they were colleagues. Uncle Shamus could sense an air of tension and did not invite Geoffrey to join them, but Geoffrey was already a step ahead and politely said, "Thanks for the recommendation. I'll sit in the other booth and await my fish pie, whilst you both catch up with each other."

Geoffrey sat across so he could see Uncle Shamus, and Richard seemed quite uncomfortable, as his uncle was talking loudly; Geoffrey picked up loads of snippets of Tricky Dicky as a lad. He also heard Uncle Shamus warning Richard not to get involved with Tommy Balls, and Geoffrey knew this name needed investigating.

What an enlightening evening, he thought. *I cannot wait to see Sarah and Shams on Sunday.*

The Seventh Inscription

Respect the Earth and All That Dwell on It

Her Majesty, a British rock band, was formed in the early seventies. The line-up included Andy May (lead guitar and vocals), Conor Parfitt (drums and vocals), Lewis Roberts (bass guitar), and their lead singer, Frankie McGinty. Their earliest work was hard rock and heavy metal, but the band gradually ventured into more conventional and radio-friendly works; in their latter years, their music had a huge impact in spreading their beliefs about respecting the environment. They influenced several groups into a wave of better living and respect amongst each other.

Over and above having a great talent in the music industry, Andy, Conor, and Lewis were extremely well educated. Andy was a bachelor of science in physics. Conor attained a first in economics, and Lewis attained a first in music. Despite their highly qualified degrees, the seventies were a very suppressed period; the stock market was in a slump with high inflation, rising interest rates, and high unemployment, so sadly, all the three boys remained unemployed.

Eventually, the three of them got together and jammed on the weekends, which was followed by the odd busking sessions in the streets of London.

Andy was raised by a single mother, who unfortunately found solace and comfort from alcohol. Agatha May, his mother, was often dragged back home by her friends (or, even worse, by strangers) after having far too much to drink at the local pub. Andy always made sure that Leanne and Jane, his younger sisters, were safely tucked up in bed so as to avoid them witnessing their mother in her drunken stupor. She would wake up the following morning, claiming her friends had spiked her drink or some excuse, other than the fact that she was an alcoholic. Other mornings, she would apologise that she needed to drink, as it was their father's fault for abandoning her. Andy's father passed away after Leanne was newly born, so the children were always confused as to why their mother blamed their father for leaving her. He had no choice in the matter.

On countless occasions, Agatha would come back from a pub, slurring, "Love, you have no idea how hard it has been for me to raise all of you. I miss your dad so much, and my only friend and consolation is my whisky. It lifts me up just for a moment to take the pain away, and for that short moment, it is pure bliss. Do not judge me, son. I can see you are going to do me proud one day, and I love you. I have no idea where you got your brains from, but now that you have your posh degree, why don't you get yourself a good job?"

It saddened Andy as he handed over every penny of his busking money; he wished she could realise how he was there for her. Suggesting that she join AA only led to her being more angry, so Andy continued to do his best for her.

Agatha smirked, "You have no idea what my life's about. Now see to your sisters and make sure they are on time for the bus. I just need another ten minutes in bed."

Andy looked at his mother; he never knew how to react or respond. His dad died when he was just twelve; he remembered him as a tyrant who brought the wages home but did absolutely nothing to help with the children. His mother was terrified of him and was never allowed to work, so Andy assumed his father's death gave his mother a new lease on life, but in a strange way, this was how she preferred to spend her freedom. Leanne and Jane were just ten and twelve and were so embarrassed about their mother. However, they thought the world of their big brother, the scientist.

When Jane came down for breakfast, she saw Andy and asked, "So have you figured out the Big Bang theory, Joe 90?"

Andy laughed, as his sister teased him about his heavy black framed glasses, which were similar to the well-known comic character Joe 90; he replied, "Don't be so cheeky, and make sure Leanne gets on the bus with you, as I'm meeting Conor at Covent Gardens and going the other way. "

Jane had a massive crush on Conor and immediately pricked her ears at the mention of his name.

"Can I come along and watch you jam?" she asked hopefully.

Andy smiled and said, "One hundred percent no. You need to go to school and get some good grades so you can look after your big brother."

Jane gave him a huge hug and said, "Just you see, you will be famous and rich, and I will marry Conor one day."

Andy gave her a gentle shove and said, "Stop being silly, and go bring Leanne down for breakfast, and then you both are straight on that 364 bus."

Conor Parfitt was also from Southwark, like Andy; he lived with his sister Kayla, his father Niall, and his stepmother, Mavis. Their mother had left Niall and abandoned them; the children only remember being brought up with Mavis as their mother. Niall worked all hours, and Mavis worked as a dinner lady at the local school. All Saints Primary School was very generous and allowed her to bring home any uneaten food. She was frugal, and in spite of their low earnings, she always ensured that Conor and Kayla had new shoes, a clean uniform, and a full tummy when they left for school. Kayla was completing her first year A levels and was very into art and music. She desperately wanted to attend the Rose Dench College, and Conor hoped to help her achieve her dream. Unlike Andy, he had wonderful supportive parents, and Conor vowed to look after them when he could afford to.

Both Conor and Andy had a great love for music and were inspired by the legends of Led Zeppelin, the Who, Black Sabbath, and Deep Purple. They were very much into heavy metal rock. Together with Lewis, they began busking in Covent Garden and absolutely loved the buzz they got from performing in the streets.

Lewis was a posh boy from Surrey who lived with his wealthy parents in a four-bedroom detached bungalow with their very own garage. This seemed like a mansion to Andy and Conor, and each time they went to jam at Lewis's, they wondered which they loved more: the massive garage or the lovely roast dinners Mrs. Roberts always prepared, even when it was not a Sunday.

"Hey Lewis, do you have any idea how lucky you are to have roast lamb on a Wednesday?" Andy asked. He added, laughing, "We just have a bag of chips all week and then Mum's amazing chicken in a bag on Sunday."

Conor laughed and said, "Well, in that case, I'm not complaining about the leftover school dinners mum brings home, but credit to Mavis, it is always a hot roast dinner on Sunday."

Mrs. Lewis was extremely kind and always made sure to give Andy a good doggy bag of leftovers for his sisters.

Lewis went to a gig where he saw a tall, eccentric singer perform; he could only describe him to Conor and Andy as unlike anyone he had ever heard.

"What does that mean?" Conor asked Andy.

Andy replied, "Who knows? You know how posh he is. Let's see what this McGinty guy has to offer when we meet him. We will be the judge as to how good he is."

Lewis was due to show up in five minutes with Frankie McGinty, and they arrived exactly on time. Conor and Andy were just taken aback as to how tall and lanky he was.

"Hey, how are you down there?" Frankie said with a cheeky grin and a thick Scottish accent.

After jamming together for an hour, Andy and Conor gave Lewis a pat on the shoulder and agreed that Frankie should be part of their band.

"Jesus, mate, you have some pipes," Andy said to Frankie.

As a child in school, Frankie auditioned for all the singing parts; always the teacher's favourite, he was given every lead role. He was very amicable and certainly had the gift of the gab. His mother made him attend opera lessons, and his teacher absolutely loved Frankie. From the early age of sixteen, he could span four full octaves, create iconic growls, and make jaw-dropping vibratos. His teacher had so much hope for him, but when he was eighteen, he told his mum he was bored of opera and wanted to write his own music and perform rock in local pubs.

Frankie was very welcomed at the local gigs, as it always brought in a huge crowd, and the locals knew that Frankie M, as he called himself, was going to be a star, putting Edinburgh on the map. However, that was not his dream. He wanted to make waves in London, and this union of four young gangly kids proceeded to become one of the most loved and respected rock bands ever.

Forty years on, and the band was still very much revered and respected. Andy, Conor, and Lewis still performed, but their beloved Frankie passed away more than fifteen years ago. However, his legacy as a music legend lived on.

Andy was proud to be an animal activist and protested against cruelty to animals, and both Conor and Lewis were supportive of all the pro-environmental and eco-friendly fundraisers he participated in.

Tonight was no exception, and they were as excited as the paying guests to see what Andy had put together for the evening.

It was Valentine's Day, and Andy May had organised a charity ball to raise funds to support the League.Org, the charity led by Barry Odie that works to stop animals being persecuted, abused, or killed. The emphasis tonight was based on the cull of the badgers, which Andy and Barry believed was inhumane and unnecessary. The dress code of the evening was black and white, with the ladies dressed in white and the men in stylish black tuxedos. All attendees had to wear a red broken heart at a small cost of twenty-five pounds, symbolising the recent cruel treatment of the badgers.

It was by no means an inexpensive affair, as each table of ten cost twenty thousand pounds. The menu was a simple three-course vegan meal orchestrated by a famous chef.

The starter, a rich, mouth-watering spicy pumpkin and coriander soup, was followed by a scrumptious nut roast with cranberries glistening in between roasted almonds. Desserts were mint-flavoured black-and-white fondant badgers or a mouth-watering vegan chocolate brownie. The feast went down very well.

With guests like Gwyneth Palmer, Alicia Silversmith, Ellen DeJeans, Stella Magnus, Tom Nunn, and several other big names, buckets of champagne, wine, and prosecco were flowing at exorbitant prices, and high-priced raffle tickets were snapped up like in a local church fair. Andy looked round, smiled, and knew that tonight was going to be a great success.

Barry, Annie, and Freddie Odie were invited by Andy May as guests of honour. Barry insisted on making a very generous contribution to the evening, to which Andy said, "Barry, your total commitment to the cause and running the league is plenty. There is no need to contribute anything. The hours you have put in and your dedicated supporters are impossible to put a price tag on. Are you ready for your speech tonight?"

Barry replied, "Thank you, Andy, that is truly very kind of you, but let us be honest, having you, Conor, and Lewis endorsing our movement has been the total icing on the cake. So we owe all of you a very big thank you."

"Pleasure, Barry, absolute pleasure; well, it looks like everyone has taken their seats, so I'll introduce you shortly."

Meanwhile, standing outside, the High Lord Luminous Snowspirit listened closely to the conversation, overwhelmed by the support these humans were giving to defend and protect his clans. It was not very long after his own saining ceremony, but he knew he had to come tonight and find out what these good men were planning.

Andy gave the headwaiter a nod to ensure that everyone had a full glass, and when the headwaiter gave him the thumbs up, he stood at his table and began to clink his glass for everyone's attention.

"Good evening, fellow supporters. Thank you very much for gathering here to raise funds for our friends of the forest. Of course, tonight we dedicate our evening to our beloved British badger. However, I refuse to spout another word, as the man most responsible for this entire movement is a dedicated businessman, entrepreneur, and philanthropist. Please stand and raise your glass to Mr. Barry Odie."

After the enthusiastic applause ended, Barry began his speech.

"I have nothing to say other than to repeat the words of a very young inspirational speaker, Mr. Lloyd Luna, who once said, 'Several times in probably countless number of occasions, we have been told to step up.' Well, to step up simply means to be better. The meaning was so easy that we also easily forgot to do it. Today, we are into stepping up. But what does it really mean?

"As a young man, I always believed that I was going to step up from where I started. I succeeded in my career and gained wealth. Yet, having achieved all my goals, I still felt empty, unaccomplished, and totally alien to my environment and what was right in front of me. I questioned myself as to whether I was better and honestly could not find myself saying yes. But one day, I was looking across the garden, watching my lovely Annie."

He turned to his beloved wife, and as she waved shyly to the crowd, he continued, "There she was tending to our garden, and whilst she was weeding, as she unearthed a few earthworms, she made sure she buried them in another patch. She carefully removed the snails and put them on our compost heap, where they enjoyed our carrot tops and potato peelings, cabbage, broccoli stems, and whatever was on that heap. She cautiously steered the slugs away from her hostas to join their close relatives on the compost heap and diligently refilled her bird feeders.

"Annie insisted that the birds did not like the fat balls and left them close to the bottom of the garden for the rats, who she insisted were still living things. Whilst working in the garden, Annie was respecting all forms of life so they could continue their own activities. I suddenly saw this better person who lived her life caring for what was around her and respecting every form of life, right before my eyes in our garden.

"At that moment, I knew I had to step up and respect my environment and our fellow living creatures. It goes without saying that my Annie leaves food for the badgers every evening, and the delight we get watching them cautiously waddle into our garden is so rewarding. The clever creatures soon realised they found a friend in Annie, and when we had learnt of the proposed cull, it became our personal mission, as we had fallen in love with our daily visitors. The horror inflicted on them was just too much to bear.

"So now, I pass on the message of stepping up and ask you to look around yourselves; have we all stepped up? Really stepped up? Don't you want to make our world a better place to live in? Thank you."

After a standing ovation, Barry Odie took his seat and gently kissed his beloved Annie's forehead.

The High Lord Luminous Snowspirit was very moved by his speech; as he stood outside in deep contemplation, he said to himself, *If my clans could only see that there are some good people on this side. It is time for me to meet with Andy May and Barry Odie. What great leaders they are.*

He looked around and began to make his way towards the woods, but as he crossed the road, he recognised a man he had seen on the big screen with another man, talking by the bus stop. The High Lord was intrigued and stood to the side. He had a keen sense of hearing and could hear every single word of the conversation.

"So Mr. Gunner, I met up with Tommy Balls last night," Richard Nicks said, "and he will meet you tomorrow at five."

"That's impressive," Ollie said. "You have organised everything so expediently. Excellent work, Mr. Nicks. Now, you made it clear that we only want the location of the badgers. I don't want the dogs going down into the setts. The badger elimination must be above board."

Richard replied, "We will make that very clear when we meet him tomorrow."

"Okay, so the Dog and Gun, at about five o'clock tomorrow," Ollie said.

"Yes, Mr. Gunner," Richard.

Ollie turned around, glad that things were finally coming together, and as he walked past a strange, pasty-looking man in a white outfit, he actually smiled and said, "Evening, sir, and a very good evening it is."

The Eighth Inscription

Respect Our Fellow Animals, and Offer Kindness and Friendship

The High Lord Luminous was in deep thought, looking at the military plans of defence that Widejaw had prepared for him. The High Lady Pure knew he was exhausted and heavy of heart, with a head swimming with different thoughts. She approached him gently, and as he looked up, he reached for her paws and drew her towards him for the comfort she always gave him.

After holding her closely for a minute, he shook his head and said, "Pure, how am I going to convince my clans that not all man are cruel and ruthless? Our warriors are so enraged and are struggling to accept my plans of defence, as opposed to a strategy of attack. Honestly, my beloved, if they could have only heard the passion in Mr. Odie's speech supporting us last night. It would make it so much easier to convince them. However, as I was getting ready to return, I overheard two men conspiring to do something harmful to us. I recognised one of them from the news flashes that I have seen on those big screens, so I need to see if there will be anything else on the screens today."

"Luminous, please, take a rest," the High Lady said. "Please stay and make your way tomorrow. You went directly after the ceremony and haven't slept at all. You are taking such a great risk going across into their world, and I live in fear of you never returning."

Still holding her paw, Luminous stood up and walked her to the entrance of the sett. He looked out and said, "Pure, we are in danger, and I cannot rest until I have secured our clans. I have been given this opportunity, and I must make a difference. Our clans are my first priority."

Pure smiled and said, "Look at our young cubs playing. For the first time in all generations, badgers of different coloured pelts are united together as one big community. You have done this, Luminous, no one else. You have even broken the feud with the hedgehogs, and look how all the rabbits, polecats, and tiny moles are all having fun together with our cubs."

With a small laugh, she added, "It would, however, help if the moles could see where they were going."

Luminous laughed aloud as he watched the moles stumble into all the other animals. He turned to his mate and said, "Thank you, Pure, for those words of encouragement. Yes, it is the dawn of a new era that we have begun. No longer are we badgers segregated; we are all animals, living now as one, including the hedgehogs. Perhaps I could go one step further and find harmony amongst man and animals. It has taken a long time, Pure, but when it is my time to go, I will be proud to leave this legacy of a new generation for our cubs and the rest of the forest."

They both began to chuckle as they could see Wisepaws struggling to prise the bunnies and cubs apart.

Wisepaws calmly ordered, "Speed, you cannot carry the small bunny in your jaws; put him down gently, and let him ride on your back, instead."

Speed Clawdigger obediently put the bunny on her back and challenged Bojana, who had a young polecat on her back, to race with her.

"I'll win you," Speed said confidently. "I'm going to be the first to get to that tree."

Wisepaws, within earshot, corrected her immediately, saying, "I am going to win, Speed."

"Whatever! One, two, three go," the mischievous minx shouted.

Bojana, who was far from giving in to the challenge, replied, "Oh no, you won't."

In half the steps that Speed needed, Bojana galloped like a champion and won the race hands down.

Laughing in spite of her defeat, Speed said, "I am going be a warrior like you one day, Bojana."

The High Lord had a soft spot for Speed; he laughed, pointed at her, and said, "I am convinced you will achieve whatever you put your mind to, young Speed."

Speed's striking green eyes bursting with joy replied, "Please tell my sisters that; they don't believe me and just laugh at me."

All the badgers continued to laugh but somehow knew that Speed was going to be exceptional when her time came.

As the cubs were play-fighting, a plump little mole pup with a glossy black coat and a tiny, gangly fawn dappled with light brown and yellow spots made their way towards the cubs. Shyly, the tiny mole pup pulled at the lanky fawn's legs, and with that being the cue, the tiny fawn cleared her throat and said, "Hello, I am Farah, and this is Mighty. Can we also join in the race?"

Speed laughed at Mighty and said he would not be able to keep in a straight line for being so blind, but Farah immediately came to his defence and said, "Actually, the moles are amazing, and we always act as a team. We allow them to sit on our backs whilst they guide us with their incredible sense of smell and hearing to protect us from danger."

With that, Farah sadly turned away and said, "We will leave, as we can see that you do not want us to play with you."

Bojana gave Speed a very angry look and jumped in front of Farah and Mighty, saying, "Please stop; it would be so much fun to play together."

Speed lowered her head and said, "Yes, it will be fun, and I am so sorry for being so mean. It was very unkind. Please stop and play."

Within seconds, everything was forgotten, and their races went on. It goes without saying that Farah won effortlessly with her graceful gait.

The High Lord began to look around for the hedgehogs, craning his neck as far as he could; disappointed, he turned to Pure and said, "I cannot see any of the hedgehogs around. We have to encourage them to come over and be part of this union. I don't want them to think the friendship treaty was purely a military alliance. I want them to integrate into our new community."

The High Lady agreed and said she would pass the message on to the High Lord Maximus Mole, who was very friendly with High Lord Henry Hedgehog.

Shams was getting ready to set off in his black Maserati Levante, when his mother, in spite of his specific instructions, came out of the large family mansion with a load of Tupperware containers filled with delectable Asian treats and food. She gave him her warmest smile and said, "Eat, son; you have been away only three weeks and look so skinny. Plenty of food for you and your friends."

Shams gave her a big hug and said, "It is impossible to be mad with you, Ammi; now go inside and keep out of the cold. I am just going to the building yard to say goodbye to Abba."

Not wanting to let him go, she gradually released him and said, "Take care, son. You do not look happy, so if this job does not agree with you, remember nothing will make your father happier than to have you work with him."

Shams smiled and drove towards the yard. His four elder brothers all worked in the family building business. The business was highly successful and had been in the Aziz family for three generations; they were one of the most successful and respected families in Birmingham. The Aziz family also played a significant role in all the local charities and was held in high esteem and respect in the community.

Shams's decision to pursue his university studies was not well received by his father. The last three years were a big strain on Shams, as his father ignored his achievements, and his brothers made him feel like a traitor. Regardless of this, Shams, being the youngest, continued to show his father and brothers respect. His father did not attend his graduation day, but his beloved mother arrived with his favourite uncle and spared no expenses, showing up with the car of his dreams.

On his arrival at the building yard site, he saw his father turn away as he pulled in. Shams took a deep breath, released a sad sigh, smiled, and came out of the car. He humbly approached his father and said, "Morning, Abba; the site looks great. I am sorry I did not get a chance to see you all this weekend. I hope you will not be as busy the next time I come home."

Without looking at Shams, Mr. Aziz replied, "Well, if you were helping your brothers and myself, we would be able to spend more time together. Look how hard your brothers work."

Shams knew it was pointless saying anything else and respectfully said goodbye and set off for Bristol.

Mr. Aziz turned around as Shams left and felt a pang of guilt that he was not more accepting of his son's choice. Furthermore, he knew he'd face the wrath of his wife on his return home, as she was very upset that he refused to show Shams any approval. She had been furious that he refused to spend any time with him whilst he was home that weekend.

Sarah came off the M6 motorway at junction 30 to have a coffee break at the Tickle Trout. It was lovely spending the weekend with her mum and dad, and she felt so good having confided in them as to how she was feeling. Her parents' exemplary marriage was envied by all their friends, as they did everything together. The anniversary party was a great success, and it was sad to say that her late grandfather's absence actually contributed to a wonderful evening. Her grandfather had never accepted her dad, but the success of her parents' marriage only proved him wrong. Even on his deathbed, he refused to accept their union and left everything to Sarah in a trust.

Sandra and David MacBain had tried for years to conceive a child, so when Sarah was born, nothing was spared to cater to all her needs. She was not spoiled with everything she wanted but was given everything she needed and always received her parents' support in all she did. They picked her up when she made mistakes and served as punching bags in times of stress. But the MacBains were always just a phone call away and never let her down.

She had just left them only two hours ago and was already missing them.

I feel so guilty ruining all Friday evening complaining about my job, she thought. *They must think me so selfish.*

She dialled their number.

"Hi guys, I stopped for an early lunch and just received a call from one of the team, who said he has some very interesting and unbelievable things to tell me."

Mrs. MacBain replied in her very posh Scottish accent, "Was this the young gentleman you could not stop talking about all of the weekend? Geoffrey?"

Sarah, faking annoyance but finding that she could not stop smiling, replied, "Mother, we are just colleagues. He's really weird and not my kind."

Her dad immediately chirped up, "Exactly what your mum said about me."

Feeling cornered, Sarah replied, "Okay guys, that's enough now. I just wanted to say how much I love you, and I'm so sorry for just moaning about my job all Friday evening. I also could have made a better effort mingling yesterday."

"Don't be daft," her dad said. "All those old codgers were just so glad to see your bonny face."

"We'd be gutted if we thought you did not tell us your problems," her mom added.

"Always here for you, kiddo," Dad said, "and don't you forget that."

"You are the best, the both of you, mmmmwahhh. I still have a long way to go, so I'll just text you when I get to Bristol. I am meeting Geoffrey and Shams at two o'clock and already cutting it fine. Love you lots."

"Sarah," Geoffrey said, "stop laughing and making me feel like I was hallucinating and making all this up."

"Okay, I am sorry, Geoffrey, but it all sounds so bizarre," she said. "What do you think, Shams?"

Shams looked at her and said with a serious expression, "Well, Sarah, I do not believe Geoffrey would make up such a tale, so let's concentrate and retrace his steps. Please go over it again, Geoffrey."

Feeling embarrassed that she had not taken Geoffrey seriously, she apologised and paid closer attention.

Geoffrey repeated his tale from the start: "Well, my family was away on holiday, so I was on my own at the weekend and decided to look out for tracks in the evening when the badgers were actually out. It was so eerie walking into the forest and not hearing any of the usual noises, but as I walked farther into the woodlands, I got a whiff of a strange scent in the air and then began to hear the most amazing animal sounds, in harmony, like a choir. I followed the sounds and then stopped in my tracks when I saw the most astonishing gathering in front of me. There must have been a thousand badgers gathered together with all of the forest animals in a massive congregation, as if in a ceremony or a big meeting. I don't know. It was just crazy."

He continued, "They were literally in a formation of some sort. I tried to make a video, but as I pulled my phone out, I stepped on a twig, and the sound alerted a huge red badger, who turned around immediately. Guys, I was convinced that was the end of me."

He then proceeded to tell them about the meeting he had observed with Richard, Uncle Shamus, and the mysterious Tommy Balls.

More composed and taking Geoffrey seriously, Sarah said, "Wow, you had a busy weekend."

"Yes, I did indeed. We need to get to the Dog and Gun pub and walk approximately fifty-five hundred steps in a south-west direction, and that will get us close to the spot where this all happened."

Sarah looked at Geoffrey, who at this minute seemed gawky, nervous, and totally embarrassed, and she suddenly thought he was actually adorable and vulnerable. She wanted to hug him and apologise for laughing at him.

"Well, let's not waste any time," Shams said. "We'll make our way there immediately, as the sun will be setting soon. We also need to call in the pub and ask if the owner knows who Tommy Balls is. I am actually starving, and that fish pie did sound delightful."

Sarah could not risk the opportunity and chirped up, "Since we are in such a hurry, shouldn't we go in the Maserati?"

The suggestion surprised Shams, but he realised she simply wanted a spin in his car, and with a little laugh, he replied, "Why not? Come on, let's go drive a real car."

As they drove towards the Dog and Gun, Geoffrey pointed out that none other than Ollie Gunner was walking through the door.

Geoffrey, Sarah, and Shams stepped back, and within a minute, a silver Saab pulled into the carpark, and none other than Richard Nicks stepped out of the passenger seat. An older gentleman got out of the driver's seat.

"Hey, guys, look," Geoffrey said. "Ollie Gunner and Richard; that older guy must be Tommy Balls. I actually have a picture of the two of them on my phone. I only knew this as the uncle kept going on about this guy owning a Saab, a silver Saab."

Shams said, "We need to get into the pub and try to figure out what's going on."

Sarah had a light bulb moment and blurted out, "The uncle, the terriers; remember Richard's big plan in our early meetings?"

Shams and Geoffrey stood frozen as they realised Sarah had hit the nail on the head.

She elaborated, "And remember when he wanted a personal word with Ollie Gunner?"

Geoffrey was now slowly zooming in his phone, making a video of Richard and Tommy Balls entering the pub.

"Let's hang back for a couple of minutes," Geoffrey said, "and use the back entrance so we're not seen. I must get a picture or video of the three of them together."

Ollie Gunner was not too happy about meeting at such a public place. He walked up to the bar and ordered himself a pint of cider. With the hood of his jumper still covering his head, he walked to the far end of the pub and waited for Richard Nicks and Tommy Balls.

He took his phone out and was just about to text Richard when he heard him shout out, "Mr. Gunner, what would you like to drink?"

What an idiot, Ollie thought. *What part of discretion don't you understand?*

He regained his composure, raised his glass, and said, "I'm okay."

Richard and Tommy approached Ollie.

Tommy reached his hand out and said, "Hello, Ollie. I am Tommy Balls."

Without looking at him, Ollie said arrogantly, "Get one thing straight, Mr. Balls. I am not interested in badger baiting; I'm only interested in your dogs tracking the location of the badgers. Have I made myself clear?"

Tommy looked at Richard and said, "Son, I don't care who this ignorant fool is to you, but I refuse to be spoken to so rudely by a kid who is still wet behind his ears."

He picked up his drink, downed his whisky in one go, slammed his glass down on the table, and made his way towards the door.

Richard looked at Ollie and forgot for a minute that Ollie was his superior; he shouted angrily, "Good grief. Do something."

Ollie, still in a state of shock from Tommy's reprisal, ran over to Tommy and shouted, "Mr. Balls, please hang on a minute."

Tommy stopped walking but did not turn around.

Ollie moved ahead of him and said, "I am sorry we got off to a bad start. I guess I am pretty nervous; can I please get you another whisky?"

Tommy looked around and could see that Dicky was anxious for him to return to the table. He told Ollie, "I don't give a toss about you, you ignorant upstart, I am doing this to help an old friend's son."

Ollie held back what he wanted to say but he thought, *The cheek of it; you'll be wanting a lot of money for doing this job.*

Ollie returned to the table with a large whisky, sat down, and using a less-arrogant tone, he said, "Firstly, I would like to apologise, but I really must reiterate that I don't want to have anything to do with badger baiting. All I want is for the dogs to sniff out a location. Richard can go along with you and note the location. He can then work with his team and legitimately forward the tracks so I can organise the culling team. The badgers seemed to have disappeared. Something very unnatural is occurring, and I cannot put my finger on it."

Tommy nodded his head in agreement and replied, "In all honesty, there are random patrols in the area, so it's important that we monitor their patrol for a week."

Ollie interrupted and said in his usual superior manner, "No, no, I cannot wait a week. We need action like yesterday. I will pay you whatever it takes. This has to take place in a couple of days."

Tommy paused for a while and said, "I want five thousand pounds, in cash and paid upfront."

Richard almost choked on his lager, and Ollie said sarcastically, "Even Dick Turpin wore a mask. I want results, or else I'll be getting my money back."

Both gentlemen looked hard into each other's eyes, and after thirty seconds, which seemed like an eternity, Ollie put his hand out, and Tommy shook on it to seal the deal.

Richard just sat by with his mouth agape, as if watching a tennis match at Wimbledon whilst the two exchanged their dialogue.

Ollie and Tommy stood up and walked towards the door, whilst Richard sheepishly followed behind.

As they left the pub, they all walked towards Tommy's silver Saab and then went their separate ways.

Unknown to Ollie, Richard, and Tommy Balls, Sarah, Geoffrey, and Shams had overheard the entire conversation. They could hardly breathe as they sat in their booth and tried to calmly eat their evening meal. It was impossible to get a video or picture of the three of them together, but they heard without a doubt that they were scheming to circumvent the DEFRA regulations.

Geoffrey carefully raised his head to see if the coast was clear, and they all heaved a sigh of relief and began brainstorming as to what they were going to with all this intel.

"Oh, my goodness," Sarah said. "I never liked Richard from day one."

Shams was taking notes down and said, "Let's ask the pub owner if he knows of Tommy Balls. Better for you to ask, Sarah. I am sure you have more charm than either of us."

The pub owner, a jolly plump man with rosy, red cheeks and a mop of unruly greasy curls, was walking towards them. He gave them a big smile and said, "Nice to see young folk in here. Did you enjoy the pie? Hope we'll be seeing you again."

On cue, Sarah put on her biggest smile and replied, "That was certainly the best fish pie I've had in a long time. Are you also the chef?"

"Certainly am," he said. "Jack D'agostino is my name; whereabouts are you from?" He wiped his sweaty brow with his not-very-white shirt sleeve.

"We just joined the office at DEFRA and are absolutely loving the countryside. Originally, I am from Scotland, Shams from Birmingham, and Geoffrey from the Northwest."

"Blimey, a nationwide ensemble," Jack said, chuckling. "I assume you are part of the cull program?"

"Yes, we are," Geoffrey said.

Jack's jolly expression faded into a sad smile as he said quietly, "Aye, my niece Melissa works there as well. I have nothing against them creatures;

part of God's world, but who am I to make comment? Please just be kind and fair to the animals."

Geoffrey, Sarah, and Shams looked at each other and did not acknowledge knowing Mel, as they were unsure who else was involved in this conspiracy.

"Oh, indeed we are," Shams said. "We have rules to abide by."

Geoffrey piped up, "Did you notice that older gentleman with the two younger guys at the table behind our booth? They sounded like they were having a heated conversation, and I thought I recognised his face, but maybe he just looks like one of my dad's mates."

"I know everyone here," Jack said. "That man goes by the name of Tommy Balls, and I doubt that your dad would have ever associated with the likes of him."

Sarah immediately grabbed the opportunity and continued, "Oh, Jack, you don't come across as one who has a bad word to say about anyone. What's that about?"

Jack slowly shook his head, heaved a big sigh, and said, "You are right, Sarah, I really do not like to speak ill of anyone, but that man is a bad egg. He used to associate with the likes of the Hardcore Terrier Men. I am convinced that he still dabbles with badger baiting, together with that nasty scoundrel Mark Ashley. Shamus Nicks and his sons were part of that mob, and they made their living setting up badger-baiting events. In fact, Shamus Junior still comes in. He not only served his time in prison, but he paid the ultimate price on that fateful night."

Geoffrey probed, "What night? That sounds like an interesting tale."

Jack sighed again, put down the plates he just cleared, and began to tell about the night that ended the lives of Shamus Senior and John Nicks.

"I can't say it was a sad tale, as what they were doing was illegal and cruel, but that John Nicks left his young son fatherless was a tragedy."

Sarah glanced quickly at the others and gently asked what happened.

"Aye, I think his mother took him to Torquay," Jack said. "I believe she married someone else, and folk say that Richard has done very well for himself, but I would not recognise him now, not after all these years. Hey, I best clear this table. Can't be chewing off my customer's ears all night, ha ha."

Sarah looked at him with a big smile and replied, "Not at all, Jack, you have been so interesting and shown so much hospitality. We won't just be coming back for the fish pie but would love to see you again."

Jack roared a hearty laugh and said, "You little charmer. Well, I do hope to see you here again."

Jack lumbered back into the kitchen with a full load of plates, and as soon as he was out of earshot, Sarah squealed, "Oh, my goodness, this is all coming together like a jigsaw. It all makes sense why Richard was so secretive about his past. This might be some kind of way of him avenging his father's death."

"It certainly is a lot to take in," Shams said, "and speak of the devil, Richard has just texted to say he cannot meet us in the morning. It's too late now to look at the spot, so let's check in at the campus first thing in the morning and come back tomorrow."

13

The Ninth Inscription

Protect the Young and Innocent, as They Cannot Comprehend Evil or Bad

On this crisp, frosty, Monday morning, Speed and Bojana were racing back and forth to the thick box hedge, close to the sett, when Bojana suddenly spotted four sets of bright, shiny eyes peering through the hedge. Clumsily and without thinking, she poked her paw into the bush, and a loud ouch was followed by a cry of a little hedgehog coming out from the corner of the hedge.

"Oh, I'm so sorry," Bojana said. "I did not realise what you were. Did I hurt you?"

The little hoglet ran back to the hedge, and a few seconds later, three other hoglets meekly peeped out from around the box hedge.

Finally, the largest hoglet came forward and introduced herself.

"It's okay," she said. "That's my youngest sibling, Split; our mama will be mad if she knows we were spying on you. We enjoyed watching you and your friend racing to the hedge. It looked so much fun. I am Maggie, by the way."

Bojana grinned at Maggie and squealed, "It's okay, I am Bojana, future warrior of the clan. Come and join us, and bring your siblings."

Maggie squealed some more and then said, "I too want to be a lady warrior, like the High Lady Dharma."

"High Lady Dharma? Who is she?" asked Speed, who missed nothing.

With a big smile on her face, Maggie continued, "She leads all the fallow deer in the forest. All the big stags bow down to her because she is in charge. Have you not met Farah? She is offspring to the High Lady Dharma."

"Oh, yes, and her little friend, Mighty. I too want to be in charge," Speed said, but Bojana jumped forward and said, "Oh, no, you will not. I will be in charge."

She playfully pushed Speed into Maggie, and within seconds, Maggie, Speed, and Bojana were in fits of giggles and tumbles.

Maggie curled into a ball and hurled herself in front of the new cubs and continued, "Maybe you both can be in charge, like the High Lady Dharma. She makes all the rules with Lady Dasha always by her side."

Bojana gave Speed a big hug, looked at Maggie, and said, "Sounds good to me. You can also lead with us, Maggie; from today forward we are calling ourselves 'BMS.'"

The three youngsters rolled around, laughing, but it was the little male hoglets who stole the show.

Without restraint, Sonny and Spiky were twisting, leaping, pivoting, and hurling about like gymnasts, and Split, their youngest sibling, who had already forgotten his sore eye, curled into a spiky ball, like his siblings. With extraordinary strength, they began to hurl themselves, leaping and bounding to see who could reach the hedge first. Spiky had longer quills than his siblings and ended up stuck in the hedge, and this caused the young badger cubs to roar with laughter.

Speed and Bojana tried to curl themselves but could only roll in a somersault, then they lay quite immobile. All the cubs had just received a lesson to roll backwards into their sett, and that was difficult enough. Speed, laughing uncontrollably, said, "I want to be a hedgehog."

Power, Sharp, and Drill came running to see what was happening, and Bojana's siblings, Mercury and Dynamite, were close behind. In no time, there must have been thirty young hedgehogs and all the cubs of the sett, playing together and enjoying the crisp winter's morning.

The badger cubs were in awe of the incredible feats of balance and agility of the young hedgehogs. Under Maggie's choreography, her siblings formed a triangle with Split at the amazing apex. Their motor coordination, strength, speed, and flexibility did not just impress the young cubs, for not far away was Widejaw, observing the dexterity of these remarkable animals. When he saw his cubs run off earlier, he made sure to stay nearby, and so did Clawdigger. A couple of the young hedgehog parents also came from around the hedge and walked meekly towards Widejaw and Clawdigger.

"Good afternoon, I am Lord Sparta, the warrior leader and responsible for those little show-offs, who are my hoglets. This is Lord Didas, who is head of our hoglet's academy."

"Pleasure to meet you," Widejaw said, "and I am very impressed at your young hoglet's skills and dexterity. I am Widejaw, and this is Clawdigger."

"Your reputation precedes you, Widejaw. Clawdigger, all our hearts have gone out to you and your family," said Lord Sparta.

"Thank you, Lord Sparta," Clawdigger said. "I am fascinated by the skills of your young hoglets. We are big and strong, but so slow and clumsy in comparison to you."

Clawdigger continued, "I honestly never thought I'd see the day when hedgehogs and badgers played together. It has been an absolute joy to watch their innocence and the absence of prejudice amongst all the young forest animals."

"Papa, please come over here," Drill and Speed called out.

Lord Sparta replied, "I have great hopes that this unity will be the final seal of all the woodland creatures bonding as one family."

Widejaw replied, "Yes, you are absolutely right, Lord Sparta. We should protect each other, and we already owe so much to all the animals who have cooperated and collaborated together in the last few weeks, eliminating our tracks and helping to camouflage our setts. The High Lord Luminous has reported that man believe we actually left our territory."

Lord Sparta turned and looked towards Clawdigger, who was now surrounded by his cubs and currently blindfolded, going around in circles in between his cubs and the other young animals.

In a sad voice, he continued, "I do not know if you are aware, Widejaw, but the High Lord Henry and I were hunting in the woods when we stumbled on the horrific site where the slaughter of your clan took place. It was a cruel, ruthless bloodbath, and it was then our High Lord felt that the true enemy between us was man. That was when he decided to make that very bold entrance at your ceremony. I hope to prove to you, Widejaw, that between our skills and your strength, we will be able to devise some remarkably interesting strategies to protect our forest."

Clawdigger walked back towards them and caught the last bit of the conversation; he nodded in agreement as Widejaw responded, "Without a doubt. I humbly admit that we have a lot to learn from your military skills, and I am very much looking forward to having a meeting. I am convinced there will be one very soon."

Lord Didas interrupted, "Clawdigger, would it be possible for me to be introduced to Councillor Wisepaws? I have heard so many tales of his exquisite mind and would be very privileged to make his acquaintance."

Clawdigger responded, "Oh, yes, he would be delighted. Do you and Lord Sparta have time to come across now?"

"Well, I was sent on a mission to locate my four little hoglets," Lord Sparta said, "and now there are about thirty here, all enjoying themselves. We best return, as their parents will be very anxious in view of the recent events. However, we will be happy to meet tomorrow and bring our families."

"That sounds like a wonderful plan," Clawdigger said.

"Well, in return for the great feast we had at the saining of your cubs," Lord Sparta said, "let us surprise you tomorrow with some of our delicacies; I am convinced you will enjoy them all."

Lord Didas struggled to pull the hoglets away, and after he got them together, he smiled to himself, anticipating a better life in the forest.

"Are you sure this is the spot, Geoffrey?" Sarah asked.

Geoffrey looked around carefully and said, "Guys, clear your minds, take a deep breath, and look around you; this is the place. Look how clean and clear of any tracks it is. It's surreal."

Sarah inhaled deeply and could smell the faint aroma of resin.

"Yes, I can smell something," she said. "Where are you going, Geoffrey?"

"Stay there, please," he said, then he walked ahead and came across a tree with several quills in it.

"Guys, come and have a look at this."

Shams came close to the tree and inspected it.

"I believe these are the quills you mentioned yesterday," he said.

"Exactly. I know I'm right," Geoffrey said triumphantly. "This is definitely the spot."

Sarah walked a few steps farther and could hear scuttling and a mixture of chirping, clucking, and barking. She peered through a bush, and her eyes lit up to see a field of young badgers, rabbits, polecats, moles, and hedgehogs, all playing together. It was such a beautiful scene, and she soon found her eyes filling up with tears. As gently and carefully as possible, she pulled out her iPhone and began to video this beautiful scene.

Geoffrey and Shams looked for Sarah and realised she was missing; they began to shout for her.

As she turned to reply, she stood frozen because out of nowhere, a large badger was just five feet from her, with his jaw opened wide. She let out a scream and dropped her phone.

"Sarah," Geoffrey shouted. "Sarah! Are you okay?"

The badger rushed back into the bushes.

Sarah ran straight into Geoffrey's arms, shaking from what had just happened.

Incoherently, and in a fit of nervous sobs, she blurted out, "I was videoing the forest animals and young badgers playing together, when suddenly, a large badger approached me. He was mad and was definitely going to attack me, but he turned away when he heard you shouting."

Still very shaken up, she continued, "I did not realise how aggressive badgers were and must admit that I was terrified."

Shams started to shake his head and said, "No, that is definitely not their natural reaction; if anything, they retreat. It's very unusual for them to approach a human and be so aggressive."

"Was it a large red badger?" Geoffrey asked.

"Yes, it was," Sarah said, "and now I am 100 percent sure that you were not making anything up. I am so sorry for mocking you."

"What are we going to do?" Sarah said. "I feel crazy saying this, but the badgers seem to be hiding from us. Come and see what I have just been watching."

As the three of them watched the forest animals in astonishment, they did not hear a small, pale man, dressed in a shabby white outfit, approach them from behind. Unknown to the three of them, the High

Lord Luminous had overheard their conversation and transformed himself when he realised they were trying to help his cause.

"I would very much appreciate if you would not share our secret to those who want to harm us."

The small voice made them jump, and the three of them turned around and looked quizzically at the strange man.

Geoffrey stood in front of Sarah, and in unison, all three asked, "Who are you?"

"Well, I doubt that you will believe me," the High Lord said, "but my clans are in so much danger, I feel I must now take the risk of entrusting you and revealing myself to you."

"Clans?" said Sarah, "You do not look very Scottish."

"I am the High Lord Luminous Snowspirit, spiritual leader of the badgers' governing clans of Brocklehurstshire."

Sarah, Geoffrey, and Shams looked at each other in total disbelief but remained speechless.

Shams said, "I am sorry, sir, but you look like you've lost your way, as you are dressed in what appears like a patient's clothes from a hospital. Perhaps we can guide you back."

The High Lord gave a small laugh, smiled, and said, "Please prepare yourself for an experience that no man has ever witnessed."

Sarah tightened her grip behind Geoffrey's back, and Shams stood frozen, not knowing what to do.

Without further warning, the High Lord knelt down and recited aloud, "Sekarang saya jadi binatang."

A bright light flashed before Sarah, Geoffrey, and Shams, and when the light faded away, a splendid badger of the purest white pelt stood before them. He no longer seemed pale and weak as before, but now the three of them saw a magnificent, majestic badger who exuded power and nobility.

The High Lord stepped back and, in another flash of light, reappeared as the pale weak man in the white soiled clothes. He smiled when he saw their bewildered expressions.

Not giving them another minute to think or take in their unbelievable experience, he calmly continued, "We need your help. Can I trust you to help? We cannot understand why man are trying to destroy us. We have been accused of spreading this disease, and I can assure you that none of us are plagued with any disease. We do not want a war. We just want to live with all the other forest animals. My warriors are upset and want to attack man, but I know there are some good people out there, like you appear to be."

Geoffrey bowed clumsily and said, "Your Majesty."

The High Lord laughed and said, "Please, young man, just address me as Luminous; you do not owe me any respect on a bended knee."

"Luminous, "Geoffrey stammered, "h-h-hear me out. We work for the department that is trying to destroy you."

The High Lord stepped back in disbelief, but Sarah came forward and said gently, "But all three of us are against the mission, and yes, we will help you. What can we do?"

The High Lord looked at each of them with piercing eyes and was satisfied that they were telling the truth. He slowly continued, "I believe a Mr. Andy May and Mr. Barry Odie are actively raising funds for us badgers. We need more help to lose our tracks, so we can stay concealed and safe whilst more good man prove we are not spreading this disease to cattle. The animals including the birds are doing their best, but our young cubs and elderlies are too confused to understand the complexities. My greatest worry is that they will lead our enemies right into our setts.

"On Friday night, I heard Mr. May and Mr. Odie's wonderful speech to support us, but a few minutes later, I heard two other men discussing how they were going to use dogs to track us down."

Geoffrey got his phone out and showed the High Lord a picture of Richard Nicks and Tommy Balls. "Do you recognise either of these men?" he asked.

The High Lord looked closely and said, "Yes, I saw the young man, but not this man. His companion is not on this picture but was all over the big screens in the shop called Currys."

"Ollie Gunner," Sham and Geoffrey said in unison. Shams continued, "Yes, you are right, Luminous, we overheard them planning a conspiracy that is going to happen within this week."

The High Lord's face dropped into a saddened expression and said, "We just found peace and harmony within our forest, and now, for no justified reasons, we are being persecuted mercilessly."

Shams looked at him and said, "We are going to do everything we can to help you."

Sarah continued, "I actually know the son of Barry Odie, and if you are willing to reveal yourself to him, I am sure he will do everything to help you."

Sarah decided not to mention that she was in total disfavour with Mr. Odie at this moment.

The High Lord smiled and said, "Please come and witness for yourselves my wonderful clan and our friends of the forest."

Lord Sparta and Lord Didas were about to leave, but they stopped in their tracks, as did all the forest animals playing in the field, when the High Lord Luminous appeared in the shape of man, walking in with Sarah, Geoffrey, and Shams.

Widejaw was instantaneously by the High Lord's side and growled at Sarah, Geoffrey, and Shams.

Calmly, the High Lord introduced Sarah, Geoffrey, and Shams to the warrior leader, saying, "I believe you already met Widejaw, chief warrior of the clan."

Widejaw did not show any signs of welcoming them, but the High Lord continued, "Family and friends." He suddenly stopped when he saw the hedgehogs. "Ahh, I see the hedgehogs have joined us; how wonderful."

He continued, "Please meet Sarah, Geoffrey, and Shams. No harm is to come to them, and whenever they need anyone's help, from the small mole to any of the birds, I implore you to assist them. They are risking everything to help us, so I ask that you trust me and cooperate. "

The animals surrounded the three humans and began to sniff them. Sarah bravely bent down and sat on the ground as she felt she wanted to express a sense of equality, being closer to their height. Shams and Geoffrey followed her lead, and in less than a minute, Widejaw came right up to them and looked them straight in their eyes. Both Geoffrey and Shams sat in complete fear of an attack and tried their best to look unperturbed.

Whilst the High Lord continued to speak casually to the visiting hedgehogs, Shams looked on in awe, as if in a dream. Geoffrey, although extremely nervous and sweating profusely, was so pleased that his friends were experiencing this amazing encounter with him. Sarah, on the other hand, had three cubs in her arms and was even tickling Speed's belly.

The High Lord turned to Lord Sparta and Lord Didas, and said, "I am so pleased that you have joined us today. We should all walk through the forest as our home and look out for each other. Please let High Lord Henry know of our new liaison with these humans. They are special and want to help protect us."

Lord Didas replied, "We have waited a long time for this moment and are glad that we are part of this new alliance. Who knows, one day we might walk alongside with man with no fear of our lives being compromised. Anyway, we need to take the little hoglets home, but we will be back tomorrow."

Sarah, Shams, and Geoffrey, feeling more relaxed and confident, began to explore the field and were impressed by how gentle and considerate the animals were to each other. The moles were frantically burrowing holes in the field, and just as they ascended, the birds swooped down to eat the worms they brought up in the loamy soil. The birds, however, left enough for a couple of older badgers, who wallowed slowly behind the moles and helped themselves to the freshly excavated treats. As Flash and his team were cleaning out their setts, they left a pile of old hay for the birds to pick from, to build their nest with. As soon as the birds picked what they wanted, the rabbits dived in and dragged the remaining hay into their burrows. You must remember that badgers were exceptionally clean and had their latrines outside their setts, so this hay was only old but not soiled. Everything was done harmoniously, with order and respect for each other. There was a natural sense of communal life, sharing and giving.

The High Lord looked at the unity in the field, and his smile broadened; he caught sight of his eldest cub, White, protectively watching over Fire, her younger sibling.

White never left Fire's side, and he in turn was never far from Speed. He was in awe of Speed, who was a little tomboy, and despite White's disapproving frowns, Speed was always pulling Fire away and dragging him into her tumbles or teasing him mercilessly. Speed was closest to Little Clawdigger, whom she missed dearly, and her other siblings would not play the games she used to have with him, so Fire was her next best alternative. He was perfect, as she always got to win, unlike Little Clawdigger, who always beat her in all her challenges.

White complained to her mother, "Mother, Speed is far too rough with

Fire; he is out of breath, and the silly cub keeps wanting more. Sometimes, I think she is a bully."

The High Lady smiled and replied, "Darling White, she just loves a rough-and-tumble; don't forget that she just lost Little Clawdigger. She sees Fire as a friend and sibling. He loves it; look how happy he is when he is with her."

White lowered her head and responded meekly, "Oh, Mother, I feel so bad; I did not look at it like that. I am selfish and jealous."

Her mother hugged her closely and said, "Not at all, my sweet cub; the love and devotion you have for your Fire is selfless. You always make sure Fire is fed first and wait till he has had enough. That, my precious cub, is not selfish or jealous. Don't ever judge yourself so badly."

The High Lord walked over to the three humans and said, "Now can you understand how important it is for us to be left to live our days, without your impending threat to cull us. You can see that none of us are unhealthy. We should not be so unfairly persecuted."

Recalling the recent tragedy, the High Lord continued, "A couple of weeks ago, many of my kin were killed in a bloody slaughter. It was meaningless, but more disappointedly, it was savage and merciless. Are man so insensitive? But I guess we are only animals. I have seen on those big screens how you kill your own kin. You have wars because of the colour of your skin. We have different pelts but would never kill each other. Sadly, it is ironic how much good has come out of this cull. It has brought the badgers of all pelts closer, and more important; the union of the hedgehogs has made the forest a complete, happy community. I sincerely hope you never lose millions of lives before you see how important it is to live in harmony, or perhaps like us, you will need a tragedy to unite."

Geoffrey, Shams, and Sarah nodded shamefully, and Geoffrey said, "I speak for the three of us; even before we met you, we already lost faith in our leader and did not like his methods of fulfilling the cull. We are in a good position to help you and will use every opportunity to stop this injustice."

Shams turned to Sarah and said, "I know this is going to be challenging, but I suggest you contact Freddie and request a meeting with Barry Odie and Andy May."

Sarah turned to the High Lord and said, "You will need to be there; please, you can trust us."

The High Lord looked at the three of them, smiled, and said, "You are three special people. I place all my trust in you, and yes, I will be there. When you have information to tell me, don't risk coming into this part of the woods, in case you are followed. Just wait at the shop which is called Currys and concentrate on my name together, and I will sense that you are there and will come and meet you."

Sarah's mind was buzzing. She was so glad of an opportunity to apologise to Freddie's parents and did not even consider how ridiculous all this was going to sound.

She turned to the High Lord and said, "Oh, I am such a believer in fantasy and destiny. I feel like I'm having the most amazing dream ever. This is all going to be fine. I promise you; we will help protect you and your clans."

The High Lord walked his three new friends to the edge of the woods; they looked out and saw Ollie, Richard, and Tommy Balls exiting the pub.

Shams said, "That explains why Richard could not make this morning's meeting. What I would give to be a fly on that wall in the pub. They are planning something. Luminous, do you think you could get word round, as we are sure that Ollie Gunner wants these dogs to find you within days."

The High Lord replied, "I will tell Councillor Claudius Crow to keep an eye out for us. I will summon him now, and you can show him that picture on your phone. You are aware that crows are highly intelligent birds and only need to register a face the one time."

As Geoffrey was swiping through the images on his phone, the High Lord intertwined his fingers and kept his thumbs straight up. He then blew in the space between his fingers and his thumbs, simultaneously lifting his fingers up and down, and a beautiful melody, as if from a flute, began to play.

Within a minute, the Councillor Claudius Crow arrived, and Luminous showed him the picture of the three men on Geoffrey's phone.

Claudius perched on the High Lord's arm, and his black eyes bored into Geoffrey's phone.

As suddenly as he arrived, Claudius flew back into the forest.

The High Lord turned to Geoffrey, Sarah, and Shams, and said, "Let us meet just before the sun sets outside the curry shop, and I will let you know of Claudius's findings. Now be safe, and return to the campus. I thank you very much for helping us. Sarah, my dear, this is far from a dream; this might get very bloody, with a loss of lives, so I hope you understand how involved you are and the role you will play to help us."

Sarah looked at Geoffrey and Shams, turned to the High Lord, and said, "We are only doing the right thing and can assure you, like you are aware, that many men will agree that your plight is cruel and unfair. We are honoured that you have entrusted us into your clan and look forward to seeing you this evening."

The Tenth Inscription

Only with Pure Heart and Repentance Can We Call on Our Ancestors for Guidance and Help

Ollie was enraged all week as he had been trying to contact Nick Panay but according to Miss D'agostino, his mother was poorly and he had to take a week off to be with her. At precisely nine am on Monday morning, Ollie could not wait a minute more before he dialled Nick Panay's number.

"Mr. Panay," he said, "I returned to the site and was extremely disappointed that you did not follow my instructions. I specifically said to reset the footholds and cages after the first trap. We could have finished off at least another one hundred and fifty badgers over the weekend. Are you aware of the target figures I need to achieve?"

When Nick did not respond, Ollie continued, "You and your team are suspended pending a complaint that I am going to lodge to the board."

Nick said, "Actually, Mr. Gunner, I do not know when you last read your emails, but as of this morning, my team has been officially transferred to Mr. Michael Richardson's team."

Ollie put the call on hands-free and tried to scroll through his emails. Scrolling down, he saw an urgent one marked as High Priority from his manager, Jeremy Fischer, with the subject "Emergency meeting immediately."

"What is going on?" Ollie shouted. "What have you done?"

Nick, confident that he had done the correct thing and relieved that he no longer had to answer to Ollie again, replied, "I suggest you respond to the email, Mr. Gunner. I have been informed that I no longer need to report to you."

A deluge of thoughts was swimming through Ollie's mind. Richard had called late last night and said Tommy Balls had some news and wanted to meet in the car park of the Dog and Gun.

He made a quick call to the office, and Miss Mel D'agostino, Fischer's attractive personal assistant, answered in her quirky Italian accent with a Welsh lilt.

"Good morning, Jeremy Fischer's office, can I help you?"

"Morning, Miss D'agostino. It's Ollie Gunner; could you please advise Mr. Fischer that I am on a site visit and will see him after lunch."

"Not a problem, Mr. Gunner," Miss D'agostino replied, "but he did seem very anxious to see you."

"Okay, thanks for the heads-up; I will be there as soon as I can."

Goodness, surely no one saw me at the Dog and Gun with Tommy Balls, Ollie thought. *Maybe that silly idiot Richard Nicks blabbed about our meeting.*

When he arrived at the car park, he looked around carefully before he approached Richard and Tommy by the Saab.

"Morning," Ollie said. "I did not expect to see you so soon. What have you got?"

"I can get the dogs lined up for Friday," Tommy said. "It's a process to starve them, and it's impossible to rush it, or else the whole project will be a waste of time."

"Oh, that's good, that's really good. What's the plan? It must include Richard, and once we have the location, the dogs need to disappear."

"Well, we will set the dogs at where your last pilot zone was successful. From there, the dogs will be able to sniff them right up to the edge of the setts, where they are hiding now."

Richard had never seen Ollie so happy, but Tommy soon wiped that smile away by reminding him that he needed the money by Tuesday morning.

Ollie nodded and said, "Yes, that is as agreed, but neither of you have mentioned anything about our meeting to anyone, have you?"

"Are you joking?" Tommy snapped. "I don't go round advertising my business. It's a word-of-mouth thing, and, should I say, only for a niche client."

"Not me, Mr. Gunner," Richard said. "I don't associate with anyone at the campus."

"Hmm, very strange," Ollie said. "I have an emergency meeting with my boss, and I don't know what it's about.

"Right, Richard," Ollie said. "I'll give you a lift back to the office and will make arrangements for the payment. I will call as soon as the payment is ready."

Just as they parted, a large crow flew in between them in a very menacing manner, making all three men jump, but none of them realised that their entire conversation was overheard by none other than Councillor Claudius Crow.

Ollie made his way to Mr. Fischer's office and was greeted by Miss D'agostino's big smile. Of a mixed Italian and Welsh heritage, Mel was extremely attractive; there was not a single guy at the office she had not mesmerised with her beauty and charm. She was in a relationship with Dale Matthews, who was part of the Kill Team, so she already heard a little gossip about Ollie Gunner. She professionally stood up and led him into one of the interview rooms, where he sat down and calmly waited for Jeremy Fischer.

After fifteen minutes, Jeremy entered the room with some files and a laptop. He did not even look at Ollie. Mel entered and asked if any drinks were required, to which Jeremy responded, "I don't think that will be necessary; thank you, Miss D'agostino."

The PA closed the door behind her, and Ollie felt his neck go red and his heart began beating like a drum.

Jeremy looked straight at him and said, "What exactly are you playing at, Mr. Gunner? I had such high hopes for you, but what I saw and heard this morning is totally out of order."

Ollie paused and stammered and asked, "Why am I h-h-here, sir? I can explain the need to use Tommy Balls and his dogs."

"Oh, my goodness, this gets worse," Jeremy snapped. "What the devil are you talking about?

Sheepishly, Ollie related all the events and encounters that he had had with Tommy Balls, but avoided mentioning Richard Nicks.

Jeremy looked at him aghast, slammed his files down, and switched his laptop on.

"I received a complaint over the weekend from your Clean Kill Team over the inhumane manner of your instructions to trap and kill the badgers. We have enough do-gooders ripping us to shreds about our humane policies, and if this coverage is leaked, the whole operation will be shut down."

Jeremy Fischer opened the laptop and found the video Nick Panay had forwarded to him.

Ollie piped up, "Sir, I achieved double the figures in one day."

"Don't interrupt me, Mr. Gunner. Come around here and identify if this is your plot CULL1."

When Ollie went to observe the screen, the video showed the entrapped badgers bleeding to death. The pictures were graphic and distressful. A close-up of a young cub was included, showing a knife slicing the helpless cub down its shoulder. The ground was steeped with blood, and the piercing cries of the helpless badgers availed them not.

"Is this your plot, Mr. Gunner?" asked Jeremy.

Without any remorse or guilt, Ollie replied, "Yes."

"So above this incriminating footage, you are also involved with Tommy Balls. The activists are making our lives hell, and if it leaks that we are associating with that inhumane monster …; I am simply speechless. I'll ask you nothing further, as you are now suspended from the department pending your investigation in front of the board."

He looked straight at Ollie in complete disappointment; he heaved a disgruntled sigh, shook his head, and continued, "I am currently only inches away from the position of secretary of state, and my recommendation to make you my undersecretary, which is the executive director of DEFRA, was in the bag until this morning. Ollie, what have you done? I cannot be associated with this footage or been seen to have an alliance with Tommy Balls."

Ollie sat frozen and felt his whole world tumbling down, whilst Jeremy added, "I have never questioned how you acquired your target for the cull, but you've worked here for the last five years and should know the procedures and rules of our Clean Kill policy. Your performance is disgraceful and inhumane, and I do not want to be associated with you at all. I am sorry, but I'll be reporting you to the board. Kindly hand over your pass and mobile phone, and leave the building immediately."

Jeremy walked out and left a frightened and bewildered Ollie in the conference room.

As Shams, Sarah, and Geoffrey walked back into the office, all their phones beeped simultaneously. They stopped to check their email; each of them had received an email from Jeremy Fischer.

The email read,

> Dear Tracking and Investigating Team Member,
>
> Please note that effective tomorrow, you are to report to Mr. Michael Richardson's Tracking training room. No response is required, but I would appreciate if you would all continue your great role in the CULL 2014 operation.

Geoffrey, Shams, and Sarah looked at each other and then turned towards Richard, who was in deep thought, staring at the floor at the end of the corridor.

Sarah approached him and said, "Richard, are you alright?"

Richard was miles away and carried away in his own thoughts.

Someone must have seen us with Tommy Balls, he thought. *Did Mr. Gunner involve me? How can I find out? What should I do?*

In a louder voice, Sarah repeated, "Richard, Richard, I am talking to you. Are you alright?" She looked at his chalk-white expression and continued, "You do not look well; are you alright?"

Snapping out of his own thoughts, Richard replied, "Sorry, I was miles away; what were you saying?"

Geoffrey looked directly at Richard and asked, "Do you know anything that you need to share with your team?"

Unable to look directly at anyone, Richard's eyes darted from one person to the next, and he began to sweat profusely. His face was drained of all colour, as he meekly responded, "I do not know anything. I last saw him at the campus on Friday, like all of you did."

"Who are you referring to?" Geoffrey asked.

Sarah gave him a stern look and turned to Richard; she put her hand gently on his shoulder and said, "Richard, are you in some kind of trouble? I know we didn't hit it off, but the three of us are genuinely concerned for you and are prepared to help you."

He angrily pushed her hand away and said, "Why should I be in trouble? What do you know about what's going on?"

Shams stepped up and said, "Listen, let's go and ask Miss D'agostino if she can fill us in."

Geoffrey broke into a smile, saying, "Any excuse to speak to Miss D'agostino."

Just as he said that, he saw Sarah turn away with a scowl.

Hmm, he thought with a smile. *Someone seems annoyed.*

Geoffrey, Sarah, and Shams headed to the office, but Richard hung back and called Ollie Gunner. The phone rang continuously with no response. He hung up and decided to send a text instead: "Mr. Gunner, I do not know what is happening, but Tommy Balls is going to want the five thousand pounds you agreed on. Please call or reply."

Jeremy Fischer was holding Ollie's phone; he ignored the calls, but after the notification flashed on the screen, he could not help but read the text.

"Goodness me, young man, what have you done?" Jeremy said, then he called his PA into his office. "Miss D'agostino, I would like you to trace this number. Do not call it back, and please note that this is in the strictest of confidence."

"Yes, Mr. Fischer," Mel said. "That goes without saying."

As she stepped out of his office, she looked up to see Geoffrey, Sarah, and Shams walk towards her, followed closely behind by Richard.

"Hello, guys," Mel said. "Nice to see all of you. You saved me four emails, as I was about to get your particulars ready for Mr. Richardson and make appointments for each of you to see him."

Geoffrey boldly asked, "Miss D'agostino, what is going on? It all seems so sudden and abrupt."

Mel flashed an enormous smile and then replied, "I know as much as you do. I do, however, know that you are going to like Mr. Richardson, who is, as they say, down with the kids. Now, you need to see him at two o'clock, but in the meantime, please give me your numbers, as it will save me getting out your files."

After they gave Mel their numbers, the four walked away, but Richard went his own way and tried to phone Ollie again.

Mel began her email to Michael Richardson, and as she listed the names and numbers of the recruits, she looked twice at Richard's and realised it was the number Jeremy just gave her. She sent the email and immediately went into Jeremy's office.

"I am sorry to interrupt you, Mr. Fischer, but I know who that number belongs to."

Jeremy looked up and said, "Whoever it is just called again; they must be desperate to get hold of Mr. Gunner. Who is it?"

"It's one of the new recruits, Richard Nicks."

"Well done, Miss D'agostino. Keep this to yourself, but please ask Mr. Richardson to see me before he meets Mr. Gunner's recruits."

Geoffrey, Sarah, and Shams made their way to Costa for a quick lunch before their meeting with Michael. Richard, as usual, wandered off on his own.

Sarah looked around and said, "I wonder where Richard is. I think we should have made a better effort with him. I feel really sorry for him. He's mixed up in some kind of weird avenge mission."

"Are you crazy?" Geoffrey asked. "Don't be so soft. I am convinced that he is up to no good with Ollie Gunner and that other man, Tommy Balls."

"I know you're right," replied Sarah. "It just kills me to see someone so lost and alone. I really want to help him."

Shams smiled and replied, "You are a kind person, Sarah. But for now, please contact Freddie and do your best to convince him and his dad of our bizarre tale. We need to act fast and make some plans with the High Lord Luminous this evening."

The Right Honourable Bill Walsh was in his office at the ministry of defence in Whitehall, London, when he received a call from Agnes Dickson, his personal assistant.

"I am sorry to interrupt, sir, but your son is on the phone and says he needs to speak to you urgently."

"Agnes, please advise Oliver to make an appointment," he said. "If it is urgent, diary him in at four this afternoon."

After he hung up, Agnes sighed sadly but disguised her tone and went back to Ollie, saying, "I am so sorry, Oliver, but your dad is in an important meeting with the foreign minister. He wants to speak to you and asked me to pencil you in at four this afternoon."

She felt a sharp twinge in her heart as she lied to Oliver. However, she felt for the young man, who was always desperate to win his father's attention but received nothing in return.

After a long silence, Agnes continued, "Oliver, I will put the call through at four, so he will definitely be on the phone to speak to you. Is that okay with you?"

Ollie politely replied, "Thank you so much, Agnes. You have always been so kind to me."

Ollie wasn't sure what he was going to say to his father, but he knew he would help him, not out of parental love but more to avoid the scandal that would inflict his own career.

Bill Walsh married Olivia Wolstenholme in the early seventies. They were deeply in love, and Olivia was a faithful, obliging wife who supported her husband throughout his political career. Oliver was born in 1978, and Olivia suspected that Bill was not being faithful to her. He was a powerful man and demanded all her attention, and the new baby was in his way of her affections. Olivia was heartbroken, as she received financial support from Bill, but he showed no love for their only son. After three years of the continued indiscretions, she decided to leave Bill. She never disclosed his infidelities to either his family, friends, or colleagues, as she misguidedly believed that was loving someone and not letting them down.

She raised young Oliver alone, and with his father's financial support, Oliver had the best education and an envied lifestyle of most children, but he never received the recognition or love he craved from his father. Any awards that he won went unnoticed, and the odd call from his dad meant the world to him. All he ever wanted was to succeed and follow in his dad's footsteps.

After his mother left his father, she married David Gunner, so Ollie always assumed the breakup was initiated by his mother due to her involvement with David Gunner. David adopted Oliver as his own child, and he and Olivia raised him as best as they could.

Olivia was always aware that Oliver was spoiled and got everything he wanted. She always blamed herself for not staying with Bill to play the model wife for their son's sake. However, the humiliation and pretence were too unbearable. Whenever Oliver had a bit too much to drink, he would lash out and make unforgivable accusations to his mother. David was a patient and kind man and knew never to come between mother and son. He always comforted Olivia, and after Ollie calmed down, he'd advise him to apologise to his mother.

Much to David and Olivia's surprise, Ollie pulled up in their drive just after eleven that morning and walked in, not looking in the best of moods.

"What a pleasant surprise, Ollie," Olivia said. "Is everything okay?"

Despite blaming his mother for his plight, he knew she loved him immensely; looking at the only two people who cared for him, he broke down and began to tell them everything.

Olivia took him in her arms and comforted him, saying, "What were you thinking of, Ollie? You accomplished so many things on your own, and yet you still felt the need to resort to foul play to get that promotion to win your father's attention. My dear son, we lost him a long time ago, and your true father, David, and I are so proud of you. I am so disappointed that I have failed to teach you what is right from wrong."

"I am sorry, Mum and David," Ollie said. "I was obsessed and lost control. I really need Dad to help me out of this. I promise you, Mum, I will make things right, even if I lose my position at DEFRA. I just want to leave untarnished and start again."

"Well, son, your father owes me a lot. 'Tarnish' is certainly the keyword. You have no idea what I could do to your dad, so let me make that call, and believe me, I won't be waiting till four o'clock. Agnes will get him on the line now."

For the first time in a long while, Ollie found himself laughing; he said, "Mum, I had no idea you had so much influence on Dad."

Ollie knew his mum protected him and looked out for him; he appreciated her love. As she marched to the phone, he went over and gave her a hug. He said, "I am so sorry, Mum. I promise I will make you proud of me one day, and if Dad still ignores me as his son, I know that you and David are here for me. You have always been here for me."

Mel picked up the phone and pleasantly answered, "Good afternoon, Jeremy Fischer's office; can I help you?"

"Good afternoon, this is Bill Walsh speaking, can I please speak to Mr. Fischer?"

Mel knew that Jeremy had only just commenced his meeting with Michael Richardson, but she also knew who Bill Walsh was; she politely responded, "Hold on for one minute, please."

Mel put the call on hold and knocked on Jeremy's door, and before he had a chance to tell her off for interrupting the meeting, she said, "The Right Honourable Bill Walsh is on hold for you."

Surprised, Jeremy turned to Michael and said, "We'll resume this meeting after I take this call."

Michael nodded, stood up, and left the office.

"Good afternoon, Minister, to what do I owe this pleasure?"

Bill minced no words and cut to the chase; he replied, "I believe that my son has got into a spot of bother with you this morning."

Confused, Jeremy replied, "I am sorry, sir, I don't recall having an issue with your son and was not even aware that he was working in my department."

Bill felt a surge of pride that Ollie had not used his name to enhance his career at DEFRA. He continued, "Ahh, yes, you must know him as Oliver Gunner?"

Jeremy froze in his seat and was quite unsure as to how to respond. He meekly replied, "I apologise, sir. I had no idea that Ollie Gunner was your son, but unfortunately, he must be held accountable for his actions, and I feel it is my moral duty to report him to the board."

Bill was expecting this response and replied, "Mr. Fischer, what my son did was immoral and callous. But I don't think we need to get the board involved at this stage. Admit it, we have all taken chances and tried to jump hoops to get there. I am not saying that he is to go unpunished, but I think we can take advantage of this situation to help all parties involved.

I am sure we can strategically work something out for all of us. After all, are we not one big family in the government?"

Without giving Jeremy an opportunity to respond, he continued, "If you reinstate my son, he can continue to do the deal with Mr. Tommy Balls under your surveillance, you know, like an undercover operation. Tommy can be arrested, as he deserves. You then look the hero, organising the setup with Ollie as your undercover person, hence trapping an associate of the Hardcore Terrier Men. Tommy Balls can tell you where the badgers have gone. If this is not seen as a straight route to your promotion, I will ensure that the right person gets a nudge from me. I am only asking you to give Ollie a chance to redeem himself and accept this as a bad mistake on his part."

Jeremy knew he was being told to do as commanded and had no choice in the matter, but he saluted the minister for his brilliant strategy and replied, "Well, I do remember being young and impetuous. Yes, I will give him a second chance. Please ask him to come back in; the timing is perfect, as no one else knows of the situation. All I can say, sir, is that I wish I had a father like you, who looked out for me when I was younger."

Bill shifted uncomfortably in his seat, feeling a twinge of guilt; he replied, "Thank you, Mr. Fischer, for helping sort out this small mess."

Jeremy put the phone down and smiled, thinking, *You practically told me what to do, but it's a winning situation for everyone.*

He called Mel in again and said, "Miss D'agostino, please reschedule my meeting with Mr. Richardson for four o'clock. Mr. Gunner will be returning in an hour. Kindly email all his recruits and tell them they won't need to report to Mr. Richardson this afternoon. Everything will revert to normal with Mr. Gunner tomorrow. Oh, and please copy Mr. Richardson in that email."

Mel looked confused, but Jeremy simply said, "Are my instructions clear enough, Miss D'agostino? And please remember to observe your position of confidentiality in this matter."

"Of course, sir. Yes, I am sorry. I'll do that email immediately."

Ollie waited nervously in the lounge to hear from his father. When his mother called his dad, Bill promised to contact Jeremy Fischer within the minute. Ollie wished he could believe that his dad was doing it for him, but the sad truth was that his mother had some strange hold on his father. He was just protecting himself.

About thirty minutes later, the house phone rang.

His mother rushed to answer it and said, "Gunners' residence. Oh, Bill; that was quick. Yes, of course he is. Hold on, please." She turned to Ollie and said, "It's your dad; he wants to speak to you."

Olivia passed the phone to Ollie, who was shaking. She squeezed his hand and walked away.

"Hello, sir," Ollie said nervously "How are you?"

Much to his surprise, his father said, "Son, I am not going to give you a hard time as to what is right or wrong. I am sure you have been shaken up enough today. Please return to DEFRA, and Mr. Fischer will go through a plan we discussed."

Ollie was in a state of shock and simply replied, "Thank you, sir."

Bill felt a flood of guilt for all the years he had not been there for Ollie. His own mother had brought him up on her own, with no financial help from his father, so until this moment, he honestly thought he had been a good father, as he had never let Ollie down when it came to financial support.

"Son?" he said and then hesitated.

"Yes, sir?" Ollie said.

"For starters, please call me Dad. I want to tell you how proud I was when I realised that you developed your entire career at DEFRA without using my name. Secondly, I would like you to come across to London and have a drink together when it suits you."

Ollie was numb with shock and remained silent for what seemed like an eternity before he mumbled, "Thank you, Dad," and put the phone down.

All three teams were bewildered as to what was going on that morning; they gathered in the foyer, speculating and asking each other questions, when Jeremy approached them and said, "Right, all of you, be grateful for your afternoon off. You are no longer kids at university, so let's see some adult maturity and make yourself scarce."

When it was just the three of them, Sarah informed Shams and Geoffrey that Freddie agreed to see her in the afternoon.

Shams looked at Sarah and knew she was terrified about facing Freddie and his family; he suggested, "Since we all have the afternoon off, let's all go in the Maserati, and we can back your story."

Geoffrey smiled and nodded, and Sarah replied, "Thank you, guys, you must have read my mind."

As they made their way to Sham's car, they saw Ollie Gunner pull into the carpark. Richard Nicks walked straight up to him, and they began to talk.

Geoffrey gently put his hand on Sarah's shoulder and said, "Still feeling sorry for him?"

Richard approached Ollie and said, "Thank goodness, Mr. Gunner; today has been somewhat of a mystery. You haven't answered any of my calls or text messages."

Ollie cringed at the thought of Jeremy reading all those messages but was glad of the heads-up Richard had inadvertently given. He had no idea how his meeting was going to go, but with a confident smile, he told Richard, "The boss wants to see me. I will call you as soon as I can. Chin up. Everything is going to be okay."

"Thanks, Mr. Gunner, look forward to your call."

15

Badger Meets Man

The crisp, frosty winter day capriciously changed into a bitter cold afternoon. The strong winds whipped through the trees, slicing mercilessly into the branches, and the rain lashed mercilessly on Sham's windscreen. It was scary driving past the curtain side of the HGV trailers, as the winds seem determined to tear through them. The heavy rains slowly turned into sleet and then into large snowflakes, reducing visibility on the motorway.

"Sarah, remind me which junction we are coming off?" Shams asked calmly, in complete control of his car.

"Junction 17," she said. "Shams, I am so glad we are in your car. I would have never survived this journey in my ten-year-old Clio."

As they came off the junction and approached Cribbs Causeway, they were more shielded from the blasting winds and snow with the avenue of tall trees and woodlands on either side of the country road. Shams carefully made his way along the dark roads until they arrived at Freddie Odie's home.

Sarah pressed the buzzer, and within a minute, the heavy wrought-iron gates began to open. On each gate was a copperplated monogram of the letters A and B.

Geoffrey began to smile and asked if what he was wearing was decent enough to meet the Odies. Shams continued slowly on the golden gravel drive, which was thick with fresh snow, and parked up by a black Range Rover with a private licence plate AB 1, which was adjacent to another burgundy one, licenced AB 2.

As they got out of the car, the snow miraculously stopped, and the dark sky cleared up, with blue patches hovering above them.

"My mum always says a blue sky after a heavy storm is a good omen, so fingers crossed, guys," Sarah said nervously.

Before Sarah could ring the bell, Freddie opened the door and stepped back, as he did not expect anyone other than Sarah.

"Wow, Sarah," he said. "You brought the whole team."

"Freddie, thanks so much for accepting my call. Are you sure your mum and dad will see us?"

"Yes," Freddie said. "I explained that you were anxious to share some beneficial information to help the badgers, and they agreed. Please do not let me down, Sarah."

The three of them followed Freddie through the huge lounge; they went into another room with an open roaring fire, which the visitors appreciated very much.

Ann, dressed in an elegant trouser suit with her thick blonde hair in an effortless chignon slumping down her neck, gave a small smile and stood up to leave the room, but Sarah politely asked if she would stay to hear what they had to say. She smiled, looked at Barry and Freddie, and said she would bring some tea and refreshments in to warm everyone up.

Barry broke the ice and asked how the cull was doing.

"So have you broken records and hitting targets as bragged by Ollie Gunner?"

Ann returned to the room with a large tray, and Sarah began, "Mr. and Mrs. Odie, Freddie, we have come here in desperation for you to help us save the badgers. We did not sign up to be cruel to the animals and were misled about them spreading disease. But we now know the truth of DEFRA's incorrect assumption of the badgers and of Mr. Gunner's selfish exploitation for his personal gain, and we beg you to help them."

Barry looked at the three of them and said, "I will do anything in my power to assist. What can we do?"

Sarah took a deep breath and began to tell the complete tale, including their encounter with the High Lord Luminous.

Sarah thought Barry was going to kick her out as he did before, but he put his hand on his chin and asked, "And you are saying that he is prepared to meet up with me and Andy? He really was outside our marquis?"

"Yes," Sarah said. "He practically repeated your speech about stepping up, word for word, to all three of us."

"I am lost for words," Barry said, "but what have I to lose, other than confirming that my son has a poor choice of friends, if this turns out to be a crazy prank." He stood up and walked over to the sideboard, picked up a decanter, and poured himself a whisky. He continued, "I know it's a little early in the day, but I think I need this."

As Sarah and the others filled Ann and Freddie about the morning they had with the animals, Barry went into the other room and called Andy May.

"Andy, I know it sounds crazy and insane, but how the hell would the kids know about my speech? The Youtube video was more interested in recording what the lovely ladies were wearing."

Barry returned after twenty minutes and casually said that Andy was on his way.

About ten minutes later, Andy arrived, and following the starstruck mesmerisation from both Geoffrey and Sarah, Shams had to discreetly break the trance and emphasised the urgency to get back to meet the High Lord.

Barry and Andy, who were still in a state of disbelief, awe, and intrigue, jumped into one of the Range Rovers and followed behind Shams's car.

Nick Panay sat across from Jeremy Fischer and was expecting to be filled in on the retribution that was given to Ollie Gunner.

"Well, Mr. Panay, I am very happy that you forwarded that video directly to me, making me aware of Mr. Gunner's unfortunate instructions. The matter has been dealt with, and Mr. Gunner has been given a disciplinary warning. You need not report to him, but his intentions were heading in the correct direction. Let's just say he lost his way. Now in the interest of everyone, I would like you to delete that video in my presence as footage like that, falling in the wrong hands, can bring down our entire organisation. The fact that you were aware that it was incorrect is testament that we do not operate under such measures."

Jeremy looked straight into Nick's eyes, and Nick took his phone out and deleted the video.

"Good lad; do you mind if I confirm that it is deleted? You must realise that if this falls in the wrong hands, it ultimately lands on my shoulders."

Jeremy took his phone, went into the deleted option, and emptied all deleted contents to ensure that the footage was not restorable.

"Can I ask if anyone else besides you, Ollie, and myself were aware of this?"

Nick responded, "Well, all the lads on duty with me were aware that I filmed the scene; they were very upset with what they were asked to do. As their section leader, I feel obliged to give them some feedback after our meeting."

Jeremy took a deep breath, reclined in his chair, and said, "Firstly, Mr Gunner will be apologising to each and every one of you, and then, you are going to take them all out for a meal, to celebrate your promotion as a conscientious member of my team reporting this distasteful incident. However, we now need to move on, and I am counting on you to make this all disappear and continue our good work. Have I made myself clear? I cannot tell you more, but the outcome of all this will make you feel proud to be part of our DEFRA team. Have you reported to Michael Richardson to assess his locations?"

"No, Mr. Fischer," Nick replied. "Mr. Richardson said to leave it till four this afternoon, but as we all know, the tracking team cannot seem to find any badger locations. We are still waiting for our next mission."

Jeremy chewed on his bottom lip and replied, "A true enigma, Mr. Panay. Well, that's down to the tracking teams; I will have a word with them as soon as possible, as the results have been disappointing. But rest assured that will soon come right, I guarantee you."

Jeremy stood up as a signal that the meeting was over, and Nick jumped to his feet. Jeremy reached out to shake Nick's hand and said, "Once again, well done on a good job. You will receive your new appointment and a healthy remuneration as an acknowledgement of your new position and responsibility. Remember, Mr. Panay, this operation is crucial for the survival of our whole department, so I am counting on you to keep this scandal airtight."

Nick shook his hand and confirmed, "Yes, sir, you can trust me to do that."

When Jeremy returned to his office, Mel said that Ollie was waiting in the interview room.

Jeremy shut his eyes, took a deep breath, and said, "Right, let's get this over and done with. Miss D'agostino, please bring a large pot of coffee and organise some sandwiches, as we are going to be in that room for quite a while, and I am starving. "

Jeremy walked into the room and saw Ollie slumped in a chair; he looked terrified. He always thought this young man always appeared smart and confident, but this whole incident had really shaken him up.

"Well, Ollie, a fine mess you've put me in. I can see how your dad made minister of defence, turning this around so we can all come out of this like the good guys. However, just how much does the young Richard Nicks know?"

Ollie turned a deep crimson red, embarrassed that Jeremy found out he was involved, and stammered, "A-a-apologies, Mr. Fischer, he is just a messed-up kid, and I wanted to keep him out. In all honesty, he was the one who set the meeting up. I think Tommy Balls is a family friend."

Jeremy looked at him and said, "Well, I did some digging, and it turns out that his late father was associated with the Hardcore Terrier Men, so I am not exactly sure what he is getting out of this, but he is to presume that we are progressing with this operation and not to know that we are planning to arrest Tommy Balls. The first thing you need to do is apologise to your previous Clean Kill team. I have gone out of my way to make sure they have been appeased, and a sincere apology from you will support my explanation that you are under caution with a disciplinary warning."

Ollie replied, "Yes, sir, I will do that after our meeting. Since it is now all out in the open about my undercover mission, could I please ask if the five thousand can be funded by DEFRA? I'm not exactly sure I'll still have a job after this and am much too embarrassed to get the funds from my family."

Jeremy replied, "Mr. Gunner, you went about it in entirely the wrong manner, but your dad has hit the nail on the head, and we can turn this around to a very victorious situation for all of us. But yes, I will organise the funds to be ready for you by tomorrow morning. I think that promotion is going to be yours, so lift your spirits up, as I need this operation to run smoothly."

Ollie felt everything he had done for five years finally paid off, getting to the position he was seeking for so long. He smiled and replied, "Mr. Fischer, I truly appreciate everything you have done to avoid exposing me. However, I do not deserve that promotion and would be very happy to see the best man get it. I promise not to let you down and assure you that the operation on Friday will be a success."

As Ollie left the room, Jeremy called Mel and asked her to call Mr. Richardson in to see him.

"Please apologise on my behalf, Miss D'agostino, and ask if he could just give me another half-hour. I will have everything put together then. I would also like you to be in that meeting, as we have several things that must be tied in together, and I cannot think of anyone more organised than you."

The mobile phone rang with its popular "Marimba" ring tone. Richard looked and saw that it was Tommy Balls.

"Hello, young Dicky," Tommy said. "Are we still good for the payment tomorrow, as I need to get the dogs prepared for Friday?"

"Yes, yes. All is well. Mr. Gunner just assured me that everything is to plan, but I am leaving it to him to contact you and await to be told when to meet up with you on Friday."

"Brilliant, my young lad. Well, on that assurance, I am going to get some mutts organised. The dogs trace back to Reverend John Russell himself. Proper little Jack Russells, with the stamina for the hunt and courage to face the badgers."

Tommy Balls proceeded to drive to visit Mark Ashley, who bred the terriers. Mark officially sold them as working terriers to help sniff out rats and foxes, who were menaces to the local farmers, but he actually trained the dogs to hunt down badgers and compete in badger-baiting events. Sturdily built with a duplicitous personality, all who knew him were intimidated by his offensive arrogance. He had shifty black eyes and flashed a set of teeth that were akin to that of a piranha, nicotine-stained from a continuously lit cigarette perching at the corner of his mouth.

Whatever the weather, he was always in a vest top, exposing overworked arms from his regular gym visits, military-styled cargo shorts, and a pair of Berghaus walking boots. He had a reputation to breed the best working terriers and advised his customers that his dogs were not to be bought as pets. Oddly, he also had a massive aviary on his farm that housed about thirty owls of six or seven different species. In spite of his arrogant offensive disposition, he actually had a passion for these birds, although no one was sure if he had a legal right to keep them in captivity. No one, however, dared to cross him and therefore left him to his own devices.

"Good afternoon, Mark," Tommy said as he got out of his car. "How's things?"

"Bloody hell, Tommy," Mark said. "Good to see you. Still in your blooming Saab."

"Absolutely, mate. You know how I love my Saabs. Right, pal, I spoke to that guy after our quick chat on the phone, and he definitely wants the dogs. It's more or less a rental for the day, as the guy only wants the badgers sniffed out. There is to be no fighting, so your dogs will be as good as new when you get them back."

"Aye, my dogs can do that. They will just stand at the edge of the sett and await instructions. Simply shout, 'Halt,' and they will stay completely still. How much are you giving me for the rental? I like that word."

"Shall we say one and a half thousand in cash?"

"No way, pal. I get two thousand per pup, and when they are trained to sniff out, farmers give me up to three thousand, and sometimes more for a bitch, as they have a stronger scent. Clever are my bitches."

He continued, "Not putting my beauties at risk for anything under three thousand pounds. I have to consider, shall we say, unforeseen circumstances?"

"Listen, Mark, two thousand is as much as I can go. I am only going to have them a couple of hours, and like I said, they will be brought back as good as new. I will need three dogs."

"Twenty-five hundred, and we have a deal. I've got to put work into them for the next couple of days, and when you collect them, they will be ready to bite the head off anything. And I want the cash before you take them."

Tommy patted his shoulder, smiled, and said he would see him on Friday morning with the money.

Mark approached his shed, where there were about ten stocky, fit Jack Russell terriers. His dogs slowly and respectfully approached him and began to lick his bare legs, submissively awaiting a command.

"Right, which of you three bitches are going to make me a proud dad? Digger, Patch, and Dainty. Come, come. Sorry, girls; I have to put you in quarantine for a couple of days, but when you come home, you will feast on fresh meat."

Mark locked the dogs in a small shed with only a large bowl of water. His dogs were used to this routine, as they understood it was in preparation of a hunt. He also left the skin of a dead badger in the shed; this began the preparation for the hunt on Friday.

As he left the shed, he saw a large black crow flying low above his aviary.

"What the hell is he doing swooping down so low?" he asked, grabbing a garden rake. "Shhossh, shoosh, or I will blow your brains out, you silly bird."

Unperturbed, Councillor Claudius Crow elegantly took flight away from the aviary, thinking, *That's alright. I heard enough of what I need to know.*

"Well, how did the meeting go?" Mick Jones asked. "Did we get rid of Ollie Dollie?"

"Right, lads, firstly, the governor said we've done a great job by bringing it to his attention, and as a reward, he wants us to have a meal out on DEFRA's expense."

"What?" Steve Foley asked. "Is this some kind of bribe for us to keep quiet about all of this? I don't like the sound of it."

Nick expected that response and said, "No, no. Ollie Dollie is coming to see us to apologise and has been given a disciplinary warning. Mr. Fischer said to trust him, and at the end of this, we will all feel proud of what we are doing, but we have to keep quiet about the incident, or else all our jobs, including his, will be in jeopardy."

"As long as I don't have to speak to that butcher or take orders from him," Mick said, "I'll be happy to have a bloody good meal on DEFRA tonight."

Steve was still uncomfortable about the whole incident, but after the others made some jokes about Ollie Dollie, he had a small laugh and decided to chill out.

"The other guys said Michael Richardson is a really sound guy," Steve said, "so I am looking forward to meeting him."

As Ollie approached the team, he got the end of their conversation and heard them talking about Michael Richardson.

"Hi, guys. Yes, you are right. Mr. Richardson is an exceptionally great guy." With his head lowered and his usual obnoxious arrogance in tow, he continued, "Er, hmmm, I wanted to come across and apologise to each and every one of you. I can offer no excuse, so I am not going to. My behaviour and management were unacceptable, and I am sorry that I put you through those instructions. There is a plan in the pipeline, so not for me, but for DEFRA, guys, we need to keep all this under the hat because the week will pan out, and all this conspiracy will work well for all of us. Maybe not for me, as I deserve to face the music for my behaviour, but believe me, DEFRA will get the credit it rightly deserves."

Nick looked at Ollie and felt sorry that someone on such a high horse has fallen so low. He looked at the other guys, who were also taken aback by this new version of diffidence from Ollie Gunner, and said, "Listen, we all have bad days and deal with personal issues. We made our opposition very clear to your management, and you've been reprimanded. No ill feelings from any of us."

All the guys took turns in wishing him luck and made their way to meet up with Michael Richardson.

Michael Richardson, a tall young man with striking blue eyes and a mob of black curls, walked in with an endearing smile; in his thick Geordie accent, he said, "Third time lucky, Mr. Fischer."

"Please sit down, Mr. Richardson. I asked Miss D'agostino to sit in this meeting, but let me be the first to apologise for the ridiculous day you've had to endure."

"Not a problem, Mr. Fischer. I am sure you will have a good explanation."

As soon as Mel entered, Jeremy began, "You both certainly have witnessed a strange chain of events today. I'll cut to the chase, and any gaps that I am not filling in, you must assume are of no relevance to you."

Both Mel and Michael looked at each other, shrugged their shoulders, and simultaneously nodded their heads.

Jeremy began, "An undercover plan Mr. Gunner and I were devising came close to being sabotaged today. However, we managed to salvage the plan but unfortunately now need more players to make it work. I decided you two can be trusted to be part of the plan."

Michael smiled and said, "This sounds intriguing. Count me in."

Mel sat down in her chair; she was quite uncomfortable, as her partner, Dale, already told her Ollie would be getting the sack, and up to the point of Bill Walsh's phone call, it was certainly looking like that.

She asked, "Is this something to do with the phone call from Bill Walsh?"

Jeremy looked at her sharply, wishing she was not as smart as she was, but he bit his tongue and simply said, "Yes, it is of a high security interest."

With the both of them completely enraptured with curiosity, Jeremy fabricated a tale to cover up the activities of Ollie Gunner.

"Have you heard of the Hardcore Terrier Men?"

Mel shook her head with a blank expression, whilst Michael furrowed his eyebrows and asked, "Are they not involved in badger baiting?"

"Bingo," Jeremy replied. He continued, "The Hardcore Terrier Men are barbaric anachronisms, and their vile hobby goes back to a time when badger baiting was a sport to be enjoyed. It's shocking, but this is still going on in the twenty-first century, and it needs to be stopped. Yes, we are trying to reduce the badger population to eliminate the spread of tuberculosis to our cattle, but we do not condone animal cruelty, in spite of what League. Org thinks of us. To get to the point, Ollie Gunner has managed to smoke out a member of the organisation and is collaborating undercover with him. I had plans to remove him from the team but decided it would work better to keep things as they were, as the newly recruited tracking team were asking far too many questions, and I did not want Ollie to be the subject of controversy when, in actual fact, he might help us redeem our tarnished image of being cruel to animals."

"Well, I take my hat off to Ollie," Michael said. "He has always been ahead of the game and certainly has great potential. He certainly deserves the promotion, Mr. Fischer."

Hmmm, Jeremy thought. *If you only knew.*

"Well, let's not stray away from our first priority in our operation," Jeremy said aloud, "and for the record, you are doing a brilliant job, Mr. Richardson.

"Miss D'agostino, please take these notes down, as I want a record of what I am going to say." He continued, "A meeting is to be held on Friday between Ollie Gunner and Tommy Balls ..."

"Tommy Balls?" Mel interrupted. "My uncle owns the pub at the Dog and Gun, and I have heard him speak ill of him, and he never has a bad word to say about anyone. Sorry, Mr. Fischer, please carry on."

"Yes, you will need to organise five thousand pounds in cash, ready for Mr. Gunner in the morning. Mr. Balls has promised to have the terriers ready to track the badgers' location. That, as we all know, has been a complete enigma, as they seem to have disappeared. Mr. Gunner has entrusted a new recruiter; Richard Nicks, who will have a tracker on him when he meets up with Tommy Balls. As soon as the location is confirmed, he will contact Mr. Gunner, and here is where you come in, Mr. Richardson. I want you and the Clean Kill Team following the same tracking devise at all points so you are at the location as soon as Richard calls Mr. Gunner. I also want your tracking team to collaborate with Mr. Gunner's team to check out the tracks, as I am not too sure how good these dogs are. At no point must either the tracking team or Clean Kill Team know what is going on.

"The officials have already been alerted," he continued, "and a young undercover agent will be joining Mr. Gunner's team as a last-minute addition. The arrest of Mr. Balls will be made on the spot, and Miss D'agostino, when I give you the go-ahead, I want you to alert the press immediately."

"Goodness, Mr. Fischer, you have been busy today," Michael said.

"That, Mr. Richardson, is quite an understatement. Friday has to be a success for us, and I am sure I can count on your discretion and cooperation."

"Yes sir," they both said, standing up, knowing that was their cue to leave.

After they left, Jeremy slumped back in his green leather captain's chair. He looked up at the Victorian ceiling rose, surrounding an extremely large, ornate chandelier, and said, "If there is anyone up there, help me pull this off. Everything is sounding too good to be true. I cannot believe I sorted out this mess in eight hours."

The journey back was terrifying, as the sun was beginning to set and the absence of road lights on the motorway (due to a ridiculous campaign launched by Highways England to switch off lights on major motorways, to save money on energy and reduce associated carbon emissions) made it impossible to see. The additional rough winter day made visibility dangerously poor, but Shams drove very carefully, although anxious not to be late to meet the High Lord.

"Take it easy, Shams," Sarah said. "I am sure he believes in us and will know we have a valid reason if we are late."

Shams got them safely back to Brockley and parked up in the Curry's carpark. It was close to half past five, and the sun was setting. They got out of the car, and Barry and Andy walked towards Curry's with them.

"We said we'd be here before sunset," Sarah said as she rubbed her frozen hands together.

Andy sarcastically replied, "Already finding an excuse for the no-show. I need my brain checked, coming along on this wild goose chase."

Sarah smiled and said, "Mr. May, I will accept your apology shortly." She walked on and said, "Please, let's hurry up."

Shams and Geoffrey were a little ahead of them and stopped short in their tracks as they passed the huge windows of Curry's. They began to walk back towards the others, and Geoffrey said, "Sarah, he is in there; walk slowly past the window, and let's wait outside."

"Who? What? Which one?" Andy asked, desperate for an answer.

"Please calm down, sir," said Shams. "He is very conscious of his identity not being revealed, and we cannot allow him to lose his trust in us."

Barry said, "This is extremely exciting. Totally agree, Shams; where should we go?"

"I suggest we walk to the end of the shop closest to the start of the woods."

The five of them huddled closely round the corner of the shop, keeping out of sight.

No one spoke; each one of them had thoughts racing through their minds. Unconsciously, Sarah, Geoffrey, and Shams began to think of the High Lord, and suddenly out of nowhere, the small, diminutive figure dressed in white appeared.

"Good evening, Sarah, Geoffrey, and Shams," the High Lord said; he then turned to Barry and Andy and continued, "I am truly honoured by your presence and grateful that you found time to come and meet me. Sarah, Geoffrey, and Shams, you are in my debt for being honest in your mission to help me and my clans."

Sarah smiled, turned to the other gentlemen, and said, "Mr. Odie, Mr. May, allow me to introduce the High Lord Luminous Snowspirit, spiritual leader of all badger clans in Brocklehurstshire."

Barry and Andy shifted very awkwardly from side to side, wondering if these young people were videoing them for a prank.

The High Lord closed his eyes and smiled. He then nodded his head knowingly as he said, "Ah, yes, of course, you doubting men have no faith unless you can see. We are favoured, as we see our ancestors every year at our annual celebration, but you have never seen your God, and many struggle to believe in him. To see, you know, is not always the answer. A good friend of mine has poor sight but had the vision to orchestrate an event which led to harmony in the woodlands. So let me satisfy what you need to see, so as to earn your trust."

Before Barry and Andy had a chance to respond, the High Lord looked around, knelt down, and said, "Sekarang saya jadi binatang."

A beautiful mist of fragrant vapor and orbs of bright white lights appeared, and as Barry and Andy stood back, the High Lord appeared out of the scented wisps as the majestic pure white badger, this time with a resplendent white coat. On his head, he wore a crown made of holly.

Sarah, Geoffrey, and Shams smiled as they could see that the High Lord was intentionally making a very impressive introduction to Barry and Andy.

The High Lord stood upright, as tall as Barry and Andy, who were not sure if they should be terrified or, like Geoffrey, fall on bended knees to this majestic presence.

As suddenly as he transformed into a badger, in one swift movement, he resumed his form as a man and smiled at the extremely mesmerised gentlemen, who now took his hands and thanked him for the privilege.

"Can we go somewhere warm where we can talk, High Lord Luminous?" Barry asked.

"Yes, of course we can," he replied, "but I have to warn you that I am not very well received by your kind."

The six of them walked into a Costa Café, appearing as a very peculiar group of friends.

After they sat down, the High Lord gave them the report he received from Councillor Claudius Crow.

"It appears that Tommy Balls has reached an agreement to supply three dogs to Ollie Gunner on Friday to sniff our location. The plan is to start at the spot where the cruel massacre of my clan happened three weeks ago, and from there, the dogs will be able to find us out, as they have hunted us down for generations. The dogs are currently in quarantine with no food. Councillor Claudius Crow said they are located on a farm called Ashley's Fine Terriers."

Barry turned and looked at the three recruits and asked, "Is this true? Are you aware of this plan?"

"We knew that Ollie was meeting Tommy Balls, but this is news to us. It's been a crazy day. One minute we were told we no longer reported to Ollie Gunner, and then we were told we are to continue to work for Ollie and given the afternoon off."

The High Lord continued, "Sadly, this is true. Councillor Claudius Crow reported that Ollie Gunner confirmed that the payment will be made tomorrow morning. He said something is indeed happening between Ollie and someone called Jeremy Fischer, but he could not hear much on the windowsill outside his office. Perhaps you can find out more."

A shudder went through the party, and Andy asked, "How can we help, High Lord?"

The High Lord looked up and despondently replied, "At the start of the cull, I was only hoping you would help conceal our tracks so we could live hidden in the forest, protected by all our other friends. But now, I really don't know how to protect ourselves from the dogs. They will definitely find us."

Barry refused to believe there was no way to help the badgers.

"To be honest, High Lord, all funds that are being raised were for the sole purpose of finding the badgers, inoculating them, and then declaring the area whitelisted. We would have tracked you down, but I wonder now how you would have understood our good intentions?"

The High Lord looked up and said, "It would have certainly been misunderstood. However, now we have met, I can prepare our clan for that step, but for now, Friday is my biggest concern."

Andy looked serious and, after a deep contemplation, said, "Surely using the dogs is totally illegal; how does Ollie Gunner think he's going to get away with this? High Lord, rest assured that Barry and I will do our utmost to avoid this. Thank you so much for taking us into your confidence and revealing yourself to us."

Andy could not stop wondering about Ollie's plan and continued, "Nah, this must be backed up by some higher level. Where does Ollie get five thousand pounds from? This other kid, Richard Nicks, is he from a wealthy family?"

Geoffrey replied, "We don't think so; we just figured out that his dad was one of the Hardcore Terrier Men."

"Jeez, that's bad news. A lot of illegal money there," said Andy. "Listen, we have three days to work as best as we can to find a solution to help the badgers. High Lord, please try to fill us in with as much as you can from Councillor Claudius Crow, and kids, you need to do some digging at DEFRA."

It really annoyed Shams to be referred to as a kid, but he could see that Sarah and Geoffrey would do anything for Andy May and were still in their starstruck dimension. He held back his annoyance, smiled, and said, "Yes, we will do our utmost to see what we can find out and keep in touch."

The High Lord stood up to thank all his new friends.

"My clans and I are truly indebted to you and your kindness," he said. "Mr. Odie and Mr. May, would you like to come and visit us as the young ones have?" The High Lord sensed Shams's annoyance at being referred to as kids and was careful in his choice of words.

Barry and Andy were so excited with the invitation, and they arranged to meet at the Dog and Gun the next morning.

"Since our reunion with the hedgehogs and stronger integration with the forest animals, we break our fast in the morning and gather for social gatherings for about two hours before going back to our setts. The cubs have easily adjusted, but the older badgers are generally half-asleep. Please try not to be late, as this is all new to us badgers."

Barry and Andy assured the High Lord that they would not miss the invitation at all costs.

The High Lord smiled and continued, "Sarah, Shams, and Geoffrey know exactly where to bring you. It's a very special day tomorrow; we are celebrating the union of the badgers and hedgehogs, and you will be our guests of honour."

Barry politely asked if he could bring his beloved Annie, but the High Lord replied, "I truly apologise, but for the moment, I need to win the confidence of my clans and forest friends before they will trust you. All in good time, Mr. Odie; please do not be offended."

"Not at all, High Lord. I completely understand."

The High Lord left his friends and made his way back into the woods.

Barry and Andy sat down and were still in a state of awe and wonder.

"Unbelievable," Andy said continuously for the next five minutes.

Man Meets Badger

High Lord Henry reluctantly left his warm burrow of thick moss, leaves, and old grass from under a stocky, thorny bramble bush and looked up to see all the sows busily preparing picnics composed of a feast of grubs, slugs, centipedes, and juicy earthworms for the badgers. The air was filled with exhilaration. Across the field, Lord Sparta was in full military dress, practising a routine with his warriors, for a parade they were going to display to the badgers. Meanwhile, Lord Didas was trying to organise all the little hoglets into formation, but this was quite a difficult task due to their shrieks of excitement.

He smiled and thought to himself, *I never believed that the High Lord Luminous's suggestion to break our fast in the morning and integrate with the other animals would work so well. But look how enthusiastic everyone is.*

His thoughts were interrupted by High Lord Maximus, who was standing behind him.

Practically blind and drawn to only light and colours, as all moles are, High Lord Maximus sniffed deeply and made his way towards High Lord Henry. For this special day, he wore his simple crown made of a tendril of ivy intertwined with acorns and berries. He was proud of his smooth skin and found it impractical to put on regalia like all the other High Lords, as he was constantly burrowing in the ground.

Assuming that he was standing in front of High Lord Henry, he unfortunately stammered, "Good morning Henry. I am so happy to see your whole array of hedgehogs happily preparing their visit to see the badgers. The High Lord Luminous has included all of the animals to be present at the gathering."

With a small smile, High Lord Henry politely turned around so he was now facing the High Lord Maximus and replied, "Good to see you, my friend. Yes, this is wonderful news for all of us to be getting together. I believe the warrior leaders are planning their strategies together this morning, as the High Lord Luminous is convinced that another attack is imminent."

Unlike the other animals, the High Lord Maximus was solely in charge of his moles, without a military leader. Although he appeared clumsy and uncoordinated, High Lord Maximus was truly a genius, organising everything from the building of their fortresses to the welfare of his moles.

He stood thoughtfully for a minute and continued, "Henry, I think we should invite the High Lady Dharma to our meeting. She is the only female leader that I know of, and although the fallow deer keep very much to themselves, she has always been very cooperative and works so well with us moles. Like me, we have the sole role to lead our kin, but don't underestimate her leadership, as she is definitely in charge of all the fallow deer, and her stags do exactly as she says."

Lord Sparta approached the two High Lords, and he could not control his urge to laugh as he saw High Lord Maximus sniffing him out and squinting extremely hard to identify him.

To avoid embarrassing the High Lord, he shouted out, "Good morning, High Lord Maximus; it's Lord Sparta. Yes, I have certainly heard of the High Lady Dharma. My daughter Maggie ceaselessly goes on about how one day she is going to be in charge of all our warriors. Speaking of which, I believe your clan are already at Brockley this morning."

High Lord Maximus proudly replied, "We have actually been there all week. The High Lord Luminous suggested that we build our fortresses there, so last week, we started inhabiting the area and secured ourselves in a slight arch, covering as many setts in Brocklehurstshire. It's part of our strategy, which I will discuss with all the warrior leaders later. I know you all have a laugh about our sight, and do not worry; we take no offence, but we can hear all the vibrations and recognise every step approaching above the ground, so Widejaw has been very glad of our presence and awareness."

Diplomatically, High Lord Henry replied, "Nonsense, Maximus, none of us laugh at you. When all is said and done, you all are the most amazing burrowers in the forest, and your hunting skills are unsurpassed."

He gently and discreetly turned Maximus in the direction of where his hedgehogs were heading and said, "Come and join us as we make our way to the sett."

Maximus thanked him graciously and proudly said, "My dear HHHHenry, you go on and continue with your array; it will be faster for me to burrow my way, and more than likely, I'll be there before you."

Under the watchful eye of White, Speed, Bojana, and Fire tumbled through the field, screeching with excitement, trying to imitate the stunts performed by the hoglets yesterday. Power and Drill came round from the tangled, prickly shrubs to summon them back to the classroom. Power, the eldest of Brit's cubs, smiled at the very shy White and said, "You have so much patience, constantly putting up with this riotous bunch."

White smiled and replied, "Like yourself, I feel I should be helping my mother to look after the younger cubs."

Power laughed and said, "Drill will not leave my side, and Sharp seems to have inherited our mother's beautiful voice; she is practising a medley with our mother, for our arriving guests. It's really Speed I am continuously trying to keep my eye on."

White laughed and said, "Yes, I think Speed is certainly making a name for herself. Fire will not leave her side."

Snowdrops and Glisten peered from around the corner, and with an approving nod from their eldest sibling, they came running towards Drill and began to imitate Speed, Bojana, and Fire.

Wisepaws was organising the class assembly of all the cubs, when he realised that several of them were missing.

"Wizz and Minx, please can you be in charge of the cubs? No one is to leave this classroom. I am aware that Sharp is practising her song with her mother, but the others are just being mischievous."

Crossing his brows together and pretending to be angry, he waddled out of the classroom and began to look for the other cubs. All the cubs began to giggle, but Wisepaws turned around, raised his eyebrows, and gave them a ferocious stare, and they immediately paid heed and sat still.

After a few metres, he could hear the little cubs' squeals and giggles. He smiled to himself, pleased that the cubs were playing altogether, but as he came from around the sett, he wiped off his smile and scolded, "Who gave you the liberty to be playing in my school time? White and Power, you should know better than encouraging your younger siblings to be here instead of the classroom. Now march on immediately to my classroom, or your parents will be getting a visit from me."

All the cubs scuttled quickly towards the classroom, but Speed looked at Wisepaws with a big, cheeky grin and said, "We were only having fun and practising our tumbles for our hoglet friends."

Wisepaws feigned annoyance and said, "Young mischief, I will decide when you are allowed to have fun; now march on like all the other obedient cubs."

Just as Wisepaws settled the cubs, Brooke, Bellatrix, and Molly came into the classroom. Brooke looked at her beloved Wisepaws and said, "The hedgehogs have arrived, and I must say, their little hoglets are behaving; I hope our cubs do as well."

Wisepaws smiled, looked at his cubs, and said, "I am sure my cubs will not let us down, so come on now, please partner up in twos, and walk out in an orderly fashion to welcome our guests."

As soon as the cubs arrived in the field, Speed and Bojana excitedly waited for the nod from Wisepaws to be able to meet their new friends. Likewise, Maggie and Spiky kept distracting their father, Lord Sparta, to give Lord Didas the signal to let them play.

Lord Sparta smiled and interrupted his conversation with Clawdigger, saying, "I think our young ones want to play."

He gave the signal to Lord Didas as Clawdigger nodded to Wisepaws, and within a minute, the cubs were doing their best to catch the hoglets. The little moles were going round in circles, trying to join in, so the young deer skipped towards them and gently lowered themselves, allowing the little moles to ride on their backs. The baby bunnies were riding on the backs of the other badger cubs, whilst the birds kept their distance up in the branches, as their young were too vulnerable to be amongst the riotous young animals. Speed was organising races, whilst Bojana selected the teams; the ambiance of innocence was such a pleasant distraction from the true purpose of the gathering.

The hedgehog sows were proudly presenting their baskets of gifts for the badgers and laying out the tasty morsels for the gathering. After the High Lady and Sally made everyone welcomed, the young ones settled in mixed groups of different animals. Brit and Sharp began a beautiful medley about the union of the forest. They sang of the end of the feud and the beginning of new friendships and expressed in their medley the gratitude of the badgers to all the forest animals for helping them in their time of need.

Whilst the celebrations were in full swing, the High Lord Luminous, accompanied by Widejaw, High Lord Henry, Lord Sparta, High Lady Dharma, High Lord Maximus, Grand Oscar Owl, and his warrior leader, Councillor Claudius Crow, left the field and made their way towards LOJAP, so they could discuss their plan of strategy.

The animals were very honoured to be privileged at the badger's sacred spot.

High Lord Luminous began, "My deepest appreciation for all of you to come together to help us in our plight. I am totally indebted to High Lord Henry, who made the first step to end our feud, and grateful that he valiantly instigated the reunion of all the forest animals. As I have said, we have three human friends who are allies, and they are going to help us, so please help them in every way you can. In fact, only last night, I met two extremely powerful men who are responsible for raising great amounts of money to help protect us by what is called vaccination, which is what they do with our relatives in Wales. I have invited them to participate in our celebrations, and they should be here shortly. Let us proceed with our plan of action so I may share this with them on arrival."

Widejaw thanked the High Lord Luminous and continued, "As red-pelt badgers, we have always used our strength and brute force to charge ahead in one strong formation as sacrificing shields, to protect the rest of the clans. However, we have never had to defend ourselves against humans, who have waged this big war against us. So having all you animals help us is very much appreciated. However, in my discussions with the High Lord, we feel it is time to recruit badgers of all pelts to help make our army bigger and stronger, and reduce the possible number of casualties of our volunteering friends. Therefore, if the other councillors would kindly get a list of volunteers from within the setts, we can commence training immediately, but I will reiterate that the red pelts will still put themselves at the front line."

High Lord Maximus stood up and sniffed hard to identify the position of Widejaw; after he located him, he said, "As you can see, Councillor WWWidejaw, I have invited the High Lady DDDharma. She is an excellent warrior. The fallow deer sometimes transport us moles on their backs across the forest, and this can act as a means of defence. We feel that the deer stampeding towards man will be far more intimidating than your admirable strong force of badgers, and they would not expect the hedgehogs leaping off the deer and somersaulting into them to knock off their balance."

Lord Sparta carried on, "As you have witnessed on more than one occasion, and following our well-rehearsed display earlier, our size and agility would cause a great distraction in preparation for the red pelts to move in from behind."

The excitement amongst the animals reached a crescendo, but Widejaw politely settled the warriors and said, "All your strategies are excellent, but please remember that humans have weapons called guns, and they will shoot us and end our lives immediately. I cannot allow you to be the sacrificing pawns open to slaughter. Do you all realise the price of your alliance to protect us?"

The High Lady Dharma stood up, lifted her head up, and looked at all the leaders present; she said, "We are warriors, and to be remembered on a battlefield, dying for a cause we believe in; is that not the highest reward and accomplishment we could ever attain?"

All the other warrior animals stood up and applauded the High Lady Dharma. Widejaw approached her and on bended knee said, "I am honoured that you have chosen to fight alongside my warriors; your reputation truly precedes you."

Grand Councillor Oscar Owl, who was renowned to be the wisest amongst all the animals, turned to High Lord Luminous and said, "Without a doubt, I will keep a vigilante watch with my parliament of owls across the canopy of the forest; we have decided to position ourselves closer to the sett, whilst this threat is impending. All the other birds will be monitoring the forest from the trees above. However, the cunning crows have devised a strategy of their own under my remarkable Councillor

Claudius Crow, and they have agreed to dart back and forth during the attack, picking up plans and discussions the humans have whilst we alert you of all approaches."

The High Lord Luminous stood up and graciously approached each leader; he thanked them individually, returned to his seat, and said, "I am exceedingly impressed with all our plans and overwhelmed how we have all come together, in such a small space of time. From this day onwards, I pledge that we are all one and protect each other, whoever we are. We have leaders within our own communities, but we need one animal to call on, fast enough to alert all of us when there is trouble. There is only one animal who is intelligent and understands the ways of man. We all know that crows are relentless in tracking down evidence, which they pass on so efficiently so that information can be attained within an hour, so I nominate Councillor Claudius Crow to be messenger of the forest, a role that will be known from here on with high regard and respect."

Councillor Claudius Crow stood up and proudly fanned his tail as all the other leaders applauded. He stepped forward, hopping and nervously bobbing his head, whilst darting his beady eyes to take account of everyone present.

As the applause simmered down, he said, "Thank you very much for your unanimous approval; I proudly accept my new position. We generally do keep very much to ourselves, but the recent tragedy was ruthless, and we are participating like all of you are, as who knows when the humans decide that hedgehogs are a nuisance, or moles are making unwelcomed holes in their gardens, and then another cull is initiated. The intelligence that the High Lord Luminous and I have gathered confirms without a doubt that we will be attacked on Friday."

A shudder of fear and anxiety went through all the warriors, and as the High Lords and councillors shifted uneasily in their seats, there was a crescendo of various comments and questions.

Finally, the High Lord continued, "Yes, my friends, on Friday, we are expecting some highly trained dogs to be set on us to track our setts. Man will be following closely by. So our main mission is to distract the dogs as best as we can and to try to mislead the humans. Our human friends should be here soon, and we can exchange all the information we have, but for now, let us return to the feast. Our sows and the young ones are anxious, and they need not be alarmed as to what is happening. When our human friends arrive, we will resume the meeting with the military leaders."

They all returned to the feast, with very little appetite but filled with foreboding thoughts and ideas to prepare for the later meeting.

As the High Lord ushered the last member of the meeting to go before him, someone cleared his throat and said nervously, "Excuse me, High Lord?"

The High Lord turned to see Bodger Badger standing tall and looking smarter than he had been in a long time; he gave him a genuine smile of encouragement and said, "Good to see you looking so well, Bodger. What can I do for you, as you are aware that I am very busy preparing for this war?"

Bodger replied without hesitation, "Firstly, I beg your pardon for my last encounter with you, but more important, we have heard whispers in the setts that we all need to help on Friday, and I would like to volunteer, and I recruited several other black-and-white pelts to join me. I also convinced our tenants, the foxes and weasels, to help participate in whatever manner they can help us."

The High Lord reached out and touched him gently on the shoulder and said, "Bodger, you have redeemed yourself today, and I am sure you will make Sally and your cubs very proud of you. Come let us enjoy the feast the hedgehogs have prepared."

Just as the High Lord was returning to the feast, he could sense the presence of his allies from the other side of the forest, waiting at the edge of the woods. He greeted them warmly and led them into the woods.

"Earlier than expected," he said. "That is very considerate of you."

Andy smiled and said, "To be honest, I did not get a wink of sleep all night, as I have been so excited for this morning."

Barry laughed and added, "Perhaps it was because we had to sleep in our car, as opposed to check into a hotel. You may not be aware of Andy's illustrious celebrity status, and we did not want to attract any attention in this small village."

The High Lord smiled.

"Yes, I believe you are renown in the music world. Perhaps I can persuade our musical talent to perform once more. Come, we have lots to discuss." He continued, "Hello, Sarah and Geoffrey; where is Shams?"

Sarah replied, "There is too much going on that we cannot seem to put together, so Shams has gone into DEFRA to ensure we don't miss anything. On our return, if there is further development, we will reach out for you and organise another meeting."

The High Lord responded, "Earlier this morning, we nominated Claudius Crow as the messenger. When you need to summon him, take this instrument and blow into it, and within five minutes, Claudius will be with you. We call it a Bluuout, and it's only audible to the forest animals. The High Lady has been extremely anxious of me going back and forth into your world, and I promised to be close by. Like myself, she can shape-shift but has a greater gift of seeing the future. Despite me continuously telling her that we will survive this, she keeps saying it will end tragically, so I need to be close to her."

The Bluuout looked like a little broken flute; without thinking, Sarah impulsively blew into it and smiled, as she heard nothing. She was about to ask the High Lord how it worked when all at once, Councillor Claudius Crow appeared. The High Lord laughed at Sarah, who apologised to Claudius, who simply bobbed his head and quickly flew off.

The High Lord then said, "Sarah, please believe me that Councillor Claudius Crow will not let you down. Tell him anything, and he will come straight to me."

They arrived at the gathering with the High Lord. The cubs and hoglets ran immediately to Sarah and Geoffrey, and they lay on the grass and allowed the cubs and hoglets to jump over them like stationary hurdles. Drill, Minx, and Polly began to put crocuses into Sarah's hair, whilst Brad and Bob pulled hard at Geoffrey's wiry red curls.

Barry and Andy were mesmerised at how calm and peaceful all the animals were. This was so different from what happened in human society when newcomers arrived. They are scrutinised from head to toe and made to not feel welcome at all.

In contrast, the animals smiled and nodded their heads and continued with their activities; it fascinated Barry and Andy, especially when these animals were preparing a defence against humans. The fact that they adhered to the good word of the High Lord made Barry and Andy wish there was one person who could influence other human leaders to eliminate the unwanted wars based on religion and the need to attain power.

Barry and Andy witnessed the natural order of responsibilities. No one waited to be served. Everyone participated in ensuring they had enough to eat and cleaned up after themselves. The only ones not doing anything were the elder animals, who were distinguished by their slower gait and older appearance. They were quite content with their honeycomb chews.

The High Lord approached Barry and Andy and said, "Can you see what a happy society we live in? We do not try to upset your side of the forest and have even made restrictions to the foxes and hedgehogs, who agreed to stay within the woods and not take your food, as we have plenty to share. However, we cannot speak on behalf of our relatives born in your side of the forest, as they are as alien to us as you are."

Barry said, "I promise you, High Lord, Andy and I will do our best to protect all the animals. We have a lot to learn from you."

The High Lord summoned the warrior leaders and then called Sarah and Geoffrey, who were looking like they were having too much fun, to come across.

"Warriors, the only information we know is that on Friday, the dogs will be tracking us down. To all our nocturnal friends, contrary to our recent regime of breaking our fast in the early hours, we will revert immediately to sleeping through into the evening, which will minimise daytime activity and reduce our tracks. The red pelts will remain vigilant at the entrance of the setts. Sarah and Geoffrey will be constantly listening to find out more information and contact the messenger."

The High Lord continued to relay the plan of defence the animals prepared; Barry and Andy were totally flabbergasted by the ingenuity of the strategies of all the warrior leaders.

Barry stood up and said, "Forest friends, Andy and I feel helpless, as we have been building up funds to buy vaccines to inoculate the badgers and prove they are free of this disease they are accused of spreading. We can clearly see that you are all healthy and never imagined we would have been given this privilege and honour to be amongst all of you. The cull that has been legislated is cruel and unnecessary; war is something we detest amongst my supporters, and we promise to try to avoid a bloodbath on

Friday. We will never divulge what we witnessed amongst you and will always look out to protect you."

All the animals nodded in gratitude, and the badgers began to scratch their paws into the ground. The High Lord explained to the guests that they were asking their ancestors to protect their new allies.

Sarah turned and saw tears streaming down Andy May's eyes. The High Lord approached him and said, "Sit down, man of big music talent; we have a very special treat for you."

The guests were led back into the field, and in a short space of time, Clawdigger managed to organise what looked like an arena with a centre stage. There was a badger with a younger cub, a small group of badgers to the right (the sett's choir), a mixture of weasels and polecats to the left, and a variety of birds swooping casually in and out.

The High Lady nodded her head, and both Brit and Sharp sang in a crescendo of sounds, backed by baritone depths of vocals from the badgers on the right and the shrill soprano notes and octaves of the weasels and polecats from the left. The birds added staccato notes with their brief chirps, and although their guests had no idea what they were singing, they could feel that it was about thanks and appreciation, which is exactly what the High Lord translated to them.

Andy sat on the grass next to Sarah, and they were both bawling like newborn babies, whilst Geoffrey was trying very hard to hold back his tears. Barry allowed his tears to flow down his cheeks, determined more than ever to succeed in his fight against the cruelty of animals.

The High Lord gently led them to the edge of the woods and earnestly thanked them for their help and support. Barry and Andy said they were grateful for being given the opportunity to experience a pure fantasy come to life.

Andy was still very emotional as they walked back to the Range Rover.

"It was incredible," he said. "It was music at different levels, but it was just one movement, so well-harmonised. A range of contrast, moods, tones. It was simply a rhapsody."

Geoffrey smiled at Sarah; he felt a new release from Her Majesty was about to be created.

The Plot Thickens

As agreed, Ollie met Tommy Balls on Tuesday morning in the car park of the Dog and Gun.

Tommy stubbed out a cigarette as he walked towards Ollie and said, "Morning, do you have time for a coffee?"

Ollie looked at his watch and said, "Really sorry, but my team is meeting me in an hour, so I need to get back."

Not interested in making chit-chat, he looked around, walked towards the woods, and took a large brown envelope out of his parka.

He told Tommy, "There is five thousand pounds in cash, as you requested, for the dogs to track the badgers. Is there any way I could see these dogs or know where they are coming from?"

"Keep your voice down, son; I'm not deaf. Sorry, but I cannot disclose the source of my dogs."

Ollie asked, "What is my assurance that these dogs will find the badgers?"

"Son, I have been doing this long enough, and you have my word. Besides, isn't Tricky Dicky meeting up with me on Friday and confirming the siting?"

"Yes, yes, of course he is. I guess it's just a lot of money to part with. I needed to know the job was in the hands of a professional."

"Professional? That's a laugh. We are just a group of bored idiots who enjoy watching the dogs and badgers have a good fight. I am a nobody, really. The big guys get their dogs from Mark, and that's what I do too. Blimey, you are pretty talkative today."

Ollie was sweating under his thick parka, which hid the wire that recorded their conversation. Meanwhile, Ady Head, a young undercover agent, was videoing the entire rendezvous from behind the bushes.

Trying to coax Tommy to say more, he asked, "Sorry, so Mark is your contact?"

"Are you interrogating me?" Tommy snapped; he started to sound uncomfortable.

"No, n-n-no," Ollie stuttered, and then he said, "I guess I am just too embarrassed to ask if I'd be able to watch a fight?"

"Whaaat?" roared Tommy. "I thought you were dead against it."

"I have to do my job as dictated by DEFRA, but truth be known, between you and me, if we need to get the numbers down, does it matter how we do it?"

"Well, they are just large vermin, as far as I am concerned, but what strong fighters. Right, if you really are interested, I'll contact the boys to arrange for you to come to see a fight, but for goodness sake, don't mention who you work for, and I do not want young Dicky involved. Must stir up some terrible memories of his dad."

Ollie looked confused and asked, "Why? I don't understand."

Tommy was somewhat surprised that Ollie did not know about Richard's past; he told him about the fateful demise of Richard's father and grandfather.

"Anyway, it's much more professional now," Tommy said, "so don't be worried about losing a leg." He laughed callously and continued, "Right, should I call you or Dicky when I have the dogs?"

"Call me please," Ollie said.

Tommy opened the envelope and took a deep breath, inhaling the scent of the new bills. With a glint in his eyes, he said, "Nice doing business with you. I will keep you informed as soon as we have a fight scheduled."

Ollie was hesitant to offer Tommy his hand to shake, as his palms were so clammy and cold with fear; he slid them into his pocket, nodded, and then turned and walked away towards his car.

As soon as Tommy's Saab was out of sight, Ady came out from the bushes; making sure that no one was around, he walked over to Ollie's car.

Ollie sat in his car, drenched of all colour, with his head slumped onto his steering wheel. He was shaking from head to toe and jumped up with fright when Ady tapped on his window.

Ollie came out of the car, apologised, and immediately ran into the woods to throw up. Ady looked at him, smiled, and shook his head. He looked into Ollie's car and saw a six-pack of Evian water in the back seat. When Ollie returned, Ady passed him a bottle and said, "Well done, Mr. Gunner. If you get tired of DEFRA, I'll find you a job with us on the force." He continued, "Seriously, are you okay? You did a fine job getting that information out of him. I'll contact my guys, and with what you got on the wire plus my video coverage, I am convinced we can nail him with the dogs on Friday. When we arrest him, hopefully he would have contacted the big boys, and we can get that number and bring them in too."

Ollie was feeling a little more composed and said, "A young recruit will be with him on Friday. Please ensure that he is not hurt during the arrest. I will come and pick him up at the station."

Ollie shuddered as he recalled how John Nicks was killed and mused, *And I thought I had Daddy issues; the poor kid.*

Ady assured him that Richard would not be hurt and said he would see Ollie later in class.

"But why, Mr. Gunner? I want to continue to be involved in this. It's something I've wanted to do for a very long time. It does not seem fair, when I have been instrumental in finally locating the badgers."

Ollie looked at this sad, disillusioned young man, who truly believed killing every single badger would avenge the death of his family.

"Mr. Nicks, you will be rewarded with recognition after Friday. You must trust me because if you do not follow my exact instructions, you will jeopardise this entire operation. But if you do exactly as I say, I promise that you will be extremely happy, but you must trust me."

Ollie continued, "I met with Mr. Balls and paid him the deposit. I don't want you to attend the tracking team meetings, but as soon as Mr. Balls gives me the signal, I will contact you to meet him. You will meet him and track the badgers together, as discussed, and as soon as you confirm a siting of their setts, you must text me your location. You must stay with him, ensuring that the dogs do not go down the setts, and wait till I arrive. In fact, Mr. Nicks, thinking about it, I would prefer you to wear a device so I can track you at all times."

Richard responded sullenly, "Well, I don't think anyone is going to miss me, but yes, of course, Mr. Gunner, I do trust you."

Ollie continued, "Keep away from the campus, as I do not want the other recruits seeing you and asking questions. Do you have somewhere to go within five miles of the area? If not, I will be happy for you to stop with me."

Richard replied, "No, I am okay. I will spend some time with my uncle. He is only a couple of miles away from here."

"Brilliant," Ollie said. "Look out for my call on Friday, and I am sure I do not need to reiterate how confidential this whole operation is. Mr. Nicks, remember that you have been key in all this."

Ollie looked at the young man, who seemed confused, lost, and broken; in a bizarre way, he saw himself in Richard.

In a softer tone, he continued, "Good work, Richard. On Friday, you will see that all will be well and that you will make DEFRA proud."

The fact that Ollie addressed him as Richard perked the young man up, and he walked away once again feeling that he was truly part of this operation.

Nick Panay, Steve Foley, and Mick Jones sat in the canteen and were about to have their lunch when they saw Dale Matthews, sitting on his own a few tables away.

Nick called over, "Hey, Dale, why didn't you come out with us last night?"

Dale looked up, raised his hand to acknowledge the comment, and continued eating.

Nick turned to the other lads and said, "What's up with him? Let's go and have a chat with him." The three of them walked over to Dale.

Nick tried again, "Hey, pal, are you okay? You seem annoyed."

Dale, a small man from Yorkshire, looked up and hesitated making a cutting retort to his immediate supervisor, but decided that he was big enough to stand up for what he thought was right. He looked at Nick and then at Steve and Mick and said, "Right, I know you are my boss, and I don't know how to put this, so I am going to be blunt and just say it."

"Say what?" they simultaneously asked.

"I am ashamed to say that you are all sell-outs. Nick, with your recent promotion, I understand you turning a blind eye to what we had to clean up that night, but Steve and Mick, a free meal and booze to move on and forget how we literally slaughtered those animals?"

Nick felt his cheeks rise into a deep flush of crimson. He was not sure if it was out of embarrassment due to Dale being right or anger for the way he announced his promotion before he had a chance to tell the lads.

Furious that Dale had actually exposed him, and recoiling with embarrassment, remembering the way he unquestionably deleted the video like a trained puppy in front of Jeremy, he snapped, "One minute, Dale; how dare you insinuate that my promotion was based on me shutting up? Is Mel telling you porkies that should not be leaving the office? Because if she is, I think the big boss should hear about it."

He turned to the lads and said, "Guys, I could not tell you about my promotion. You know the red tape. Things go well, and yes, I get promoted, but if things went bad, I'm the one who gets it in the neck."

Steve and Mick looked at him; Steve said, "When did it go well? It was a disaster."

They began to walk away, but Nick stopped them and said, "Listen, I've been told there is some kind of conspiracy going on; something's going to happen on Friday, and we are going to make the news. I have not been told anything other than I need to keep my guys happy and ready for Friday. Dale, I am sorry. I should not have said those things about Mel, and I am sorry you think I'm a sell-out, but I have superiors to report to and am just doing my job. Can we shake on it and move on, please?"

Dale stood up and shook his hand. He continued, "Guys, I am sorry, but I cannot take back what I said. I appreciate we all need our jobs, but Nick, I will be handing in my resignation after Friday. There is nothing that could redeem how I have been feeling since that evening. I cannot think of one reason that could make me feel proud of working here."

He turned and walked away, leaving Nick, Steve, and Mick in silence with very mixed emotions.

Mick finally said, "Well, that really makes me like a hypocrite. Nick, can you tell us more? Ollie Gunner should have had the sack."

"Guys, give me a break, I am just another pawn in this whole operation, and I have told you exactly what Mr. Fischer told me, so cut me some slack. I need this job and was not going to mouth off my opinion, especially when he told me there is some big confidential plan."

Mick took a deep breath; he sighed, nodded, patted Nick on the shoulder, and congratulated him on his promotion.

Steve had been silent throughout the conversation; he looked at Nick and Mick, and as he left, he said, "Not good, is it? Congrats, Nick, and I hope you are right about all of this."

Ollie took some time to freshen up in the gents; he took a deep breath, straightened his tie, ensured that his hair was in place, and walked towards the tracking team's meeting room. As soon as he entered, he saw Ady Head sitting next to the beautiful Rita Mosina, making conversation.

"Morning, I see you all have met Mr. Ady Head. Mr. Head has joined us with exceptional credentials and has a history of successful tracking capabilities. Unfortunately, Mr. Nicks has resigned from his role, and Mr. Head will be replacing him as part of Mr. Aziz's team. As a result of Mr. Head joining us, we have made tremendous progress and believe that Friday will be the day we finally secure the location of the vanished badgers."

Puzzled murmurs and questions were exchanged amongst the teams, so Ollie raised his voice and continued, "Mr. Head, would you like to introduce yourself to the teams?"

Ady stood up and introduced himself. Originally from Worthing, the handsome young man had a thick head of black hair and the brightest blue eyes, curtained by a thick pair of dark lashes. Beth, Jade, and Rita could not stop ogling at this fit guy with the cutest dimples and cheeky smile. They did not take in a word of what he was saying, but Sarah looked at him suspiciously.

He is much older than us, she thought. *How has this happened in less than twenty-four hours? Let's see what he has to say to us when we can have him to ourselves.*

The tracking teams left and went their own way, whilst Ady walked confidently towards Sarah, Geoffrey, and Shams.

"Nice to meet you guys," he said. "I believe I am Richard's replacement. Hope I can fill his shoes."

Sarah smiled and replied, "Interesting, and is that what Mr. Gunner has led you to believe?"

Ady laughed and said, "Oh dear, have I said something wrong?"

Geoffrey said, "Take no notice of her; the lad was alright, just kept very much to himself."

Much to their surprise, Ady seemed to be interrogating them, and they genuinely struggled to get anything out of him.

Close to the point of infuriating impatience, Sarah blurted, "Ady, excuse my bluntness, but how have you managed to assure Mr. Gunner that you can track the badgers on Friday? It sounds bizarre. Have you some sort of crystal ball?"

Ady laughed at her and replied, "That would be asking, wouldn't it? I officially start on Friday, so you'll just have to wait and see how the experts do things."

Ady walked away, chuckling to himself, but he couldn't help thinking how striking Sarah was; she looked quite beautiful when she got annoyed.

"Why, I never," Sarah snapped. "Richard, come back; all is forgiven. What an arrogant so-and-so."

Shams and Geoffrey tried to calm her down. Shams said, "Something just does not sit right. We know for sure that Ollie, Tommy, and Richard have met. We know definitely that the dogs are going to track the badgers on Friday, so why has Richard resigned? Why does Ollie boast a definite location on Friday, thanks to Ady Head. Did you notice in his conversation just now, he doesn't know that the badgers are usually asleep in the day?"

The three of them decided they must see the High Lord, and when they were in a safe vicinity, Sarah got out the Bluuout and blew into it gently.

Within two minutes, Councillor Claudius Crow arrived.

"Claudius, we must meet up with the High Lord," Sarah said. "Goodness, I don't know why I'm talking to you, as you cannot even respond to us. I am going crazy with worry now."

Much to their surprise, Claudius began to caw, and all three of them understood exactly what he was saying.

"I witnessed Ollie Gunner with a new gentleman this morning," he cawed, "but could not understand what they were doing. However, he later told Richard that he is not to return to DEFRA but will meet Tommy Balls on Friday. There is much unrest amongst the sett, so leave the High Lord to his clans, but they will need your help on Friday. I will follow the new gentleman and help you find out who he is."

As Councillor Claudius Crow flew away, Sarah turned to the other two and burst into a flood of tears.

"I am so worried," she cried. "What are we going to do? There is some sort of conspiracy out of our control, and we are going to fail the badgers."

Geoffrey took her into his arms whilst Shams rather stiffly patted her back; he said, "Sarah, it's okay. We will not let them down."

Barry Odie requested an emergency meeting at his office, and without delay, his team of staff, donors, and supporters showed up promptly at lunchtime, extremely thrilled to see that Andy May was also present.

Barry started the meeting by saying, "Morning, guys, thank you very much for getting here so promptly. Both Andy and I are aware of something happening at Brockley on Friday but are not at liberty to tell you more, other than to ask you to trust us and gather as many supporters to protest against a possible shoot that day."

A cold shiver ran through everyone at the meeting, and a staccato of various voices questioned how it was possible that Barry was given this information.

Barry stood up and tried to quell them, continuing, "This information has been given in the strictest of confidence, and a leak could jeopardise the careers of three recruits working for DEFRA. We are working very closely with them, and they have passed on confidential information to us and have asked that we help stop a possible slaughter on Friday."

The members all looked at each other, confused but excited that they were going to partake in such an event.

Paul Lingwood, one of the very generous donors, asked, "Exactly what can we do, Barry? What progress are we making to obtain the vaccines for the poor animals?

Barry responded, "It's a tough one, Paul. We are convinced from what these recruits are saying that the badgers are not even infected. However, the immediate problem is to prevent the shoot. Our next plan of action is to prove they are not the cause of BTB. For now, please gather as many supporters as possible, and I will let you know exactly where the shooting will be targeted. This is going to be very dangerous, so I don't want any children around."

Andy stood up and reiterated, "This is truly a matter of confidentiality. No one must know of the possible shoot. Like Barry said, we cannot divulge our sources and ruin the trust of these three recruits, who only want to do what is right for the animals. Have your phones ready for a call to be given the location, and once again, thank you for all your continued support."

A terrible atmosphere of anxiety and fear befell the animals as they realised they were preparing for the unknown. What they were sure of was a definite possibility of the loss of lives amongst their friends and clans, but each leader bravely brought their family and friends to make home, closer to the setts, in preparation for the attack.

Widejaw and Clawdigger liaised with all the military leaders to strategically relocate all the animals in front of the setts so the dogs would have to come through all the forest animals before reaching the badgers. The deer rambled east and west of the moles' linear row of fortresses they already established, with the High Lady Dharma at one end and Lady Dasha at the other.

The birds hovered at lower heights in the trees, with the owls canopying as the main lookout whilst the crows were closest to the ground, constantly darting in and out, passing messages to the various leaders. The hedgehogs made new homes by the bushes closest to the deer, whilst the foxes, rabbits, and weasels were positioned very close to the setts.

The young animals were super excited and totally oblivious of the impending danger. They were just so thrilled that everybody was so close to play with. Wisepaws, Lord Didas, and the other academic leaders had a very difficult job explaining to the young animals the importance of complete order and discipline for Friday, without alarming them of the true danger.

As the day went by, half of the forest was now abandoned by the animals, as they were all congregated as close to the setts as possible. Widejaw and the leaders of the foxes and weasels had a couple of days to disguise their setts as badger setts to distract the dogs, but Widejaw was fully aware this was only a ploy to gain but a few minutes before the dogs realised the trickery.

The High Lord Luminous came out to see how busy the animals were and was impressed by their bravery and dedication to protect the badgers.

He walked over to High Lord Henry and High Lady Dharma and said, "Thank you once again for your overwhelming support."

The High Lady raised her head and said, "It could be us one day, and I am sure you would participate as we have."

High Lady Pure peered from the corner and said, "You are truly an inspiration to the young female animals, and I am so impressed by your bravery."

High Lady Dharma smiled and replied, "My dear High Lady Pure, behind High Lord Luminous, I see a strong partner who is a pillar of his strength and support for everything he does. That, too, my dear friend, is bravery."

The High Lady Pure smiled and then walked over to the High Lord and said, "I know I have been very anxious and needy these last days, but I just keep seeing a troubling vision, and it saddens me so. However, I know you need to go to the other side to meet with your human friends, so go ahead, but please make your visit short."

The High Lord said, "Pure, everything is under control, and Claudius is keeping a close watch on any developments. He is my eyes and ears, and my place is here, to keep everyone strong and reassured. Let us go and check on our setts."

As the High Lord and High Lady walked towards the setts, he noticed Councillor Claudius Crow in a very serious conversation with Grand Councillor Oscar Owl.

Grand Councillor Oscar Owl, who was generally of a tranquil

demeanour, was bobbing his well-groomed head of finely chiselled features in a very distressed manner.

The High Lord said, "Why, Grand Councillor Oscar, what has ruffled your feathers? I have never seen you so upset."

Grand Councillor Oscar Owl looked at the High Lord and angrily spluttered, "It's no joking matter, High Lord."

Grand Councillor Oscar continued to tell the High Lord how Claudius discovered that several owls were being kept in captivity by this man called Mark Ashley, who was the same man who was preparing the dogs for Friday.

A cold shudder ran through the High Lord, who immediately said, "What can I do to help them?"

Claudius responded that they were secured in cages; only a human could unlock them and release the birds.

The High Lord turned to the High Lady and said, "I must return the favour and help these owls. I will return as soon as possible."

The High Lord transformed himself into a crow and immediately took off after Claudius and Grand Councillor Oscar; they flew towards the Ashley farm.

Grand Councillor Oscar Owl flew quietly into the owl enclosure and spread the word to all the captive owls to keep very quiet whilst they planned their escape.

The High Lord, now transformed as man, unlocked the cages and carefully removed the bindings and long chains attached to the owls, who were perched on stands. He carefully lowered the chains, and after half an hour, all the owls were released and flew off with Claudius and Councillor Oscar. The High Lord was just about to transform back into a crow and fly off but decided to check out the surroundings. The dogs began barking, and within minutes, a big man came out of the house with a shotgun in his hand.

He gruffly shouted, "Who's there?"

But he was immediately distracted as he saw a whole flock of his owls flying away from the farm. He rushed into the owl enclosure, shouting a series of abusive curses, and came out pointing his shotgun from one angle to another, ready to shoot anything that moved.

The High Lord resumed his form as a badger, and the dogs were yelping and barking ferociously, as they could smell his scent outside. For once in his life, the High Lord felt cornered; he could sense Mark approaching him, but just then, five or six owls swooped down and knocked Mark to the ground. The loud report of his shotgun was heard as it went off when Mark fell down, and the owls immediately pounced on him, pecking mercilessly on his face whilst their talons tore at his chest. They could only think how cruel he had been to them, chaining them in the cages and not feeding them for days when he was laid out drunk.

A woman came out of the house, screaming; she ran over to the kennels and opened one up, and the dogs rushed over to Mark, who was under the owls. The birds took off, and the dogs were unsure as to what to do, as the evening was like a bonfire night gone wrong, with frenzied barking of the dogs in the shed, a screaming woman, and feathers everywhere, settling on Mark's bloodied chest.

The High Lord wasted no time and fled back into the woods.

Mark was furious and shouted to his wife to stop screaming. He was angry, as he could not report the loss of his owls to the police, and annoyed that he could not go to the hospital to explain an attack by owls, but more than anything, he was livid, as he had organised an exhibition of his owls the next day, which was now impossible, and that meant a full refund to all the guests arriving.

"I can't explain how this happened, but I swear on my mother's grave, I'll get each and every one of you owls back," he snarled through gritted teeth.

Grand Councillor Oscar Owl was perched stealthily in a tree close by and simply said, "Not under my watch will you have another owl in captivity." And with that, he flew off to meet the other animals.

On returning to the forest, everybody applauded the High Lord for his bravery. However, the bullet from Mark Ashley's gun had skimmed the High Lord's shoulder, which was a very close shave. He bravely assured the animals that he was fine and together with Grand Councillor Oscar welcomed the new visitors, who expressed their gratitude for their freedom.

What started as a dismal day filled with gloom and despair ended with a feeling of victory against all odds, and the animals slept safely, confident that they were in good hands and looking out for each other.

The Final Preparations

The young ones, wide-eyed with grins from ear to ear, were so excited. They did not understand why they were all huddled together but thought it was so much fun that they were allowed to sit with together with whoever they wanted. Maggie, Mighty, and Spiky sat on Farah's back, whilst Bojana, Speed, and Fire placed themselves in front of the fawn, not wanting to miss anything. Lord Didas was teaching today, and he was explaining how the forest animals were preparing for a new way of life and that it was very important for the warriors to protect them.

However, he continued, "As young animals, you also play a big role, and it's most important that you keep out of the way, stay safe, and not be mischievous or break any rules."

The little ones sat mesmerised, not quite understanding what he was saying, but Speed, with her eyes welling up, raised her hand and asked, "Has this got something to do with why my Little Clawdigger was taken so early by the ancestors?"

Lord Didas looked at Wisepaws. who lumbered to the front of the class and replied, "Yes, my dear Speed. Sadly, some man want to cause some trouble, but as you have seen for yourself, there are also good man like those you met, who are helping to protect us from the bad ones. So for the next two days, we are going to train all of you to help. It is going to be like a huge hide-and-seek game, but you cannot come out unless you hear either Lord Didas or myself give you the command. This is a serious game, and no one must break the rules. Do you all understand?"

The little ones were all slumped over with their heads down, but they immediately sat up straight and shouted attentively, "Yes, Councillor Wisepaws."

"Very good, in an orderly way can each young fawn take a hedgehog and a mole on their back, whilst the others partner up in twos. Fire, I know you love to be with Speed and Bojana, but you'll need to be with White at all times, and both of you closest to me. Is that clear?"

Fire nervously looked at Speed and Bojana, and both of them mouthed, "It will be okay," and he then turned to his sibling, squeezed her hand, and replied, "Yes, Councillor Wisepaws."

Wisepaws and Lord Didas sensed that the young ones were getting anxious, so they took them out to take a break and play some games, before they commenced the drill that they both choreographed for Friday.

After the young ones finished their break, releasing all their energy spinning, somersaulting, jumping, hopping, and skipping; Wisepaws and Lord Didas shouted for them to line up. They gathered in the field under five towering pine trees, surrounded by several hawthorn trees almost in full foliage. Thick gorse bushes with hints of yellow buds waiting to burst into bloom squeezed in between the hawthorn and pine trees, and on closer observation, there were three setts built between the tall pine trees.

As the young ones were lining up, Speed, who was out of breath from playing, raised her hand and asked, "Councillor Wisepaws, why do all those trees have laurel leaves with strings of berries on them?"

Wisepaws looked at Lord Didas and rolled his eyes in amusement; whilst shaking his head, he smiled at Speed and replied, "You don't miss a thing, do you? Well observed, Speed."

When all the young ones were settled in an orderly fashion, he asked them to sit down and continued, "As Speed noticed, we have assigned certain trees and bushes with laurel leaves and a certain number of berries tied to its branch or trunk. This is going to be our big hide-and-seek game. Behind us is the hiding place you will all go to on Friday when Lord Didas and I give you the signal. We are now going to give you a laurel leaf with the exact number of berries as seen on each tree. The first practice is for you to look for the tree or bush that matches what you have in your hand. You have to keep the leaf and berries safely with you unless you can remember exactly where you need to go. So now, you need to run around and look for your matching leaf and berries."

The young ones jumped up, screeching and squealing. With much excitement and good fun, they found where they needed to be and proudly stood at attention at their designated spots, waiting for their next command.

Wisepaws and Lord Didas cheered loudly and praised them for their victory. Lord Didas continued, "Well done. Now that you have found your spots, come back to the field, and we'll do that once more, but this time, with no squealing or any noise. You must not forget it is an important hide-and-seek game, and no one must hear you. Instead of Lord Didas or myself shouting you back to the field, listen out for the Bluuout three times to return to the assembly field. Do you all understand?"

"Yes, Councillor," they all sang in unison. The little ones were so enthusiastic to please their teachers, and as instructed, they quietly found their spots once again.

Wisepaws praised them again, and they stood at their assigned positions, filled with pride. He said, "Tremendous. Now all with a laurel leaf and three berries, please look down on your right. Those with a laurel leaf and six berries, look behind you, and the ones with two laurel leaves and one berry, look in front of you. Are you all in position?"

"Yes, Councillor," they repeated.

"Brilliant. Now for all those with three laurel leaves and no berries, you are perfectly in your correct position." He smiled as he saw the young fawns camouflaging amongst the gorse bushes. The birds with one laurel leaf were nestled in the heavily foliaged hawthorn trees, and with another big smile, he continued, "Yes, for all our fine feathered friends, you are also in the correct position. Well done."

Lord Didas stepped forward and said, "Whilst the fawns and birds stay in position, can the badgers, rabbits, hedgehogs, and moles run down the setts that you can see by your position. Young foxes and weasels, please go behind the fawns in the gorse bushes."

The young ones did exactly as they were told, and Lord Didas and Wisepaws looked at each other and congratulated themselves on such a brilliant choreography, as the animals were completed hidden and camouflaged within the bushes and trees.

Wisepaws blew into the Bluuout three times, and they all came out and ran back to the assembly field, where their teachers praised them.

"We are so proud of you today. Tomorrow, we need to practise this drill all day, and the goal is to keep as quiet as possible and be faster each time. In the morning, we will signal and blow twice. You must stop anything that you are doing, even if it is breakfast, and instead of coming into the classroom, you must assemble here. You can only come out of your hiding places when you hear the Bluuout three times and return to this field. Do you all understand? There will be a lot of noise and unusual sounds. You must not come out to find out what is going on, unless ..." Wisepaws nodded and opened his palms to the children for them to complete his sentence

"Unless we hear the Bluuout three times, Councillor Wisepaws," the children sang out.

The young ones were dismissed to return to their families, with every single one beaming with pride, and not one of them understanding the true reason of their drill. It was certainly not a game.

On Wednesday morning, Richard arrived at Moss Lane, which had a row of ten rustic, medieval cottages, each with a hipped thatched roof and a tall old chimney, spouting off the welcoming odour of burning logs. It was impossible to park close to the cottage, with its cobbled road indented with potholes here and there, so Richard parked in an open field like everyone else and carefully walked towards his uncle's cottage. It was a lovely winter's day with a clear blue sky; some of the neighbours sat outside, whilst others were weeding their garden plots across their homes, making room for the bulbs that were ready to burst through the grounds to welcome spring. Uncle Shamus sat on a sturdy black wrought-iron garden chair, smoking a cigarette. He stood up carefully with his crutch and hobbled towards Richard when he saw him approaching.

He proudly shouted to his neighbours, "Everyone, my nephew Richard. He is working for DEFRA, you know."

Richard was so embarrassed as he proceeded to shake all their hands and answer silly busybody questions, but he did not take offence, as he could see that his uncle and neighbours meant well and were just very curious. Uncle Shamus started to wave him into the house with his crutch, so Richard politely nodded goodbye to everyone and walked into the cottage.

Ivy cottage, aptly named, boasted a rich blanket of thick ivy lobes, tightly hugging and wrapping the walls; they were neatly trimmed to avoid the troughs. It was bursting with thick clusters of red berries, much to the delight of the birds, as evidenced by a couple of robins darting back and forth. As he entered the room, a very old-fashioned décor and a charming wood burner welcomed him. On one side of the wood burner were uniformed chopped logs, and on the other side, an old black wrought-iron bucket of coal sat in front of a traditional fireplace tool set. Uncle Shamus waved him in as he reached out for the poker to make room to add another log in the wood burner.

Richard marvelled at how his uncle just got on with whatever he needed to do, despite his disability, and wished he had spent more time with him since he was released. He looked around, and Uncle Shamus had an old, red Chesterfield with distressed arm rests, cracked with age. By the charming wooden window, there was a Parker Knoll wing chair with a matching ottoman that was used as a footrest. Another wing chair was in the corner by his old-fashioned telephone on a tall stool. A mahogany coffee table incorporating a nest of tables was in the middle of the room on a heavily patterned rug, and a sideboard against a stone-faced wall was filled with pictures of the family, crowded untidily, in various sized frames of different colours. The wing chairs looked threadbare, but when Richard sat down, he found it one of the most comfortable chairs he had ever sat on. He stood up and looked at all the framed pictures of his lost family, and his eyes began to well up.

As his uncle returned with a chunk of Victoria sponge and a mug of piping hot tea, he looked up and said, "Uncle Shamus, they are incredibly comfortable chairs."

Uncle Shamus smiled and replied, "Oh aye, this was your grandparents' home, and all this was my ma's. She had good taste she did. Your dad was born here. We all lived here, and this will be yours when I am gone, but I would be more than happy if you wanted to live here now. Richard, you are my only flesh and blood, so believe me, you mean everything to me."

Richard patted his uncle on his shoulder and genuinely believed him.

He felt he was paying homage to the family he had lost. His family, mercilessly slaughtered by those vermin. He looked around and as his emotions began stirring up, he thought to himself, *Dad, we are finally going to get them. I hope to kill every single one of them.*

Uncle Shamus ushered him to sit down.

"Sit down, son. I cannot tell you how pleased I was when you said you were taking a couple of days off to spend with me."

He filled Richard in on the family history and all his dad's escapades, not realising he was actually fuelling Richard up for what was going to happen on Friday.

Bellatrix was not too happy with Widejaw's dismissal of the female red pelts being part of the military strategy.

"This is ridiculous. I cannot believe that you are refusing to accept that I am as good a warrior as any of your army."

Widejaw, a proud strong badger and one not gifted with kind, soft words, simply replied, "Please, Bellatrix, this is no reflection on you being less important or less strong. I need you to supervise the elders and young ones. I cannot understand why you are trying to complicate things."

Her eyebrows narrowed into a furrow, and still very much in a sullen mood, Bellatrix continued, "You seem absolutely fine brainstorming strategies with the High Lady Dharma."

Widejaw stepped back and looked at her in bemusement. Completely surprised, he said, "Bellatrix, do I detect a hint of jealousy?"

He continued clumsily, "Come here, my fiery warrior; there is no one I admire more than you as my sow and mother of my cubs. Take it as the highest compliment that I am not assigning anyone other than you to protect our cubs and the young animals in their hiding spot. Please, let's agree on this, as I truly need to know that you are happy and aware,

He hesitated and then continued, "Aware that you are very important and my number one reason for coming back safely."

Bellatrix was very taken aback, as she had never seen this side of Widejaw. It unnerved her, as it showed that even Widejaw was anxious about what might happen on Friday. She could read the urgency of his fear in his eyes to protect their cubs and knew she was being unreasonable and perhaps a little jealous, so she nodded and replied, "Widejaw, you are right as usual, and I am being ridiculous. Go, go, you have lots to do. I am okay."

As he left, she shouted a little louder, "You are my number one as well."

Widejaw turned around and smiled, feeling more determined to ensure that all the animals were prepared to defeat their enemy.

Brad, Poppy, and Polly had Bodger limply surrendering and completely out of breath in a corner, pretending to be their prisoner. Without warning, he stood up and growled at them, roaring, "Which one of you cubs am I having for my dinner?"

The cubs shrieked and ran away, but he managed to grab all three of them and tickled their bellies mercilessly.

Sally smiled as she came to see what all the commotion was about. Bodger looked at her, turned to his cubs, and said, "Oh, I think there is a bigger feast to have with this badger; let's all get her."

The cubs ran towards their mother to protect her but knocked her down instead and then began to smother her with cuddles and kisses. They screamed at Bodger, saying, "No, no, you cannot have Mama for your feast, but you can come and cuddle her."

Sally sat up and reached her arms out to Bodger.

"Come here, there will be no one feasting on me. Help me up; I need to go and help the sows with the food packs."

Bodger pulled her up, cleared his throat, and said, "Sally, I have not gone near any decayed fruit for a few weeks now and have told the High Lord that I would like to volunteer in Widejaw's army."

Sally didn't know whether to express her pride for him giving up the forbidden fruit or her fear for him volunteering. She looked at him lovingly and said, "I am so proud of you on both counts."

He said, "Could you ever forgive me for all I've put you through? Can we start all over again?"

Sally was so happy and felt her heart surging with joy as she said, "I have never given up on you, Bodger. You are a wonderful father, and I knew someday you would find your way back to my heart."

He held her close and said, "Thank you, Sally. I won't let you and the cubs down; I'll make all of you very proud of me. I must see Widejaw in an hour, so please get back as soon as you can."

All the female animals were busy stocking up food for the cubs and the elderly. The High Lady Pure, Brooke, Molly, Sparkly, and Brit were busy making packs as Bellatrix came out of the sett and walked towards them.

"Sorry, ladies, what can I do to help?"

The High Lady looked up, smiled at Bellatrix, and said, "Sally should be here shortly, but Bellatrix, you know your place is not here with us. Could you please liaise with Wisepaws and Lord Didas, as we all want you to be part of the drill with the young animals."

"Certainly, I believe Widejaw is going to be addressing us shortly."

Sally arrived shortly, beaming with happiness, and was welcomed by the other sows, who asked her no questions but were so glad to see how happy she was.

The sows and other females filled the hide-and-seek destination with food down the setts and in and around the gorse bushes. They made sufficient packs for the elderly and stored them carefully where they would be hiding. There was no drill required for them, as they were quite happy to be told where to go, as long as there was plenty of honeycomb to chew on.

With all the animals pitching in, the food rations were prepared in no time, so they all made their way to the meeting of the councillors and various leaders.

Widejaw, Maximus Mole, Lord Sparta, and the High Lady Dharma stood in front of all the female animals, and as soon as they were comfortable and settled, Widejaw cleared his throat and began, "As you all know, I am not too happy with your involvement on Friday, as I feel your place is more with the young ones and the elderly."

A loud murmur of discontent waved through the crowds, loud enough to show disapproval at Widejaw's comment.

Bellatrix shot him a look that could have knocked him down immediately, and the High Lady Dharma cleared her throat loudly.

He continued, "However, the four of us have discussed your request to help and have decided that as soon as the Bluuout is signalled for the young ones to go into hiding, Bellatrix and other female volunteers should accompany Wisepaws and Lord Didas. I will shortly give you instructions as to what you should do. This would free up the warriors of all the animals to be at the front line, as we are quite sure you will be able to look after the young and the elderly. Is this an agreeable suggestion?"

The High Lady Dharma stepped forward and said, "Thank you, ladies, for coming together this morning. I cannot believe how quickly you sorted the food rations, but it only goes to show you will have no trouble taking care of the young and the elderly. There's no need for any of us to give you instructions, as I am convinced there is no greater warrior than a mother protecting her offspring."

She looked at the warrior leaders, who were ready to announce their instructions, and continued, "The warriors will proceed with our plans and allow you ladies to discuss your own plans. It would be appreciated if a couple of ladies come and join in our meeting so as to be made aware of what is going on; perhaps Lady Dasha could listen to your meeting, so that all of us are aware of what you are doing."

High Lady Pure smiled and said, "Very diplomatically presented, High Lady Dharma. Brooke and I will attend your meeting, while Brit will head the meeting with all the ladies, and we will be most honoured for Lady Dasha to be present."

Bellatrix's lips curled into a small smile, as she had never witnessed anyone so casually and subtly take over a meeting from Widejaw. She could not resist the smallest chuckle to see Widejaw stand with his mouth quite agape.

Sarah, Shams, and Geoffrey arrived and parked just outside the Ashley Terrier Farm, awaiting Barry and Andy.

"Claudius could not have given us more specific directions," Geoffrey said as he looked up at the watchful crow perched up in the branches.

On arrival, the three of them noticed that crowds of people were walking out of the farm; they wondered what was going on. However, Barry and Andy pulled up in Andy's blue Maserati MC20, and they were soon distracted, or rather, Shams was soon distracted, and he immediately walked over to the beauty. Andy came out of the car with a big grin; he smiled, patted Shams on the shoulder, and said, "Did not want you to think you were the only fan." Geoffrey and Sarah had never seen Shams break into a smile so quickly, and within minutes, he was behind the wheel, checking out all the gadgets.

"Okay, boys, let's catch up before we go in," Barry said to Shams and Andy. He continued, "Are you sure this is the farm?"

Geoffrey simply pointed up to the tree, and both Andy and Barry automatically looked up and gave Councillor Claudius Crow a polite nod.

Andy smiled and softly said, "Follow the crows; that's what they say."

Councillor Claudius Crow cawed and flew down, perching on Sarah's shoulder. After a few caws, he flew back up, and Shams said, "Not sure if you understood that, Andy and Barry, but Claudius was elaborating that the dogs were in a shed and also that the man who owned the farm is not a pleasant man at all."

Barry led the way into the farm gates, saying, "Let's see how unpleasant he is."

When they entered, Mark was in a deep fluster, looking like he was chasing chickens around a coop. He was very dishevelled and looked annoyed. As usual he was in his regular attire of a vest and combat shorts, making his bruises very visible. His wife followed behind him like a puppy, looking very concerned about him, and in a gruff tone, Mark called out, "Sorry, folks, the show had to be cancelled. Unfortunately, I am not issuing refunds, but if you give me your numbers, I will contact you when its rescheduled."

Without hesitation, Barry gave him a random number and then asked, "What happened here? Looks like you were attacked or burgled."

Looking at the bruises on his face, Andy continued, "You look like you're hurt."

Mark grunted, "You would not believe the tale if I told you."

His wife interrupted and said in a meek voice, "I'm sorry, but your number does not appear on my list; could I have your name instead?"

Barry quickly replied, "Oh sorry, I should have said, a friend of yours said I could just come along and get some tickets."

Mark looked hard at Barry, tilting his head to one side, and with his chin raised, he squinted his beady eyes and asked, "Which friend? What's their name?"

As Barry hesitated, Sarah quickly jumped in, saying, "Tommy Balls."

Karen, Mark's wife, went a blanche colour, whilst Mark said without flinching, "I have no idea who you are talking about. I do not know a Tommy Balls. Now, I don't know why you're here, but I'd like you to leave or else I will kick you off my farm."

Sarah defiantly stood her ground and continued, "Dogs, he said you sold terriers, and my dad and uncle," she looked at Barry and Andy, "have just bought a farm. We overheard him mentioning your farm whilst we were at the Dog and Gun. So technically, we do not really know him, and I guess, we should not have said he was your friend."

Mark was quiet for a while and finally said, "I'll have no pups for at least another six weeks. Fully trained to hunt, I can let you have them at sixteen weeks old. Vaccinations will be included, but the full package will cost you a bob or two. I do not sell my pups for pets. They are working dogs."

"What's a bob or two?" Andy asked, as he noticed that Karen was giving him a very hard long stare.

Mark spat out the cost abruptly: "Three grand."

"Wowzers," Andy said. "Well, for that amount of money, could we look at mum and dad?"

Mark took a deep breath, gave them all another long look, and turned to Karen. With a snarl, he said, "Take them to see Hugo and Shira, but they are not to touch them. Just outside the kennels." He turned to Andy and said, "If you are still interested, you'll have to pay 50 percent upfront in cash."

Andy nodded his head, shrugged his shoulders, and said, "Yes, of course. It will have to be tomorrow, as I don't have the cash on me, but happy to pay you by card."

Mark began to march off and muttered rudely, "Kaz, sort it out and get their names and numbers."

As Karen led them to the kennels, she looked at Andy and said shyly, "Has anyone ever told you that you look so much like Andy May?"

Andy looked straight at her and replied, "I have no idea who that is."

Karen giggled and continued, "Goodness, how could you not know Andy May of Her Majesty?"

Sarah thought this was a great opportunity to humour Karen and continued, "Oh, my Karen, you are absolutely right. I cannot believe that I never saw the resemblance before."

She turned to Andy and said, "Uncle Albert, you are the spitting image."

Karen was beaming and giggling and so glad that someone agreed with her; for the first time in her life, someone made her feel that her opinion mattered. She laughed and said to Sarah, "Your uncle just does not know good music, obviously."

Sarah found her moment and changed her giggling tone to one of concern and said, "Karen, what happened to your husband? He looks like someone stabbed him and beat him in the face."

Karen looked around cautiously and whispered, "The owls got free last night, and the scariest thing happened: They all swooped down and pecked him. I was sure they were going to kill him. I told him I saw a man in white in the owl pen, but he told me I had too much to drink."

She giggled again and continued, "Probably did; it's my only treat in the evening, my one bottle of chardonnay."

Andy smiled and asked, "Why are those dogs barking and whining in that shed?"

"They are being trained for a hunt; we cannot go anywhere near them, but come here. This is Hugo and Shira."

A beautiful tan male and lovely white and tan female walked lovingly over to Karen. She turned around and said, "These are my babies. Shira generally gives us about eight pups, and there's never a runt. They stay with her a good ten weeks before Mark starts the training, and both Hugo and Shira train their pups with him, so they will be ready by the time they are with you."

Sarah smiled and examined the dogs, who looked perfectly innocent and adorable. She could not believe they could hunt badgers down. She turned to Karen and asked, "Do you just breed from these two beauties?"

Karen proudly replied, "Oh no, three of the bitches are in training for a hunt, and the other males are in another kennel."

Barry smiled and said, "What other kind of training do you do?"

Karen went white in her face as she realised she had said too much. She stammered, "What do you mean, what other training is there, other than preparing the dogs for the farmers?"

The conversation went very uncomfortable, and Karen led them back to the gate without another word.

Andy tried to break the ice and said warmly, "Well, we certainly want one of these beauties. Thank you for your time. We'll be back in the morning with the cash."

This time, Karen did not smile or respond but watched all of them walk towards their fancy cars, closing the gate behind them.

When they were clearly out of earshot, Claudius swooped down once again and landed on Sarah's shoulders. He filled them on the progress the animals had made, explaining the contingents they had formed. Claudius continued that it was a certainty that the dogs would track them and asked what progress Sarah and her friends had made.

Barry understood everything Claudius said and replied, "We have had meetings with all our supporters, and we are going to be there on Friday morning. Hopefully, we can disrupt the shoot. We intend to make camp and will not be moving."

Geoffrey continued, "Sadly, we have no news from our end. We know for sure that Ollie Gunner is convinced that he will find the location on Friday, but other than that, we are not privy to any other plans."

Councillor Claudius Crow thanked them for their support and said, "The High Lord was slightly injured last night; he is absolutely fine, but I am sure you have already guessed that he was instrumental in releasing those owls from captivity."

Geoffrey looked surprised, so Claudius elaborated on Mark's illegal captivity of various owls. He continued, "The High Lord would like to invite you tomorrow evening for their ceremony to their ancestors to beseech their blessings for Friday. He has asked that you meet at your usual spot. He will personally escort you in."

Sarah told Claudius, "We will be most honoured and privileged. Please do not sound so despondent. We are going to do our utmost to protest and disrupt the shoot, so as to buy us time to expose DEFRA for using baiting dogs. Barry and Andy are going to organise an investigation to save your friends. It will all be alright; please trust us."

Councillor Claudius Crow looked at them, bobbing his head up and down, and said, "It is without a doubt we believe and trust your goodwill and honesty. Whether it will be enough will all be revealed on Friday." And with that, he flew off into the forest.

The Calm before the Storm

Just before dawn, Lord Didas stood in the field and blew twice on the Bluuout. He stood by Wisepaws's side, both hoping that the young ones would respond without be awoken by their parents, and much to their pride, they saw the Clawdigger cubs emerge from their sett. Power led Sharp and Drill out, whilst Speed was running into the other setts, getting the others. The Widejaw cubs were rounding up the little moles and hedgehogs, and the Snowspirit cubs rounded up the little fawns, foxes, and weasels. Showing perfect discipline, the little ones gathered in the field, and within half an hour, they completed the drill, and when they heard the three Bluuout signals, they carefully came out and assembled in the field. When they returned to the assembly field, all the cubs were bleary eyed, yet ready for their next command.

Wisepaws stood proudly and beamed with approval; he announced, "I have only good news for you little ones. Firstly, you did a marvellous job. Well done. Secondly, there is no school today."

Before he could continue, they all cheered.

He smiled and said, "You can all go back to bed, but there will be drills all day. We are not going to say how many, but be on the alert for the next drill, and do it each time with less noise and faster. You have all been marvellous, and remember, you are all our future, and this exercise is going to be one of the most important things you will do in your lifetime. The most important part to always remember is to wait for the third Bluuout signal."

Lord Didas and Wisepaws, both weary themselves, also returned to their homes, as they knew there was plenty to do before the ceremony that evening.

Sarah, Shams, and Geoffrey went for their tracking meeting and could not believe the change they saw in Ollie Gunner. He was completely relaxed and chilled, and he casually announced that there was going to be a successful track and shoot tomorrow.

Showing none of his usual discontentment with his team, he continued, "We should know by lunchtime, and if you have the stomach for it, you can all come along and witness the Clean Kill Team in action. It's humane and effective."

Geoffrey raised his hand and asked, "Mr. Gunner, I do not mean to dampen your spirits, but why are you so sure that we are going to find a location tomorrow? We haven't seen any tracks for weeks."

Everyone in the meeting room nodded their heads.

"Mr. Gunner, aren't you suspicious how Mr. Head will miraculously identify a location, when we have struggled?" Martin Caton asked.

Sarah boldly asked, "What method has he been using? Everything we have been doing has been unsuccessful." With a small smirk, she looked around the meeting room and added, "Unless he is using dogs, I cannot see how he will locate tracks."

Sarah was sure everyone in the meeting room saw a deep flush rise in Ollie's cheeks.

A sudden coughing bout came over Ollie, and after he composed himself, he said, "I do apologise, ladies and gentlemen. I have no idea where that came from." After clearing his throat, he continued, "I can only reassure you, as I said earlier this week, that Mr. Head is like a thorough investigator. I am sorry if you feel he has showed you up, but instead of picking faults or trying to doubt him, why don't you all look forward to a successful day tomorrow? The government has been putting a lot of pressure on our department following the farmers' protest, so it will be nice to quell that unrest and earn some respect for DEFRA."

Pushing a little harder and confident that she no longer respected her boss, as she was going to find herself another job, Sarah calmly asked, "What about quelling the unrest of the animal activists?"

This time, Ollie did not look embarrassed; his crimson cheeks were more the result of rage.

"Miss MacBain," he said, "I believe when you first enrolled, the topic of animal activists was covered, in the sense that it was not up for discussion. If you support them, your resignation is welcomed."

Sarah looked around the room, hoping the others would voice their opinion, and much to her surprise, Rita, Jade, Darren, and Andrew also said they were upset and were constantly abused at social gatherings when they mentioned their jobs. They would appreciate more substance to support that what they were doing was morally correct.

Shams and Geoffrey gave each other a small smile, as they could see that Sarah had started something and was obtaining a wave of support from the others, much to Ollie's exasperation.

Ollie stood in the centre of the room, took in a deep breath, and raised himself on his toes, as if to increase his height. He came down on his feet, pursed his lips, and in very measured tones said, "Can we please have some order?" When no one listened, he hissed louder, "Order in my meeting room, or should I call it a classroom, since you are all behaving like infants."

This time, everybody sat up and kept quiet. He looked directly at Sarah and then at the others on his team and said, "You all enrolled in this scheme, fully aware of what you signed up for. No one's arm was twisted, and we did not promise you baby badgers for pets. Basically, your job was to help track down the badgers to eliminate them. If you have had a change of heart or feel that you've been misled, please leave this room immediately. I will not have anyone witness our success tomorrow unless they feel they are part of the mission to eliminate the badgers that have caused havoc to the farmers."

Ollie's words hit Sarah, Shams, and Geoffrey to the core, as they felt so guilty that he was absolutely right: They had signed up to eliminate the badgers. They wished they could leave but wanted to be there in case they found out anything that could help their friends tomorrow.

Ollie looked right into Sarah's eyes and said, "Do I make myself clear, Miss MacBain?"

"Yes, Mr. Gunner, but …"

He viciously interrupted her and said, "If there is a but, please leave this minute."

He stared hard at her, and she returned his gaze with one of her own hard unbreakable stares. She did not utter another word, but it was Ollie who looked away first.

Everyone felt very uncomfortable, but Ollie simply composed himself and said calmly, "Unless there is anything else, see you promptly at nine in the morning, and I can reassure you that you will be proud of DEFRA tomorrow."

As Shams, Sarah, and Geoffrey left the meeting room, Sarah was shaking uncontrollably; she just said, "Keep moving, we are nearly out of sight."

"I could ring his neck. That smarmy little upstart. How on earth are we supposed to be proud that we are going to kill those badgers tomorrow?"

Shams was in deep thought, trying to piece everything together, and said, "There must be something going on. How can he be so confident that he is going to look good? Well, we know for sure that he is going to use the dogs, so we need to expose him tomorrow. Don't forget, guys, we are ahead of them, as they have no idea how much we know. Let's get some rest before we meet the High Lord this evening."

Jeremy Fischer asked Mel D'agostino to round up Ollie Gunner, Michael Richardson, and Nick Panay for a quick update.

While he waited, he skimmed through his notes. Content that he had ticked all the boxes to cover up Ollie's involvement with the badger baiting and the nasty slaughter he ordered, Jeremy slumped back into his captain's swivel chair and waited for his team.

When they arrived, Michael knocked politely on the door, and Jeremy ushered everyone in. He looked over at Mel and said, "Miss D'agostino, please grab a chair and join us, as you have been instrumental in all the details. We'll go through the plan for tomorrow."

Nick politely jumped up and offered his chair to Mel, then he nipped out and brought in another. Mel did not bother to thank him, as Dale had told her what he had said about her.

Jeremy had a big smile on his face and said, "Tomorrow is going to be a spectacular day, and since some of us here have not been made aware of the complete picture, I thought we should go through everything together. However, every word said in this room is highly confidential. But to ensure a successful day tomorrow, it is time for me to be completely transparent so you all understand the plan."

Aware that Ollie could not deny anything he was about to say, he continued, "We cannot explain the unusual phenomenon of the missing badger tracks, and not just one team, but all six teams have struggled, and hence, our target number for the cull is miles behind, causing much pressure from above. I caught wind of an existing badger-baiting society, and with the help of Mr. Gunner and his young recruit; Richard Nicks, we have engaged the services of a Mr. Tommy Balls to assist us."

Michael and Nick looked absolutely aghast, but Jeremy ignored their protests and continued, "Yes, yes, let me continue. The young Richard Nicks is actually the son of one of the members of the Hardcore Terrier Men, and I guess he wanted to teach these immoral people a lesson, so Mr. Gunner and him joined with Mr. Balls to obtain some dogs to lead us to their setts, on the reassurance that they will not go down the setts. The Clean Kill teams will then take over, and I think in one day, we will easily make up our loss numbers."

He looked at Miss D'agostino and continued, "We have already notified the authorities; hence Mr. Ady Head, an undercover agent, whom I believe you know as a new recruit, will be present tomorrow. On sight of the dogs, Tommy Balls will be arrested on the spot. Mr. Gunner has also managed to obtain details of the source of the dogs on tape, and over and above that, we also have video footage to confirm this information, so an arrest of the man who breeds these dogs will also take place. It's a win-win situation, thoroughly well organised, and we just need to ensure that it goes precisely to plan."

Michael folded his arms behind his head, smiled, and said, "Genius! We put them away, gaining the approval of the activists for putting an end to the baiting in our area, and we meet our numbers to appease the farmers. Well done, Mr. Fischer. Ollie, I hold my hat up to you; this has been thoroughly masterminded."

Ollie blushed, looked at Mr. Fischer, and said, "I was only following orders."

Jeremy smiled and said, "Don't be modest, Mr. Gunner; you have been very instrumental in all of this." He continued, "Miss D'agostino has also alerted the press that at a precise time tomorrow, we can offer them exclusivity on a story that will be worth publishing. In return, we want them to give DEFRA good PR and several comments from the farmers. They are to avoid interacting with the activists. We are here to do a job, and I am sick of us being painted the bad guys."

Jeremy then turned to Nick and said, "Your promotion commandeering all the Clean Kill Teams has been approved. I will send an email to all the supervisors as soon as this meeting is over with a note that they are to meet you in an hour to discuss what needs to be done tomorrow. Nothing must be disclosed other than the fact that they must be ready at a minute's notice tomorrow. Can you confirm how many marksmen will be available tomorrow?"

Nick thought for a moment and then replied, "If you want to include every single one, we can present up to forty marksmen."

"Why wouldn't I?" Jeremy replied. He continued, "I want every single one ready. As a measure of encouragement, tell them they will be involved in an overwhelming achievement tomorrow and will all be rewarded with a bonus."

Jeremy stood up, a signal they all knew and accepted as a dismissal. He politely thanked them all and sat back in his chair. He sighed, put his hands under his chin, and thought to himself. *Well, if this goes to plan, I can see my promotion confirmed. The big decision is who I give my job to. Michael is just too by the book, but he's a great lad. I have Ollie in the palm of my hands; he'll do exactly what I say for this elaborate coverup. Besides, Bill Walsh owes me a favour now, so I'm in a great place, and things are certainly looking up."*

Feeling very pleased with himself, he slumped further into his captain's chair and propped his feet on the desk. With a grin of contentment, like a cat who got the cream, he reached for his phone and called his wife. After she answered, he said, "Winnie, book us a meal at the most expensive restaurant for tonight. We have a lot to celebrate. I'll tell you when I get home."

Ollie left the meeting, feeling very disillusioned and uncomfortable that Jeremy had such a big hold on him. However, he was grateful that it had all panned out well, although he felt a pang of guilt that Richard would not like it that Tommy Balls was going to be arrested. However, the badgers will be eliminated, and that was the essence of his mission, so all in all, a good result.

He got his phone out and called Richard.

"Hello, Mr. Nicks, are you okay? All prepared for tomorrow?"

Richard looked at his uncle and said, "Excuse me, Uncle Shamus, my boss is on the line." He walked outside and continued, "Sorry, Mr. Gunner. Yes, I haven't heard from Mr. Balls, but he did say that he'll call you tomorrow, and I have no reason to doubt that he will."

Ollie replied, "I am counting on tomorrow being a success. We cannot afford for it to go wrong. Could you discreetly just touch base and ensure all is good?"

"Will do, Mr. Gunner."

"Very good. Are you enjoying your couple of days with your uncle?"

Richard was quite taken aback by Ollie's interest and replied, "Yes, thank you. It has been very nice. I will call Mr. Balls now and get straight back to you."

Richard looked around to ensure that his uncle was still in the house and dialled Tommy's number.

"How are you doing, young lad?" Tommy said. "Your uncle tells me he has a visitor."

"Yes, I am keeping away from the campus, as my boss wants to avoid any leaks about tomorrow. Is everything on target?"

"Yes, as far as I am concerned. Mark's pretty miffed about someone breaking in and letting his owls out, but he said the dogs will be ready. I'll call your snorty boss in the morning, like he asked, and I'll meet you at the farm. By the way, I am meeting up with your uncle later; he might be wanting to drag you along."

"Ah, thanks for the heads-up. Well, if he does, I will look forward to meeting the infamous Tommy Balls. See you later, I guess."

Richard could see his uncle standing by the door, and so he waved his hand, gesturing one minute. He sent a quick message to Ollie, confirming that all was okay and saying he would wait for his call in the morning.

White, Snowdrop, and Glisten were getting ready for this evening and busy helping the High Lady Pure, whilst Fire was out with the High Lord, preparing for the upcoming ceremony. Snowdrop and Glisten soon made themselves scarce, and with a big smile on her face, the High Lady Pure walked towards White and said, "You have done enough now; go out and have some fun with your sisters and friends. You are truly a remarkable, dedicated little cub, and I will be lost without you, my little shadow. As I said before, you have the makings of a future High Lady, and I will be so proud to see that day."

"Thank you, Mother; if you are sure, I will meet up with Power and Minx. We said we will stay together, looking out for the drills and helping alert the others. Wisepaws has specified that Fire needs to be by my side, which means that Speed and Bojana will be included."

The High Lady laughed, "They are inseparable; how ironic that they each have different pelts but have bonded so well."

"Mother, are we in danger? Please tell me the truth. I am your eldest."

The High Lady heaved a big sigh, took White into her arms, and said, "The High Lord and all the warriors have everything in hand. You will be protected. Your main role is to be vigilant and follow all the instructions."

When she was completely on her own, the High Lady sank to her knees and gently clawed the ground. "Ancestors, I am aware we will beseech your blessing tonight, but please pay heed to my own request, for me to be strong for my High Lord and our clans."

Fire stood by the LOJAP with the High Lord, who was in deep conversation about the importance of LOJAP, when they both turned at the rustle of some leaves, to see Widejaw approaching with Mercury and Dynamite. The cubs were excited and asked Widejaw to tell the tale of Widejaw the Great.

"Cubs, you must have heard the tale a thousand times; come on, I promised you a quick look at LOJAP, but your mother will be wanting you back."

Mercury set himself into a warrior position, pretending to pounce on Dynamite, and said, "Father, will I be Mercury the Great someday?"

Widejaw laughed and said, "You have every chance to be exactly what you want to be, my little cub."

Fire laughed and added, "Bojana said that she is going to be Bojana the Great, but Speed insists that it will be her."

The High Lord laughed and said, "Nothing will surprise me with Speed or Bojana."

The High Lord and Widejaw looked at the positions organised by Clawdigger and once again marvelled how well he had positioned everyone.

"That badger is a genius. He has ensured that all the badgers of the Brockley Clan will feel as important as each of us in tonight's ceremony."

"Why, thank you, High Lord," said Clawdigger, who walked over to the LOJAP with Power and Drill. "It's nice to be appreciated."

"I wanted all the badgers to feel equal and as close to LOJAP as possible," the High Lord said. "They are all very anxious, and those who volunteered need to be reassured that they will receive the blessings of the ancestors."

Widejaw looked in deep thought and said, "Very brave and much appreciated. This marks a new era; we will henceforth train everyone in the setts, including the sows and the cubs."

"Yes," shouted Mercury, who was immediately silenced for interfering in an adult conversation.

The High Lord smiled at Mercury and said, "Yes indeed, tomorrow will mark the dawn of a new era. We have seen so many changes since you cubs were born; you will be the generation to ensure that the changes will make a difference. "

High Lord Henry and High Lord Maximus were dressed in their ceremonial regalia. The ambiance was different from the previous grand saining ceremony. This time, there was an air of anxiety and tension, with all the animals whispering amongst each other about the unknown tomorrow.

The High Lady Dharma elegantly approached them, with her antlers enhanced with cones and berries, with braids of white crocuses tumbling down her neck.

She smiled and said, "I wish you both could look a little more optimistic. There is going to be a war tomorrow, and if you look like we have already lost it, how are we supposed to uplift the animals? I believe the badgers will be singing one of their magnificent medleys by Brit, Sharp, and their choir; have you organised any of your amazing hedgehog gymnastics for entertainment?"

"Oh," said High Lord Henry, "I did not think that would be suitable under the circumstances."

"You would; you're a male. I'm not surprised. Everyone needs a lift; can you perform at short notice?"

"Of course, we can. Let me speak to the High Lady Pure, as I do not want to tread on anyone's toes."

"Be assured she will say yes," the High Lady Dharma said. "We females know how to diffuse tension and anxiety."

The High Lady Dharma observed the High Lord Henry in conversation from a distance and when she saw the High Lady Pure's face light up with appreciation, she smiled and walked towards her stags.

It was a very cold, frosty night, with a strong bitter wind, but the cruel bitterness of the night was compensated by a beautiful gem-studded sky. with rays of starlight hovering over the animals huddled together in the cold. It was worth enduring the bitter cold to witness the magnificent blanket of stars.

The councillors encouraged all the animals to help themselves to the treats prepared by the sows and ensuring that everyone was comfortable before their High Lady made her entrance.

The High Lady Pure walked in with her cubs, and every animal gasped at how magnificent the High Lady and her cubs looked. They were dressed in magnificent gowns of gossamer on a bed of what looked like ebony black crow feathers, and they each had a cuff of a red pelt around their necks. She walked into the crowd proudly, announced that they were waiting for the High Lord to bring in their honoured guests, and requested that they make themselves comfortable.

Sarah, Shams, Geoffrey, Barry, and Andy felt very embarrassed when the High Lord arrived. They had not changed since the morning and were so impressed to see the High Lord, resplendent in his glistening gown of pure white on a bed of crow feathers, like his family. His red pelt around his neck also had hedgehog quills delicately weaved in and out, and his crown was made of laurel and holly leaves with berries that was made to resemble that of a stag's antlers.

"Oh, goodness, High Lord, should we have dressed for the occasion?" Sarah asked sheepishly.

"Not at all," said the High Lord. "Tonight, it's all about honouring our friends and family."

No sooner had the High Lady spoken, the High Lord Luminous walked in with his five guests. The High Lady approached him, advising him of the entertainment that the hedgehogs were providing, and he smiled broadly in approval as he stood by his High Lady.

The guests were made comfortable, and much to their surprise, they watched an unexpected treat as the hedgehogs presented a magnificent display of their skills and dexterity. Four stags stood in a row on opposite sides, face to face, so that their antlers met and formed a base for the hedgehogs. The hedgehogs began to build a foundation on the stag's antlers and formed a magnificent pyramid, similar to what Sarah recalled in her cheerleading days. Every animal gasped as the triangle increased and took form; they waited with bated breath to see which hedgehog was going to complete the apex.

The hedgehogs were on the antlers and in complete synchronisation, moving from left to right and singing to a drumming beat they created. As the drumming beat increased, out of nowhere, little Maggie leaped into the air and gracefully completed the peak. The crowds cheered, and she beamed with pride as she stood at the top of the apex.

With outstanding adroitness and agility, the top of the apex rolled down and bounced off the stags until all the hedgehogs were safely on the ground; the stags gracefully took a bow and returned to their places.

The applause was overwhelming; the young cubs were screaming and cheering at Maggie for her magnificent bravery. She took a bow and ran back to the arms of her proud dad, Lord Sparta.

The five guests were applauding louder than anyone else. Andy and Sarah once again were in a flood of tears.

The High Lady thanked the hedgehogs for such an outstanding performance before she introduced Brit, Sharp, and their choir.

Brit meekly smiled and said, "We don't think we can beat that performance, but thank you for starting the evening with such excitement. Tonight, my lovely cub Sharp, the clan's esteemed choir, and I are going to do something very different. Tomorrow is a day of the unknown. We have spoken all week, addressing tomorrow as the day of the unknown, and none of us know how it will begin or end. However, tonight, we celebrate the union of all animals, the support of all animals, and for this reason, we will sing a song of victory, a song of unity, and whatever happens, we will be champions in each other's eyes."

Next came not the usual sad ballad, commemorating the ancestors or elders that had passed, but a wonderful upbeat song filled with joy and encouragement from Brit, Sharp, and their choir. The animals could not help but get up and dance. The five guests found themselves swaying from side to side, and once again Andy May was enthralled by the rhythms he was hearing. The High Lord Luminous was filled with so much pride. He was not expecting anything like this; he looked at Brit and gave her a nod of absolute approval. When the entertainment was over, everyone sat down to listen to the High Lord's Speech.

"Well, Brit, what can I say? You took the words out of my mouth. The hedgehogs? Everyone, are they not just outstanding, and are we not blessed for having them on our side?"

The crowd applauded loudly, and it took the High Lord some time to quiet the audience down.

The applause finally simmered down, and he continued, "Tomorrow, we all stand together to defend ourselves. It is heartbreaking that we have been unable to avoid this confrontation, but we're confident that our friends will help us avoid the elimination that man are so eager to proceed with. Tonight, I hope you noticed that my family and myself have paid tribute to wear all the colours of our pelts within our clans. The black crow feathers not only symbolise our thanks to the crows and all our fine feathered friends, but also as a recognition of our friends the moles. The quills embedded within my cuff are a tribute to the hedgehogs, and of course, my crown in the shape of an antler is a poor imitation of stately deer antlers. If we have not adorned ourselves with any semblance of our new friends, please believe that all animals within this forest are now true friends and part of our family. On the day of the unknown, yes, we will be exposed to something we hope we are prepared for, but taking Brit's wise words and singing to that marvellous melody, we are united, and we are champions, whatever happens tomorrow."

The whole forest was lifted with an air of positivity. The High Lord began to lead the badgers towards LOJAP, the other animals and the five guests held back, and when all the badgers were settled, they circled politely around the badgers and waited quietly to witness their ceremony.

High Lord Luminous raised his arms and cupped his palms towards the starry sky. In earnest, he fell on his knees, followed by all the badgers, and in a rhythm, they all began to scratch their strong paws into the ground. The dust lifted was not unpleasant but filled with wafts of lavender and the musky scent of regdab. The intensity of their paws increased, much to the astonishment of the five guests, who looked up to see four silhouettes of robed badgers in the sky. They looked like four new constellations, and the light they radiated was blinding. Sarah, Shams, Geoffrey, Barry, and Andy had to shield their eyes and looked around to see all the animals illuminated with brightness.

The radiance began to dim away, and all four forms slowly disappeared into the sky. There was a great sense of enlightenment amongst the animals. They looked calm and brave.

The High Lord stood up and simply said, "Go and rest, my friends and family. We will face tomorrow with the strength and pride that has been bestowed on us tonight."

He walked towards his five guests and thanked them for coming.

"The honour is truly ours, High Lord Luminous," Andy said, still bewildered by what he had experienced.

High Lord Luminous walked his five guests to the edge of the forest, and as his friends left, he fell once more on his knees, looked up at his ancestors, and said, "Whatever happens tomorrow, I will take as your will. I only ask for your guidance to help me make the right decision."

Day of the Unknown

The cubs were awakened by an early morning drill. They slowly dragged themselves out into the field, but their sleepiness disappeared when they saw the soft white snow on the ground. Without a minute's hesitation, the cubs and young animals began playing in the snow but were severely reprimanded by Councillor Wisepaws.

"Is this the instruction on hearing the Bluuout?" he said. "Don't you realise how important this exercise is? We are very disappointed. Now get to where you should be."

The young animals jumped up, dusted the snow off themselves, and scuttled to their positions.

Wisepaws felt very upset for being cross with the young animals, but his anxiety about the unexpected drove him to make the young animals realise how precise they had to be. He was very surprised to see the snowfall, as snow never followed a starry night.

Wisepaws did a quick headcount to ensure that all the animals were in the assembly field, and when he was satisfied, said, "You have all done extremely well. There will not be another drill today, but the next time you hear the Bluuout twice, it will be for real. You will have to be faster and quieter, and under no circumstances must you come out until you hear the Bluuout three times. Are you all very clear on this?"

"Yes, Councillor Wisepaws," the animals sang in unison.

"Very good," he replied. "Back to your homes now."

Speed shouted, "Please, Councillor Wisepaws, can we play in the snow for a while?"

Wisepaws pretended to look cross and then said, "Not today, Speed. Today is not a day to have fun. It's a day to be safe and not leave tracks on the snow, so back to your homes, and it is all about being alert and listening for the Bluuout signal. Make sure you have your breakfast, and go back to have some rest."

Wisepaws felt bad that he had to remind the young ones that it was not a day of fun. His young boar cubs, Wizz, Clev, Gene, and Bril, raced to him and grabbed him with a big hug, pinning him to the ground.

"No, boys, we honestly cannot play now; you must go back for some rest."

Wizz looked at his father and said, "Papa, you look so worried. Is everything going to be alright?"

Wisepaws hugged him, drew his other three cubs into his arms, and said, "Our ancestors will be looking down on us, and they will protect us. Promise me that you listen to the instructions and do everything you're told."

After the cubs were out of sight, Lord Didas joined Wisepaws, and they carefully swept away the tracks in the snow.

Tommy Balls arrived at Mark Ashley's farm at nine in the morning. He was surprised to see the gates locked and rang the bell. It seemed to take ages before Mark finally arrived to open the gates. In spite of three inches of snow, Mark was once again in a vest top and camouflage combat shorts. Mark didn't recognise the four-wheeled drive vehicle, so Tommy opened his window and shouted, "You didn't think I was going to put your mutts in my Saab, did you?"

"Ha ha, I never seen you drive anything else."

As Tommy pulled in, Mark continued, "By the way, I have a bone to pick with you. Some swanky sods came around yesterday and said they heard you mouthing off at the Dog and Gun about me selling dogs. Information like that can fall in the wrong hands, you know."

Tommy pursed his lips, raised his brows, and simply said, "Mark, I like you, but you are certainly not a topic I discuss over a pint. Weird, but

I cannot think of any other occasion that I mentioned the dogs, other than the time I was with John Nicks' son, and that conversation was practically a whisper because his boss was paranoid to be in my presence. Anyway, speaking of dogs, are they ready?"

Mark smiled and cheekily replied, "Have you got my brass?"

"Certainly."

Tommy reached into his coat pocket for an envelope and handed it to Mark. Unknown to both of them, Ady Head, along with Becky Smith, Bob Ainsley, and Mike Martyn, were hidden in some bushes, filming the whole scene. Ady and the others had tailed Tommy all the way to the farm and were simply waiting for the next move.

Mark led Tommy to the kennels. Tommy could not believe what three days of starvation could do to a dog. Digger, Patch, and Dainty looked gaunt at their haunches, and their expressions were feral in comparison to what he had seen on Tuesday.

Mark walked towards them to put their harnesses and leads on, and as he stroked them, he said, "Good girls, are you going to make your daddy proud?"

He grabbed the three dogs, picked up the dead badger skin, and made his way out of the kennels. As he helped Tommy put them in the old Land Rover he had rented for the day, he said, "Well, I generally starve them for a whole week. But I can rely on my girls to do the job. They know exactly what the abstinence means."

Mark began counting his bills in the envelope but quickly stashed a wad in his combat shorts just as Karen appeared around the corner. He told Tommy, "Now I know you know what to do, but the magic word is 'Halt.'"

He smiled, turned to his wife, and handed over the envelope, saying, "The tight so-and-so has only given us a thousand, but what are friends for, if we cannot do each other a favour?"

Mark turned to Tommy with an expression which seemed to say, "If you utter a word, I will set my dogs on you myself."

Tommy looked away from Karen and simply said, "Well, I hope to have them back in the afternoon."

As Tommy drove off, he gave Ollie Gunner a call.

"Right, I have the dogs. What's next?"

Ady and his team slipped away and returned to their cars; two of them remained to serve Mark the search warrant, and Ady began to follow Tommy down the road.

Ollie was in the meeting group, discussing the next assignment of DEFRA, planning to welcome back more hedgehogs into the forest after the cull of the badgers.

"As you are aware, hedgehogs won't inhabit badger territory, and I am looking forward to bringing our furry little iconic friends back into the woodlands community. We are planning to build little ginnels and train the hedgehogs to use the passages instead of the roads, reducing the risk of them being victims of roadkill."

Sarah saw a brief glimpse of kindness in Ollie and was impressed by his vast knowledge of forest animals and their habitat. She had to laugh to herself, as he had truly no idea of the newly formed alliance of the badgers and hedgehogs.

Just to annoy Ollie, she could not resist asking, "Mr. Gunner, do you not regard the badgers as an iconic member of the English countryside?"

Just as Ollie was about to answer, his phone rang. A large smile beamed on his face as he walked out of the meeting room.

Sarah, Shams, and Geoffrey shuddered and felt sick to their stomachs, as they knew this was the start of the wheels in motion.

"Excellent, Mr. Balls," Ollie said. "I will text you the co-ordinates of the last positive location and let Mr. Nicks know as well, so he can meet you there. Once your terriers locate the badger's location, our Clean Kill Teams will be notified, and you and your terriers can leave the premises."

Ollie contacted Richard and advised him of the meeting point with Tommy and told him to switch his tracker on immediately. He then contacted Michael Richardson and Nick Panay, telling them that Richard was going to be on the move and to synchronise his tracking device on their gadgets.

He stood in the corridor, took a deep breath to compose himself, and walked over to Jeremy's office. He knocked on his door, as Mel was not to be seen anywhere, and peeked his head in.

Jeremy was on the phone and gestured for him to come in and take a seat.

"Sorry about that," Jeremy said after hanging up. "I was actually on the phone to your dad, who called to ask what progress we had made. I was surprised you had not filled him in."

Ollie looked at Jeremy, not wanting to explain the true relationship he had with his father, and simply said, "It has just been so busy, and I assumed your emphasis on confidentiality also extended to family members."

"Very good, Mr. Gunner. I appreciate that attitude. Are we on schedule? I am assuming that is the purpose of your visit.

"Absolutely. Mr. Richardson and Mr. Panay have also been alerted, and Mr. Nicks is en route to meet Mr. Balls as we speak."

Ollie took his phone out to show Richard's tracking details of his exact location.

"Fantastic," Jeremy said, interlacing his fingers into a prayer position and continuing, "As soon as we know the location, I want to make an appearance for the press, so keep me posted."

Whilst Ady and Becky followed behind Tommy's Land Rover, Ainsley and Martyn from the RSPCA approached Mark Ashley's gate.

They rang the bell on the gate and were soon greeted by a very disgruntled Mark Ashley.

"Not interested," he snapped and began to close the gates on them, continuing, "Wish you Jehovah witnesses would leave people alone and get on with your own lives."

"Good morning, Mr. Ashley," Ainsley said, forcing the gate open and entering the property. He continued, "We are actually from the RSPCA and have a warrant to search your premises."

As Ainsley introduced himself, the other police arrived, and officers began the search, much to Mark's disapproval and protest, but he was cautioned and had no choice other than to cooperate.

Richard was already at the location when Tommy arrived. Ady could see Tommy slowing down to pull over, so he casually continued on the lane and parked out of their sight.

The Land Rover pulled up, and Richard ignored the driver, when all of a sudden, he heard a gruff voice saying, "Well, Trick Dicky, you found it faster than I did. You youngsters and your techy devices; not sure if I envy you or feel sorry for you. But here I am."

He jumped out and casually walked towards the car boot. Fortunately, the dogs were still on their leads, as they jumped out and were immediately foaming at their mouths, noses buried into the ground, tracking the scent of the badgers.

Tommy shouted to Richard, "Get hold of them whilst I get some bits out of the car."

Richard timidly held on to the dogs but soon found out that he needed all his strength to hold on to them.

Tommy took over, passing him a bag with water and bowls for the dogs, saying, "I'll take over, as they will rip a badger apart if they found one now. These girls are brilliantly trained; watch this."

Tommy shouted, "Halt," just the once, not particularly loudly, but in spite of their howling and whining, the dogs stood at a complete standstill, awaiting their next command.

"Move on."

And with no hesitation, as they began to pick up the scent of the badgers, they began their tracking, with their noses picking up the familiar scent in spite of the snow-covered ground.

They must have walked a mile, and Richard who understood tracking very well, said, "It's so eerie, all this snowfall and not a track to be seen. It's like the animals all decided to stay indoors."

"Right," Tommy said. "I have to let them go, as they are pulling like mad, or else I'll fall on my behind at this rate. Are you ready to keep up with them?"

"Is it safe?" Richard asked.

"Well, if they get a badger before we get there, does it matter?" Tommy said callously. "Only me and you are here; at least it will slow them down."

Ady and his colleague Becky were trying their best to keep up whilst filming Tommy and Richard ahead. It was not the easiest task, and unfortunately, Becky slipped and fell on some branches causing a noise.

Tommy stood still and said, "Did you hear that?"

Richard had his hands full with the dogs; he said, "I didn't hear anything; come on, I don't want to lose the dogs, and no one is going to be in the forest on a day like today." In a panic, he shouted, "Halt."

The dogs stopped, and Tommy took the harnesses and leads and put them back on the dogs. "Sorry," he said. "I cannot afford to lose these dogs. I'd rather be in control of them."

About a mile into forest, the dogs began to howl and bark. They began to cause a loud din, and Tommy said, "This must be it."

"Do we let them go, or do we call my boss?" said Richard.

"For all my years of hunting the badgers, I can assure you that this is it. You give him a call, and let's have a little fun before he arrives."

Tommy took the harnesses off and shouted, "Move on."

In a frenzy, the dogs began to snarl and whine relentlessly. All at once, a flock of birds swooped down and tried to scare them off, but they simply growled and disregarded the disturbance and barked at the entrance of a sett, foaming at their mouths.

Tommy shouted, "Halt."

The dogs kept still but were whining, so Tommy walked towards them with a bowl of chicken that they devoured immediately.

Richard explored where the site the dogs found and called Ollie; he said, "Yes, Mr. Gunner, we have a positive location."

Tommy picked up the empty bowl and said, "Well, lad, I'll be off now, as my part of this mission is accomplished. I believe it is over to your boss now. Pleasure doing business with you, son."

He began to harness the dogs up, and as he started to walk away, a stern sharp voice shouted, "Not so fast, Mr. Balls."

Tommy turned around to see Ady and Becky approaching him, showing their identification badges to him.

"We are arresting you on grounds of illegal badger persecution and collaboration with the Hardcore Terrier Men."

Within minutes, cameramen were filming the whole arrest, and reporters were all over the place. Jeremy Fischer was in the midst of it all, speaking to the leading reporter. Richard looked aghast at what he was witnessing and turned to see Tommy Balls, who shouted at him, "You two-timing little rat. You'll pay for this."

Richard stood in complete shock and horror, unaware of what was going on. Sirens were blaring, and in less than five minutes, the whole place was swarmed with police, reporters, and members from DEFRA. In a panic, he ran over to some bushes and tried to hide. His phone was ringing, and he could see it was Ollie calling, but he was afraid he was going to be arrested, so he ignored the call and switched his tracker off.

Suddenly, he saw several little animals, including badger cubs, scuttling ahead of him and rushing deeper into the forest, but he did not dare move, as he could also see three or four badgers very close by. He stood as he watched the police arrest Tommy Balls, whilst Jeremy and Ollie were both talking to reporters and having their pictures taken.

He also saw a large group of activists who had arrived at the scene and were yelling, "End the kill. End the cull. No shoot today. End the kill. End the cull. No shoot today. End the kill. End the cull. No shoot today."

Jeremy, aware that the press was watching him, sported a big pretentious smile on his face as he turned to Ollie and demanded, "What the hell are these activists doing here? How the hell did they know we would be here?"

Ollie replied that he had no idea, but as he turned around, he saw Sarah, Shams, and Geoffrey standing relatively close to Andy May and Barry Odie. He walked over to the activists, ignoring his recruits, and said, "Ladies and gentlemen, could I please address the leader of your protest?" He looked around, pretending not to be aware that it was Barry Odie.

Barry walked over to Ollie and put his hand out to him, saying, "Mr. Gunner, wish I could say it was a pleasure, but I am Barry Odie, head of League.Org, and these are my supporters against your cull."

Ollie replied, "I am very sorry, sir, but this official mission is going to be carried out, which may cause severe distress to your activists. Furthermore, you might put their lives in danger, as there is going to be a shoot within the next hour. We actually have the police at hand right now, who will forcibly remove you, but I really don't want to go down that road. May I ask who revealed this highly confidential mission to you?"

He looked over at Sarah, Shams, and Geoffrey, who slowly edged away from the activists.

"My sources are obviously reliable but their identities are totally confidential," Barry replied, looking down at Ollie and hoping that his hard stare would unnerve him.

Ollie looked at his watch, glanced up at the crowd, disregarded Barry, and walked up to Ady.

"Mr. Head, the Kill Team will be here in an hour; can you please remove those activists?"

While Ady called his office, Jeremy approached him. He put the phone down and said, "We have a unit arriving in fifteen minutes, Mr. Gunner, but officially I'm not too sure if I can restrain them."

Jeremy replied, "No worries, Mr. Head, I just spoke to the minister of defence, and he will be sending in some troops to hold off this crowd away from the site. We also have an official warrant to arrest them for disrupting official government activity. As a police official, if you could advise them to voluntarily get out of the way, pending the troops who will force them, that would be much appreciated."

"Brilliant, Mr. Fischer. You certainly are a force to be reckoned with. I will just wait for some backup and see to it as soon as they are here."

Ollie was infuriated. He assumed that Sarah, Shams, and Geoffrey had something to do with this conspiracy and walked over to them, saying, "Do you have any idea how the League.Org just happened to be here?"

All three unanimously responded, "No, Mr. Gunner."

Sarah added, "How could we? You kept this very much to yourself."

The police backup arrived, and despite Ady's cautionary warning to the activists, they refused to move and fixed themselves to the ground while they continued to chant.

The Clean Kill Teams arrived, and Nick and Michael told Ollie and Jeremy they were concerned about the activists being so close to their target, but Jeremy calmly smiled and said, "It's under control; they refused to listen to the police, so the troops are on their way."

The animals were keeping as still and quiet as possible. They were all aware of the presence of all these men, loud shouting, commands, and various noises going on, but remained still. Wisepaws and Lord Didas were grateful that the Bluuout signal had successfully positioned all the young animals where they should be; the plan was merely to hold out in their own habitats and make no presence, as the High Lord had assured them that Ollie made it clear that no dogs were to go down the setts, so it was going to be an evening of hide-and-seek.

The troops arrived in threatening tanks through the forest. The captain in charge walked over to Jeremy.

"Nice to meet you, Captain Mitchell. Thank you so much for coming so quickly."

Captain Mitchell smiled and said, "Only following orders, Mr. Fischer."

"Well, before you remove the activists, I'll tell the press to leave, as you know how dangerously they can manipulate reports, and this is a mission that cannot be jeopardised by bad press."

"Absolutely, Mr. Fischer."

Jeremy walked towards the reporters. It was beginning to get dark, and some were already setting up their lighting equipment on tripods. Jeremy smiled in his extremely diplomatic manner and said, "Guys, your fun is over. I promised you dibs for the news, but we have some serious work to do now that is life-endangering; that's why the troops are here to remove those activists. I must urge you now to leave, as what we are about to do next is official government business and not for publication."

Kirsty Nicholls, the reporter for the *Brockley Daily News*, asked, "Could we just get some pictures of the troops removing the activists? I promise we will be out of your way."

"No, Miss Nicholls, you have prime news about the arrest of Mr. Tommy Balls, and I held my part of the deal. You are now causing a delay in the progress of our mission, and I request once again that you pack up and go."

Jeremy said this with a Machiavellian smile that unnerved Kirsty, knowing that if she had tried to argue, she and her team might also end up being removed by the troops.

"Understood, Mr. Fischer, once again, thank you for the story. As agreed, we can also have the story on your success tonight, and on behalf the *Brockley Daily News*, good luck. I look forward to speaking to you in the morning."

As soon as Kirsty and her team were gone, Captain Mitchell walked towards Barry Odie and presented him an official warrant.

"Good afternoon, Mr. Odie. I am sorry, but you are trespassing on an official mission authorised by the government. In the interest of health and safety, I am asking you to please remove your activists and yourself to a safe distance away from this area."

The activists continued to chant their protest, and Barry simply said, "We are not moving."

Captain Mitchell took in a deep breath and continued in a stronger tone, "No disrespect, sir, but have you no conscience or moral responsibility? There are children participating in this dangerous activity, and rifles could misfire."

Barry followed his glance and was knocked back when he saw about ten children, he had not noticed all day.

"Please give me a minute, Captain."

Fuming, Barry walked towards Paul Lingwood. With no attempt at being polite he snapped, "Didn't I specify no children?"

"Barry, my kids stand for what I believe in," Paul said, "and so do their friends."

Without answering, Barry rounded up the activists and said, "We have to move; the kids could be endangered with the gunfire. The troops will forcibly remove us, and I don't want the children to remember this as something that will frighten them for the rest of their lives."

He looked at Paul, remembering that he was one of the biggest donors, and said calmly, "I understand Paul wanting his kids to see first-hand what we stand for, but now we need to show them nonviolence in action. Furthermore, if they proceed with the shoot, and it looks like they are going to, it's certainly not something I want children to witness."

A hum of agreement went through the crowds as Paul started to round the children up and made his way to the minibus they arrived in. He returned and apologised to the group, saying, "I'm sorry, guys. I never thought the day would be so severe. I'll wait with the kids in the van, and when they start to get bored, we will make our way home."

The others followed Captain Mitchell, and once all the activists were a safe distance away, the troops positioned themselves in front of them, barricading them from the site where DEFRA were going to commence the shoot.

Ollie, Michael, and Jeremy went to inspect the site and all agreed that the setts were definitely inhabited. Jeremy walked back to Nick and said with a cruel tone, "Get your teams lined up because soon as the sun sets, the badgers will come out, and it will be like shooting sitting ducks."

Sarah was beside herself in a flood of tears. The atmosphere was like a scene out of a film. Police cars had their lights flashing brightly in the fast-approaching evening. The tanks were now positioned with beams of light projected onto the site to assist for better vision. The activists had not surrendered their cause and still continued their chants. The troops were going in and out amongst the activists, prohibiting anyone from using their mobile phones. Any activists not complying were forcibly escorted to the edge of the forest.

Several farmers had heard what was going on and began to congregate at the opposite end of the activists. The ambiance was tense and anxious. The silence was so eerie, one could hear a pin drop. Sarah watched as at least forty marksmen lined up in a row with their rifles ready to shoot, and she burst into tears.

"Shams, Geoffrey, what are we going to do?" she cried. "Do you think the animals are aware this is waiting for them? We must try to warn them."

"I don't know, Sarah," Geoffrey said. "The High Lord must have some plan; besides, what can we do?"

"The Bluuout. I have the Bluuout; I will let Claudius Crow know."

Sarah watched how still the whole scene was. Everything was perfectly quiet, motionless and unmoving. She looked around to ensure that no one was watching her and blew once into the Bluuout. Not confident that it was sufficient, she blew another two times.

In less than a second, Claudius dived down from nowhere and cawed angrily, "What have you done, Sarah? You have signalled to the young that all is well."

Sarah fell on her knees as she watched how the stillness unfolded into a nightmare.

The innocent young deer gently galloped by, with the moles and hedgehogs on their backs, and the cubs raced by to see who could make it back into the field first. Wisepaws and Lord Didas were so confused as to who gave the signal but quickly blew into the Bluuout twice again, causing a lot of confusion to the young animals. The adults, in fear of what was going on, started to come out of their hiding. Sensing that this was not going to plan, the High Lady Dharma gave a signal to the moles, and since they were located roughly under the standing marksmen, the moles shuffled and burrowed faster than ever before, knocking the marksmen off their balance.

The marksmen could not understand what was going on and stood up to regain their positions. However, one had lost his rifle and could not find it. Unknown to him, Richard Nicks, who was hiding in a bush nearby, had grabbed his rifle.

No sooner did the marksmen regain their composure than the deer began to approach them in an alarming, terrorising manner, as if they were a pack of wolves.

Nick shouted, "Hold your fire, we cannot shoot the deer, as we have no licence to do so."

The marksmen were terrified and began to retreat. The deer continued to approach them, which was not in their nature. A minute later, they were all struck by what seemed like spiky balls and began to scream.

"Ouch, owww, ouch, arrrgggghh," Mick Jones shouted. "The hedgehogs are attacking us."

He reached down to confirm that they were hedgehogs, and when he looked up, dozens of stags had formed a line, brandishing their large antlers threatening to charge into them. They were followed by foxes, weasels, and an army of badgers, led by Widejaw in a contingent ferociously moving towards them. Above the animals, a murmuration of birds swooped down at a low level, with crows cawing and weaving in and out between the animals.

Petrified by what they were witnessing, Ollie and Jeremy sought the safety of the farmers, who were protected by the troops. The troops were not authorised to participate in the shoot, but like the activists and the troops at the other end, they were totally mesmerised by the scene.

Nick Panay looked for Ollie and Jeremy; he shook his head when he saw them hiding amongst the farmers like cowards.

"Mr. Fischer, this is not to protocol," Nick said. "We cannot shoot these other animals. Permission to abort the mission."

Jeremy had turned white with fear and suggested timidly, "Couldn't we shoot round the animals and target just the badgers?"

"No, sir, we must observe protocol, and the men will insist on following the rules, especially after the last slaughter of a mission."

Jeremy reluctantly nodded his head.

Nick ran back to the teams and shouted, "Abort mission. Retreat. I repeat, retreat."

The stags stood up boldly, creating a fortress in front of all the animals, and watched the men retreating. The hedgehogs on their backs bounced up and down and sang out, "They are going. They are retreating."

All the animals started rejoicing, and Speed, Bojana, and Fire came rushing out before the Bluuout signal. From out of nowhere, a gunshot was fired.

Richard had been standing on the side of the forest, watching the young animals return to the field. He raised his rifle and took aim at Fire, but just as he was about to pull the trigger, Bodger galloped over and knocked him down. The gunshot flew wide, missing Fire, but went straight into White's heart, and she was killed immediately.

The marksmen ran to see who had fired the shot and saw Bodger attacking Richard Nicks. Steve took aim and fired at Bodger, and in the chaos of the animals dispersing and not understanding what was happening, the High Lady screamed. She rushed over to see Fire, sitting by his sibling and crying; she was no longer answering him. She rushed to her lovely White, took her into her arms, and wailed so loud, with a cry filled with deep pain, agony, and anguish, that both the animals and humans could hear her grief.

The badgers began to scratch their strong paws into the ground, and the air was filled with dust and the scent of their ancestors granting them all the strength they needed. They galloped towards the humans with mighty strength and determination, with Widejaw leading at the front. They were totally enraged and had only one thought: to kill the humans. The stags supported the badgers all the way, intimidating the marksmen, who could not shoot the deer.

About a dozen marksmen stood, trying their best to shoot as many badgers as they could in between the deer. The eerie stillness of the night was now transformed into an evening of terror. There were screams from the activists, who were held back by the troops. The farmers stood in fear of their lives as they watched the badgers and deer violently attack the marksmen, and they left the area. The troops began to prepare themselves for an unexpected combat.

The animals were wailing and howling, and the ground was trembling with the fiercely galloping badgers and deer, and forest animals all moved towards the humans. As the badgers fell one by one, no one expected what came next.

A loud shriek came from the sky above, as the High Lady Pure shape-shifted into a magnificent white dragon. Her eyes burned with rage as she plunged down, wailing like a banshee, scorching the forest with flames that created a gorge between the marksmen and the animals. She circled and hovered, shooting out more flames and diving to grab as many badgers as she could before flying back to the other side. Still in a rage of grief and despair, she swooped once more and dived down, scorching the humans with more flames and continuing to wail. All the animals lamented the tragedy of the night, howling and whining with shrill reverberations of sadness and despair.

Sarah was sobbing uncontrollably. She cried, "Councillor Claudius Crow asked me, 'What have you done, Sarah?' Oh, God, what have I done?"

Shams stood completely still, and Geoffrey took her gently in his arms and said, "What has man done, Sarah? What have we done?"